THE SILK R

Volume 3 of The Silk Tales

A NOVEL BY

JOHN M. BURTON QC

EDITED BY KATHERINE BURTON

This book is sold subject to the condition that it shall not, by way of trade or otherwise, be lent, resold, hired out, or otherwise circulated without the author's prior consent in any form (including digital form) other than this in which it is published and without a similar condition being imposed on the subsequent purchaser.

FOR MY DAUGHTER SOPHIA WHO DESPITE HER TENDER AGE HAS SHOWN US ALL, TO CONQUER ADVERSITY, YOU JUST HAVE TO KEEP TRYING!

TEXT COPYRIGHT © JOHN M BURTON, 2015

ALL RIGHTS RESERVED

John M. Burton has asserted his right under the Copyright, Designs and Patents Act, 1988 to be identified as the author of this work.

This novel is a work of fiction. Names and Characters are the product of the author's imagination and any resemblance to actual persons, living or dead, is entirely coincidental.

First Edition 2015

Books by John M. Burton

The Silk Brief, Volume 1 of The Silk Tales

The Silk Head, Volume 2 of The Silk Tales

The Silk Returns, Volume 3 of the Silk Tales

The Silk Ribbon, Volume 4 of The Silk Tales

The Silk's Child, Volume 5 of The Silk Tales

The Silk's Cruise, Volume 6 of The Silk Tales

Parricide, Volume 1 of The Murder Trials of Cicero

Poison, Volume 2 of The Murder Trials of Cicero

The Myth of Sparta, Volume 1 of The Chronicles of Sparta

The Return of the Spartans, Volume 2 of The Chronicles of Sparta

The Trial of Admiral Byng, Pour Encourager Les Autres, Volume 1 of the Historical Trials Series

Treachery, The Princes in The Tower.

TABLE OF CONTENTS

Contents

CHAPTER 1
MURDER IN MOULSECOOMB 12
CHAPTER 2
THE INVESTIGATION 18
CHAPTER 3
THE SUSPECTS 22
CHAPTER 4
A PEACEFUL WEEKEND 26
CHAPTER 5
THE CLERKS' ROOM 31
CHAPTER 6
THE JUNIOR TENANT 39
CHAPTER 7
THE OLD SILK 43
CHAPTER 8
THE SENIOR CLERK 50
CHAPTER 9
A NEW MAN 57
CHAPTER 10
CHAMBERS' POLITICS 63

CHAPTER 11
THE OLD TENANT 70
CHAPTER 12
THE CONSULTATION 74
CHAPTER 13
NEGOTIATION 86
CHAPTER 14
WEEKEND OF MURDER 99
CHAPTER 15
RENEWING AN OLD ACQUAINTANCE AND
MAKING A NEW ONE 109
CHAPTER 16
THE PHONE CALL 118
CHAPTER 17
AN EVENING DRINK 124
CHAPTER 18
FURTHER EVIDENCE 131
CHAPTER 19
A FURTHER CONSULTATION 139
CHAPTER 20
THE DOCTOR'S NOTE 143
CHAPTER 21
SUCH A ROMANTIC EVENING 150

CHAPTER 22 ....
YET MORE EVIDENCE 156
CHAPTER 23 ....
A FURTHER CONSULTATION 160
CHAPTER 24 ....
ARILLAS, CORFU 172
CHAPTER 25 ....
BACK TO REALITY 177
CHAPTER 26 ....
THE FIRST DAY OF THE TRIAL 182
CHAPTER 27 ....
THE PROSECUTION OPENING 189
CHAPTER 28 ....
THE FIRST WITNESS 201
CHAPTER 29 ....
THE EXPERIENCED WITNESS 215
CHAPTER 30 ....
THE 'LEAVING CARE PERSONAL ADVISOR' ... 221
CHAPTER 31 ....
ALL ABOUT THE TIMING 232
CHAPTER 32 ....
THE NOSEY NEIGHBOUR 242

8

CHAPTER 33	
THE NEIGHBOUR'S SON	259
CHAPTER 34	
THE PATHOLOGIST	271
CHAPTER 35	
EYEWITNESS TO MURDER,	280
CHAPTER 36	
CROSS EXAMINATION OF THE EYEWITNESS	287
CHAPTER 37	
THE CO-DEFENDANT'S CROSS EXAMINATION	301
CHAPTER 38	
THE GIRLFRIEND	306
CHAPTER 39	
THE PRISON SNITCH	322
CHAPTER 40	
THE PRISON SNITCH CONTINUES	340
CHAPTER 41	
THE BAD CHARACTER APPLICATION	346
CHAPTER 42	
THE RELUCTANT WITNESS	353

CHAPTER 43
THE RELUCTANT WITNESS IS CROSS EXAMINED 360

CHAPTER 44
THE PROSECUTION CASE CLOSES 373

CHAPTER 45
THE DEFENCE CASE 383

CHAPTER 46
PAUL MORRIS CROSS-EXAMINED 397

CHAPTER 47
PAUL MORRIS CROSS EXAMINED AGAIN 405

CHAPTER 48
MICHAEL WARD GIVES EVIDENCE 418

CHAPTER 49
MICHAEL WARD CROSS EXAMINED 428

CHAPTER 50
THE PROSECUTION CLOSING SPEECH 446

CHAPTER 51
THE CLOSING SPEECH FOR PAUL MORRIS ...458

CHAPTER 52
THE CLOSING SPEECH FOR MICHAEL WARD 473

CHAPTER 53
THE DELIBERATIONS 482

CHAPTER 54 ....
THE VERDICT 492
CHAPTER 55 ....
THE SILK RETURNS...499

CHAPTER 1

MURDER IN MOULSECOOMB

It had been a long night for Richard Brook and he had only just managed to drop off when he was jolted awake by loud banging and shouting directly outside his flat. He briefly looked at his clock, muttering to himself that he would never get to sleep. He put his glasses on and walked to the window, rubbing his swollen blurry eyes. Who was making all this noise at 1am this Tuesday morning, a work night?

He lived in a small flat in Saunders Road in Moulsecoomb, near Brighton. It was Tuesday 6th May 2014 and Richard had enjoyed a relaxing bank holiday Monday but now he had to get up early for work the next day and he needed his sleep.

As he began to push aside the curtains to peer outside, he heard a loud voice shouting, "You almost brained me the other night, let me in or I'll fucking kill you."

He did not recognise the voice but he recognised the tone and stopped himself. He knew it would be coming from number 4A, where that new tenant, Danny Williams lived. Danny had only moved in a couple of weeks earlier, but Richard had already been woken in the middle of the night several times by similar outbursts and loud noises.

Richard had noticed that since Danny moved in, his flat had attracted a large number of undesirables. He assumed drugs were involved. To him, Danny's visitors often exhibited signs of serious degeneracy. He had witnessed the debris outside Danny's flat on a number of occasions. Frequently, there were empty beer bottles and cans, discarded take-away meals and, the other day, broken glass from two of Danny's windows. At least those had been boarded up now but the area was becoming like a slum.

He thought it best not to look out of the curtain just now. He waited a few seconds before hearing more banging, as though someone was trying to smash through Danny's door. He also heard someone shout in a gruff, loud voice, "You owe me, you little shit!"

He wondered whether he should phone the police. This part of Moulsecoomb was an area known all too well to the police, supplying a considerable number of clients for the local criminal solicitors' firms. Richard knew it was probably better to keep out of it and not have police cars visiting him in the middle of the night with this lot around. He imagined objects coming through his own windows and unwelcome late night visitors banging on his doors. He decided to wait a few more minutes and hope they would go away.

Sure enough, after a few more futile attempts to gain entry to Danny's door, Richard heard sounds of people leaving, swearing loudly in frustration as they did so. He sighed with relief and felt grateful it all seemed to be calming down out there. However, before climbing back into bed, curiosity got the better of him and after waiting a few more minutes, he peered out from behind his curtain.

Danny's flat was directly opposite his own in a street of terraced houses. He could see the boarded-up windows, and he noted that the lights were on indoors and assumed that Danny must be home. He noticed three men walking away from the flat. He recognised one, a black youth with a large seventies Afro hairdo. He had seen him at Danny's a number of times. The other men he did not recognise and could see very little of them as they were wearing their hoodies up, covering most of their faces. However, he thought they were both white, but could not be certain of this as he squinted at them through the glass.

He watched the men leave and decided not to call the police. After all, nothing had really happened. He moved back to his bed, took a sip of water from a glass on his side table and slipped back under the safety of his warm covers. He had an early start and needed to get some sleep. He pushed a couple of large bright orange foam earplugs into his ears, which a close friend had bought him for Christmas. He never thought he would find a use for them, but they had come in very handy recently!

Other neighbours had also woken from the loud noises. Shereena Bennett lived next door to Danny's flat at number 4 and she looked out of her bedroom window to see three men at his door. She was sure they were all black men and she recognised the one with an Afro haircut as she had seen him there many times before. He stopped to take a call on his phone and as he was doing so she thought he looked up at her. She moved quickly back behind the curtains and out of sight.

Her son Lloyd was less afraid and he looked out of his bedroom window which was next to his mother's room, and also saw three youths. He too recognised the black one with the Afro, but could not recognise the other two, although he was sure they were both white males.

Shereena had had enough of these nocturnal visits and, after the boys left, she discussed the matter with Lloyd who had come to her room to make sure she was alright. Both knew this was an area where helping the police could result in undesirable attention from other residents, so reporting it was not an easy decision to take. Shereena poured herself a couple of stiff drinks, large tots of dark rum from a bottle she kept near to her bedside. She listened to her son Lloyd who tried to encourage her not to get involved. Mind your own business was his view, otherwise things could get worse for them.

As she drank the second glass of rum, she heard someone outside shout, "I'll fucking kill you". She immediately went to the curtains to see what was happening.

Looking out, she beckoned quietly to Lloyd, "Come and look at this."

Lloyd peered out cautiously and saw what both he and Shereena were sure were the same three men facing a fourth youth who was backing away into an alleyway about twenty yards from Danny's flat. She was sure the retreating youth was the new tenant, Danny.

Again she closed the curtains. These kinds of incident were happening more frequently, she thought. Only the other day she had heard some smashing of glass coming from Danny's flat and then seen two men running away, one of whom she was sure was the boy with the Afro hairstyle.

A few seconds later both heard a high-pitched scream, so loud it made Shereena jump with fright and spill some rum onto her nightdress. They continued to watch and saw two men running from the alleyway followed shortly by another youth who staggered behind them for a few yards, and then collapsed before their eyes.

Shereena had no doubt what to do now, and as Lloyd ran out of the house to try and help Danny, she phoned the police. "Come quickly," she cried, "I think my neighbour has just been stabbed by some black youths!"

CHAPTER 2

THE INVESTIGATION

Detective Sergeant Mark Crook came on duty at 9am that Tuesday morning. He stood at a heady six feet four inches tall and weighed eighteen stone. He had long ago become weary of jokes from other police officers that he was the 'biggest Crook in the police force.'

He had twenty-six years' of service in the force behind him and was looking forward to a long retirement when he would soon complete his thirty years of service. He would enjoy a respectable pension, a life of golf, beer and decent, or at least semi-decent, Scotch.

Today he hoped for an easy day, as he was nursing a headache from last night's drinking session with his squad of detectives. They had been celebrating a successful day, as the decision to charge a suspect in a murder case they had been investigating for months, had finally been made by the Crown Prosecution Service. Although he had to recognise that the evidence was purely circumstantial in this case, he was sure they had got the right man. However, along with this good result, now came the news that there had been yet another murder on his patch. He would be busy on another investigation even before his hang-over wore off!

He checked the notes that had been made by the officers on duty last night. The victim was a young lad of eighteen, Danny Williams. He had some previous convictions for petty theft and drugs possession but nothing major. Apparently there were witnesses who had seen him stabbed and a 999 call had been made to police from a person called Shereena Bennett. The call was logged at 1:23am that morning.

Police officers and an ambulance had been despatched to the scene to find that Danny Williams had died from a single stab wound to the heart.

Although he would rather be doing anything else at the moment, the case was not likely to be too difficult. The locals had recognised one youth with an Afro hairstyle and there were not that many people in the Moulsecoomb area that matched that description.

By 3pm he was starting to feel human again. The four aspirins and several cups of tea had helped, and the two pints of bitter at lunch time, the 'hair of the dog' had provided an excellent hangover cure.

The Danny Williams' murder investigation was progressing well. A local police officer, Police

Constable Foster, had volunteered to him that he had investigated a report of criminal damage in the Moulsecoomb area on the previous Sunday, 4th May. Neighbours in a street near to Danny's flat, called Neville Street, had reported that a youth had put bottles through a window of a neighbouring house.

Police Constables Foster and Richards attended the house, which they discovered was rented by a David Morris. Foster recalled that the occupants had been slow to come to the door and they had heard the flushing of an upstairs toilet before they gained access. Both officers suspected that the occupants had been flushing drug paraphernalia down the lavatory, but as they had no search warrant and nothing but the barest suspicion, they did not search the premises.

The officers were allowed into the house, at number 24 Neville Street, by a young black male who had a large afro haircut. He had given his name as Michael Ward but refused to answer any other questions about the broken windows. The other occupant was a white youth who had given his name as Paul Morris, the son of David Morris. He said he knew who had thrown the bottles, but claimed not to know why. Paul took them to the suspect's address, but the youth was not home or not answering the door. Paul Morris supplied a name for them to follow up later. The name given was the deceased, Danny Williams of 4A Saunders Road, Moulsecoomb.

CHAPTER 3

THE SUSPECTS

It did not take long for Mark Crook to make enquiries around the area and obtain statements from a number of witnesses. Many were neighbours of Danny Williams who gave detailed accounts of the deterioration in the neighbourhood in the few short weeks since Danny had arrived. Some gave accounts of the night itself and what they had seen and heard.

Mark's next move was to have police officers check the CCTV from the street cameras and local shops in the vicinity to see what they could reveal. It was soon discovered that no CCTV covered the area around the alleyway but some did cover the surrounding streets. One was situated about two hundred yards from the alleyway and showed a man walking quickly away from the direction of the alley. Another man was seen to run up to him and they walked off together, presumably talking. They were then caught passing by a parade of shops on the shops' security videos. They were shown close up, deep in conversation. The videos were timed between 1:25am and 1:32am which the police officers thought fitted in nicely with the timing of the 999 call.

Mark Crook had asked Police Constable Foster to view the video. Foster recognized the first man in the video as Paul Morris and the second as a local drug addict, Charlie Dickson. Only one video picked up someone with an Afro haircut. That was from a street in the opposite direction to that taken by Morris and Dickson. He too was seen to be running away from the scene. The CCTV only showed his back so Foster could not be 100 per cent certain, but he thought it was the other male he had seen at 24 Neville Street, Michael Ward.

Within three days of Danny's death, both Ward and Morris had been arrested and were in custody on suspicion of his murder. Dickson had not been found yet but Mark was sure it was only a matter of time before he surfaced, probably when he needed his next fix.

Mark soon discovered that Ward and Morris were no strangers to police stations. Apart from some histrionics on arrest by Morris, both remained silent, other than to ask for their regular solicitors. Ward asked for Roger McCauley who had an office in Brighton.

Mark knew that Roger had done a good job for Ward in the past. He had been acquitted of a number of minor offences that Mark, having read the Court papers, had no doubt Ward had committed. Morris asked for someone called

Jimmy Short. He was apparently an ex-policeman, which in Mark's opinion was bad news. They knew too much about how the system worked in a police station.

He was told that Jimmy Short's firm had recently taken over a firm in Brighton, expanded their practice and moved this Jimmy Short in to 'front' the new 'improved' practice. He knew his case against Ward and Morris was at best circumstantial and it would help to have these two provide some answers in interview. However, as the two solicitors arrived at the station, he realised that was not likely to happen.

It was Jimmy Short who took a lead in the discussions. Mark had to provide some disclosure to both, briefly summarising the evidence he had to date. Jimmy listened as it was read out to him and then snorted when he realised the extent of the police case.

"Is that all! Why have you even bothered arresting my client? I can tell you now, I'll be advising him to say nothing so you're wasting your time interviewing him."

Roger McCauley had practised as a solicitor for over 30 years in Brighton and saw no advantage in adopting a confrontational approach with the police as he had to deal with them daily. He was aware how interviews could suddenly be cancelled by officers, which simply wasted his time. Confrontation had its proper place in the courtroom, not here in the police cells. He simply thanked the officer for the written disclosure and asked to see his client.

As if to reward his more cooperative stance, Mark announced he would be interviewing Roger's client, Michael Ward first.

Jimmy complained about the wait but apart from receiving a cup of luke-warm instant coffee with powdered milk, his complaint was ignored. He was able to see Paul Morris when a cell became free and he gave his usual advice, regardless of the strength of the evidence, "They've got nothing on you Paul, keep your mouth shut in interview and I'll get you out of here. They probably won't even charge you and if they do, I'll get you the best brief there is and you'll walk."

CHAPTER 4

A PEACEFUL WEEKEND

David woke up early on Saturday 10th May to the sound of the birds singing away happily in the garden. He could have continued to sleep but there were worse ways to wake up and he smiled as he turned to his right, where Wendy lay next to him, sleeping and looking peaceful and radiant. He enjoyed these moments so much, waking up on a beautiful day, the sun shining gently through the blinds forming stripes of sunlight on Wendy's curled up body.

As it was a Saturday there was no need to think about work or the multitude of problems currently facing his Chambers. The weekend was his to spend lazing with Wendy in some sublime and stress-free way. What could be better?

He thought of last year. After the Charlie Holmes acquittal a year ago, he had received a card from Mrs Holmes along with a bottle of vintage champagne thanking him for "obtaining justice" for her son Charlie. Despite his own misgivings about whether 'justice' had been obtained for Charlie Holmes, he had dearly appreciated the gesture and recalled that he and Wendy had also thoroughly enjoyed the champagne. He had not expected any gift as it was rare for clients or their friends or relatives to show any real gratitude for the hard work he carried out on their behalf. Whilst many were thankful at the time the jury delivered an acquittal, their gratitude usually did not reach beyond the doors of the courtroom.

Since Charlie's case, he had conducted a few other murder trials and a three month fraud case, which represented a small improvement in his practice. Still, he was nowhere near as busy as when he was a junior barrister, before he took Silk. Nor, sadly, was he paid as well owing to the reduction in legal aid fees. He thought for a moment how he had witnessed something this year that he never thought he would see. Barristers at the Criminal Bar had gone on strike for two days, refusing to attend court, they had also embarked on a campaign of refusing to cover other barrister's returns, which had meant that if a barrister was engaged in one court and another case of his was listed to be heard elsewhere, no one would represent the other client. This led to the Government's latest proposed reduction in legal aid fees to be put back for one year. These were interesting times indeed for the profession.

David recalled a case he had recently been instructed on. It was another murder case, this time in the Old Bailey, the famous criminal court where many of the most heinous historical trials had taken place. He had received a call from his clerk, John Winston, on Wednesday, 26th March, saying that the case was a late return. It was listed the following Tuesday on 1st April.

The papers were delivered that day to his Chambers and the following day, Thursday, 27th March, he had appeared in the Old Bailey to ask for a short adjournment, so that he would have a few days to fully prepare the defence. Apparently, the client's previous Queen's Counsel had, just two days earlier, been taken ill on a train on the way to visit the client in prison, so it was nobody's fault and David had no doubt that a reasonable judge would allow his application in these unforeseeable circumstances.

However, his application was not listed in front of a reasonable judge, it was listed in front of his old pupil master, His Honour Judge Tanner, and on discovering this, David's optimism had disappeared. Indeed, His Honour Judge Tanner had seen things a little differently to David. On hearing his application, Judge Tanner had commented that the case had been listed for months now and that there was a long backlog of cases waiting to be heard and he refused the application with a sarcastic comment that, "you will just have to work over the weekend". As if David did not do that anyway, when he was instructed on a case! Tanner had been as he called it "generous" in saying that there would only be jury selection and a prosecution opening on the Tuesday and no witnesses would be called before Wednesday, giving David, "plenty of time to prepare your cross-examination."

David had thanked the Judge for his "generosity" and enjoyed Tanner's look of uncertainty in response. Tanner obviously decided not to pursue the sarcasm and the case was adjourned to the original trial date, the following Tuesday.

The following day David had gone to visit the client in Belmarsh prison in South London, only to discover that the client was a devout Muslim who had chosen to attend Friday prayers in preference to a consultation with his Queen's Counsel. David had not objected, he only wished the client had communicated the fact before he arrived at the prison gates after a long drive battling through London's rush hour traffic!

The case had begun on time on Tuesday 1st April and finished on Wednesday 18th April, just in time for Easter. The client was found guilty in less than two hours. It had not helped his defence that he was seen on CCTV in a pub car park viciously beating the victim to death with an iron bar. His protestations that he was acting in self-defence had not convinced the jury, nor had David's speech on 'reasonable doubt'.

29

David had felt nothing about the case. Having watched the CCTV in Chambers he had thought the self-defence plea was nonsense. He thought to himself that it was ironic how the cases which were overwhelming caused him little stress. It was those cases about which he had a personal doubt about a client's guilt that caused him more concern. It was a horrible thought that an innocent man might spend years in prison for an offence he had not committed. He wondered if the general public would understand that. After over thirty years in practice he was still frequently asked at dinner parties, "How can you represent someone you know is guilty?" Easily, thought David. It's the innocent ones that are difficult to defend. The stakes are so much higher for them!

David returned to Chambers to hear John Winston talking about more work "in the pipeline" from that solicitor because of the "spirited way" he had fought a hopeless case. The cockney solicitor had even expressed that he thought David was, "the dog's bollocks". An expression David had learnt some years ago was actually meant as a compliment!

Yes, life was good, he was in a happy loving relationship that was getting stronger and his career was heading in the right direction and further reductions in legal aid payments had been curtailed for the moment. What could possibly go wrong?

CHAPTER 5

THE CLERKS' ROOM

Two weeks later on Monday 26th May, John Winston was in Chambers feeling particularly harassed. No one else in the clerk's room could tell there was anything wrong. John sat at his desk drinking a cup of tea and talking to Jimmy Short on the phone. Jimmy had not instructed Chambers for over a year and so the conversation was a little forced.

"I know how you feel Jimmy, but you can't really blame Mr Brant."

Jimmy had explained that he had moved from London to the Brighton office of Rooney Williams LLP and picked up a murder case. He had decided to instruct a junior barrister and a Queen's Counsel from John's Chambers which was great news. Jimmy explained that they had given notice to their in-house junior barrister, Charlotte Williams, and he was also unhappy with the service he was receiving from the set of Chambers he regularly instructed and was removing all his briefs from them. However, Jimmy was also adamant about one condition, he did not want David Brant on this case or any case.

"I don't want that bastard representing my clients. He doesn't fight cases!"

John knew he was referring to the wine fraud that Jimmy had instructed David on over a year ago. Why it was that solicitors like Jimmy Short have such long memories when something goes wrong, but seem to immediately forget when things go right!

John tried to explain that David could hardly fight a case when the client wanted to plead guilty, but he knew he had to tread cautiously. He wanted the briefs coming into chambers again, so he was not going to fight David's corner too strenuously, despite him being the Head of Chambers.

Jimmy' interrupted John's thought process as he put him on the spot, "OK John, who've you got to do a murder case in Lewes, probably around September?"

John thought for a moment before answering, "I'd still like to recommend David Brant. He has an incredible success rate in murder cases. He's just had another great success."

He decided there was no need to mention that David's last murder case had resulted in a conviction, as to him, it was still a 'great success' if the solicitor thought David had done a good job regardless of the actual result.

Jimmy was having none of it. "I don't care if he's got a phenomenal success rate, it's no doubt because he only fights winners!"

"You know that's not true Jimmy."

"I've told you I don't want David Brant. What about that new bloke, Tim Adams?"

"I agree Jimmy, he would be ideal, but for the first time I can recall, the Crown Prosecution Service has beaten you to it. This is the case of Paul Morris isn't it? They've told me they want him to prosecute this one."

"What already? The CPS don't usually instruct silks until a couple of weeks before trial, if then!"

"I know Jimmy, it's not clear to me why they have instructed him so early on, especially as they rarely seem to instruct silks these days, even on murders, but they asked him to give a preliminary advice and said the brief was his."

"What was the advice about then?"

John coughed uncomfortably and answered, "Now Jimmy, you know I can't tell you that."

There was a pause at the other end of the line which could only mean that Jimmy was thinking, always a dangerous thing in John's opinion. Jimmy quickly worked out his next move and a few seconds later raised his voice as he shouted down the phone, "You mean you've got silks in your chambers advising that my clients get charged!"

John raised his eyes to the ceiling, "It's not like that Jimmy, and to be fair we didn't know he was your client."

Jimmy paused again before continuing, "Alright, what about 'Wantmore' then, is he back in harness yet?"

"No, I'm sorry Jimmy, we don't know if Mr Wontner will ever be back full-time. He has been doing some minor cases, private pleas and the like, but he doesn't want any long trials at the moment. His wife is understandably worried that the stress might bring on another heart attack."

John thought for a few seconds before adding, "I was thinking Jimmy, you won't need a silk yet. Why don't I fix you up with a leading junior in the short term and we can talk about a silk nearer the trial?"

There was no pause now as Jimmy immediately responded, "Yeah, right! You think I was born yesterday. No I don't want you trying to fob me off with a leading junior now and then telling me nearer the time there's no silk available but your leading junior will do a good job! I want to know what silk you have got for the trial now and then we can talk about the junior."

John inwardly groaned as he thought, why was it Jimmy Short who always gave him such grief?

He took a deep breath before continuing, "That's fair enough Jimmy, you know we have a good relationship with your firm and we wouldn't want to do anything to jeopardise that."

"You should tell that to your Head of Chambers. Bloody 'No-Balls Brant'. Have you got a silk or not for this case?" he demanded.

John had tried all he could to get David the brief. There was only one choice left.

"Well, I do have a very experienced silk available. I'm just checking his diary on the computer as we speak."

He paused for a few seconds and then put the earpiece of his phone near his computer keyboard and made suitable clicking noises as he moved through a list of available Cruise ships that he could sail on in a Caribbean holiday he was planning to take with his wife.

After a few seconds he stopped clicking, "Yes, I'm happy to say he has a gap in his diary at that time and will be free in September. That's good news, I've got William Bretheridge QC available."

Not surprising, thought John, he hasn't had a brief for about five years!

Jimmy Short was quizzical, "I don't know him, will he fight cases?"

"Oh yes, he will fight your case. He hasn't pleaded a case for years."

At least that's honest, thought John, smiling to himself.

Jimmy's tone seemed to change, "Good, now as for a junior, what about that Julian Hawker, the 'ladies' man'. He's a good brief."

John paused before replying, "He's no longer with us, he left over a year ago, but I have an excellent senior junior in mind. You know Graham Martin, he's an excellent brief."

Jimmy ignored him. "Where's Hawker gone then?"

"I'm not sure."

John knew exactly where he had gone but he had no intention of giving the name of a rival chambers and potentially losing the junior brief in this case. "Knowing him he's possibly in prison now."

Jimmy laughed, "Yes, I heard he'd had a bit of a problem."

"Well the less said the better. No, Graham Martin is the man for this job Jimmy."

As far as John was aware, Julian Hawker had managed to sort out his problems and was still practising after a reprimand from the Bar Standards Board, but he saw no reason to mention that to Jimmy.

Jimmy pondered for a few seconds, "I know Graham Martin don't I? He's the one that's always pessimistic about his client's chances, a bit like his bloody Head of Chambers!"

John put on his most soothing voice, "Jimmy, Mr Martin has been a bit pessimistic in the past but he has changed and we know that when he fights a case, he is superb and I can assure you, he will fight yours."

There was silence for a few seconds, then Jimmy spoke, "All right, I'll send the papers to him and once he has read them he can do me a short advice so we can extend the legal aid to get your silk on board, what's his name, Bretherash?"

"William Bretheridge QC."

"Whatever."

John thanked him and they exchanged the usual promises to have a pint soon before John put the phone down. He lent back in his comfy chair thinking to himself, how his job was getting more and more difficult. Solicitors used to beg for silks to do their work because there were so few around and there was so much work. Now there were far more silks and far less work. He felt that selling silks to solicitors was like selling ice to Eskimoes in the middle of a deep freeze!

He smiled at his own humour as he turned to Nick, his first junior clerk. Nick had joined chambers recently when John's former first junior, Tony, had left to join a commercial set of chambers for almost double the pay. John noticed that Nick had a large smirk on his face.

"What are you smirking about? I'll let you take the next call from Jimmy Short, that'll wipe the smile off your face."

Nick's smile did not diminish as he replied, "Do you want me to tell Mr Bretheridge that he has a new brief, his first in five years?"

John smiled back, "No thanks, I'll tell him. That's not the hard part. It's telling Mr Martin he's being led by a silk who hasn't seen the inside of a Courtroom for five years and I'm going to leave that news for you to deliver!"

CHAPTER 6

THE JUNIOR TENANT

"You have got to be joking."

Graham Martin slammed his papers down on his desk as John broke the news. He had changed his mind and decided that it was probably too early to introduce his first clerk to one of Graham Martin's tantrums.

It had started well. Graham was overjoyed when John told him that he had been briefed in a murder, but his joy immediately turned to dismay when he heard it was for Jimmy Short and then to horror when he learnt he was to be led by William Bretheridge.

"David's the man to lead me on a murder, not Bill. Bill was good in his day and I do have the greatest of respect for him, but he's not conducted a case in years, you cannot give him a murder trial!"

John nodded, "Between us sir, I agree. As I told the solicitor, Mr Brant has a phenomenal record."

Graham looked at him closely, he was surprised that John knew the word, "phenomenal", he decided that John must have taken up reading something other than the tabloid newspapers recently.

John continued in the same breath, "But, the problem is Jimmy Short doesn't think Mr Brant's a fighter."

"What? And Bill is a fighter? A man who has not fought a case in years. Even in his day he had a reputation for pleading out cases that should have been fought."

"That was some time ago, in any event, the solicitor would not accept Mr Brant in any circumstances. We obviously needed to provide them with a silk otherwise there was a risk that both the silk and junior briefs would go elsewhere."

Graham quietened down a little at the thought of losing this brief that had only just arrived. He paused before continuing, "I could do the case as a leading junior and we could bring another junior in from chambers?"

John shook his head. "No, I'm afraid I suggested that and Jimmy rejected it. He is adamant that we provide a silk and the trouble is that, as he won't accept Mr Brant, the only one I could offer at the moment was Mr Bretheridge."

Graham thought for a few moments. He could make a stand and refuse the brief unless another silk was instructed, but then he had received very few cases recently and was struggling to pay his mortgage. He really could not turn down a murder brief whatever his misgivings about the leader.

"Ok, well I suppose I have to think of the client and at least I have got a murder brief. When are the papers coming?"

John smiled, he had thought it might be a little more difficult to persuade Graham to take the case with William Bretheridge as his leader. Times were clearly changing. A few years ago Graham Martin would have thrown the papers back at him with a resounding, 'No way!'

John had wondered for a few years now just how much time he had left in this game. Oh well at least I'll be able to retire to my villa in Spain, play golf all day and drink beer.

His thoughts immediately changed to concentrate on his plans for the following day. He had arranged to play golf all day with a London solicitor and then entertain him at the 'nineteenth' hole with lunch and a few beers - all, of course, at Chambers' expense.

He thought for a few moments and realised, he did not want to retire yet, he would have to pay for his own golf and beer, and he was not sure that he was ready to retire yet. At least not whilst Chambers paid for regular sessions of beer and golf!

CHAPTER 7

THE OLD SILK

The clerks found it difficult to find William Bretheridge QC. After all, in the last five years the only time they had to contact him was when his tailors or other creditors phoned about an unpaid bill, or even less often, an old friend tried to contact him to arrange lunch in the Middle Temple Hall.

William had been at the Bar for over fifty years. He could still remember when murder cases carried the death penalty in the early 1960s. Indeed, he remembered the last executions were carried out on his 27th birthday. At 8 am on 13th August 1964 Peter Allen and Gwynne Evans were hanged for the murder of John West, Evans at Strangeways Prison in Manchester and Allen at Liverpool's Walton Prison. He recalled those days fondly. The pressure not to make a mistake in a murder case was something the youngsters today could not understand - Although he conveniently forgot that he had not actually conducted a murder case himself in those days.

William, Bill to his friends, had not adapted well to modern practice. The concept of using 'newfangled' devices like a computer or a smartphone, were lost on him. He had reluctantly purchased a basic mobile phone but rarely turned it on and certainly struggled to actually use it. He seldom gave the mobile number to anyone. These days the only people who wanted to contact him were chasing some bill or other. As a barrister, he had long ago become accustomed to waiting over a year before getting paid for a case and he could not understand why these impatient 'tradespeople' were not willing to wait the same amount of time.

Despite the complete lack of work in his diary, he had a set daily regime. He still regularly arose at 7:30am, got dressed, put on his black waistcoat and jacket, and prised himself into the ever shrinking grasp of his grey pinstripe trousers. He was sure the dry-cleaners were constantly shrinking his trousers and dismissed with contempt, his wife Jane's suggestion that he might be putting on weight.

He would then make his way to chambers at 8:55am arriving just before 9am. He and his wife had a flat in the Inner Temple, a couple of hundred yards from chambers so it was not a difficult journey to work.

Jane had become used to his routine and sent him off with a healthy packed lunch. She was concerned about his health because of his age, so she made sure that only the best ingredients went into his sandwich with plenty of salad. She could not understand why he was still overweight when she had put him on a strict diet for some time now.

Bill would arrive in chambers, say hello to the clerks and then make his way to the silks' room. Taking a seat behind his desk his first task of the day would be to open his sandwich, have a cursory look at the contents and then consign it to the waste bin before planning which wine bar to visit for lunch that day. He chose wine bars at least a tube ride away from the Temple. In his opinion, it was not appropriate to be seen drinking wine at lunch time around the Temple as some instructing solicitor might see him and get the ridiculous idea that he had a drinking habit, or worse still, that he had no work, and that would not help his reputation or his career.

On this day he had gone to one of his favourite wine bars, 'Vino Veritas' near Mansion House tube station. He was well known there and he ordered his usual steak baguette with half a bottle of claret. After all, he didn't want to overdo things at his age.

He would return to chambers at 4pm having consumed a glass of vintage port with a small selection of cheese. He missed finishing his lunch off with a good cigar, damn the British nanny state, he thought bitterly, it prevented a man enjoying a good cigar with his lunch.

Today he returned at 4pm and put his head round the door of the busy clerks' room and announced to John that he had returned and would be in the silks' room if he was needed. Long ago he realised this was pointless, but it had become part of his daily routine and he did not bother to wait for an answer. Today though, when he was already on his way to the silks' room, he heard John Winston acknowledge him for the first time in years.

"Mr Bretheridge, I hope you've got no plans for September as I've managed to get you a murder brief."

Bill stopped in his tracks, was his clerk, John, really speaking to him, he wondered. Surely he had misheard him or it was one of John's poor jokes?

"Pardon, John? What did you say?"

"I've got you a murder brief for September. It's from the firm, Rooney Williams. You'll be leading Mr Martin from Chambers. It's at an early stage, it's only just been transferred to the Lewes Crown Court from Brighton Magistrates Court. Once Mr Martin has seen the papers he'll do the

47

necessary advice for legal aid and you'll be instructed."

Bill smiled, "Lewes you say, I wonder if it will be in front of my old pupil, His Honour Judge Jamie Sinclair?"

John looked at him quizzically. "His Honour Judge Sinclair retired two years ago. Didn't you go to his retirement party?"

Bill's cheeks reddened slightly before he replied, "Of course, yes, you're right. We gave him a great send off. Thank you John, contact me immediately when the papers arrive, I shall want to work on them straight away."

John gave a wry smile, "Of course you will sir."

Bill continued his journey to the silks' room. He would have to read up on current law as he was a little rusty. This was despite the fact that he continued to carry out the Bar's compulsory twelve hours of 'continuing practice development' each year.

He was aware that some barristers carried out something called "online quizzes" to earn their CPD points. He had no idea what they were. His 'continuing practice development' had consisted of attending two six-hour lectures each year, although he confessed to anyone who was interested, he usually dozed off during them and never took a single note and had less idea what they were about at the end of the lecture than he had at the beginning.

He decided he had better go and ask David whether there had been any recent developments in the law of murder that he should be aware of.

David looked up from his work as the door to his room opened and Bill walked in.

"Hello Bill, enjoyed one of your long lunches? I'm surprised that Jane hasn't discovered what happens to her sandwiches by now."

Bill smiled and took a seat before replying, "My dear boy, I have learned over the years to be somewhat circumspect in these matters. It's for Jane's own good really. She worries too much and she enjoys preparing my lunch. It gives her something to do and I would hate to take such a joy away from her."

David smiled back and then looked down at his papers. He was working on an appeal in a case involving allegations of rape twenty years earlier. It did not look hopeful to him however and he was struggling to find any arguable grounds.

Bill interrupted his thoughts, "David I wondered if you could spare me just a few minutes of your time? I have just been told by John that a firm called Rooney something or other, are going to instruct me in a murder case for trial in September this year. Are there any recent Court of Appeal or House of Lords cases on murder that I should be aware of?"

David looked up from his papers and could not hide the surprise etched all over his face. Rooney Williams? A firm which had instructed him regularly, and for which he had obtained good results, but which had not instructed him for over a year, were now sending a murder trial to Bill? Of all people? Bill didn't even know that the House of Lords had been replaced by the Supreme Court in October 2009! David was shocked. His own diary was empty for September. Why hadn't he been instructed in this murder, he wondered? He would have to go and have a private word with John.

CHAPTER 8

THE SENIOR CLERK

David gave Bill a potted history of the recent decisions on murder cases but, as neither knew the facts of the case, he was unable to suggest any particular ones that might be relevant to his case. So, after the briefest of lessons, David returned to reading his appeal papers, unable to shake the image of Bill's smug expression as he had sat across from him earlier. He thought it would probably be about time to take John out for a drink soon, just to see how chambers was doing generally and, more specifically, how his own practice was looking!

At 6pm, David wandered casually into the Clerks room and took one look at John who was still seated at his desk and suggested they catch up over a drink, "Not to discuss anything specific, just to discuss general matters."

John smiled and nodded in agreement, knowing full well what 'general' chambers' matters David wanted to discuss!

A new wine bar had opened in Fleet Street, somewhat unimaginatively called, 'Briefs'. Within half an hour, David and John had occupied one of the red leather booths and were sipping a couple of glasses of passable house claret.

David looked around and recognised a few faces around the room including His Honour Judge Tanner, who was standing at the bar talking to a couple of senior criminal barristers. As the judge looked in his direction, David gave a slight nod in acknowledgement. It doesn't hurt to be polite, he thought, even if it's not genuine. Tanner just ignored him and looked away. No change there then, thought David.

He chatted with John about irrelevant matters, such as the weather, holidays and families before broaching the subject he was really interested in.

"So John, how are things in Chambers?"

John smiled and took a sip of wine before replying. "Everything is reasonably good. We've been a bit understaffed recently. As you know Tony left us to become a first junior clerk in a commercial set of chambers but we were lucky and soon replaced him with Nick Gobright."

He frowned thoughtfully as he continued, "It's taken a little time to train him in our ways, and coupled with that, it hasn't helped that Asif has taken quite a few days off ill recently."

He then continued with a grin, "Apart from that, chambers is busy, although our income is down on last year due to the last round of legal aid cuts ..." He paused before continuing, "and of course we lost Mr Hawker, who was a high earner for chambers. We still haven't found a suitable replacement for him yet have we?"

David ignored the reference to Hawker, John knew full well he had been asked to leave chambers because of his unsavoury and unprofessional behaviour.

"That's good to hear." David took a sip of the claret before continuing. "Tell me, are all the tenants busy?"

John smiled, "Well, it's like always, some are very busy, a lot are busy, one or two are struggling, but the clerks' room does its best to get work for everyone."

David was starting to become irritated. It was obvious to him that John knew exactly what he was talking about and was avoiding answering the question, forcing him to be more direct than he wanted to be.

"How are our regular firms of instructing solicitors? Are we still getting the same amount of work from them?"

John had known all along where the conversation was headed and was enjoying himself but he realised it was time to deal with the subject head on.

"Yes, most of our regular firms are still sending their work to us. Some have taken on in-house solicitors and barristers, so the junior work has decreased but other firms are finding the cost of employing them to be too much and they are letting their in-house people go. That means they are referring more work to us."

He was about to continue, but David interrupted, "Are you referring to any firm in particular?"

John smiled. "Yes, Rooney Williams has just made one of their in-house people redundant, even though they have opened a new office in Brighton. Consequently, they are sending a murder brief into chambers for both a silk and a junior."

"Oh that is good news. Who are they sending that to?"

"Well Mr Martin has the junior brief. You'll recall our conversations in the past about him needing some more work and I'm happy to say I secured the murder brief for him."

David could wait no longer, "And who is getting the silk brief?"

John looked directly at David and took a long sip of the claret, holding the glass at an angle as if to check the viscosity and assuming the look of a true oenophile.

After a significant pause, he returned to the glass to the table. "Rooney Williams have instructed Mr Bretheridge on that."

Finally! David thought before adding, "A murder for Bill, that's good for him ..." He paused before continuing, "... although he hasn't really done much recently has he?"

John observed David's expression with a slight smirk before adding, "No, he hasn't but I'm sure it'll come back to him. It's like riding a bike isn't it?"

David paused before replying. He was going to have to be more direct. "Not quite! I know you clerks tend to think all we do is just turn up at court and read out a set of facts, it's not actually as easy as that."

He paused before continuing, "I've conducted a lot of good work for Rooney Williams in the past. I notice I've not had a new brief from them in ages. Do you know why that is?"

55

John took a further sip of his claret and acknowledged a clerk from a rival criminal set before replying, "Well sir, I think you know, everyone in the clerks' room knows you're an excellent brief, but solicitors can be difficult about such things. Jimmy Short still has not got over that business with the 'wine-fraud' and, quite frankly, he's not willing to use you at the moment."

David's smile turned into a grimace. John continued before David could say anything, "But don't worry, sir, I'm working on him and I'm sure he will send something soon. Just bear with me."

John noticed David's expression change to one of annoyance, "Not willing to use me? I've done some excellent work for that firm. The client in the wine-fraud case wanted to plead guilty and so he did. What has that got to do with anything?"

John looked down at his empty glass of wine and poured himself another and topped up David's glass before replying. "You know what some solicitors can be like. Jimmy Short is not an easy man to get on with. He thinks you should have fought the wine-fraud. He lost a lot of legal aid income from that plea. We both know that the client wanted to plead guilty but Jimmy conveniently forgets that. He now says he doesn't want to use you because you're not a 'fighter'. His words, not mine. Don't worry though, I know that's not true and I'll take Jimmy out soon for a long lunch and I'll put him right."

Another bottle of claret appeared and they both moved onto other chambers' issues before leaving.

David took a taxi back to his flat in the Barbican feeling slightly down. Everything had felt good just a short time ago. Now he had discovered that one of his former major instructing solicitors would not use him because they thought he was not a 'fighter'.

Great, that's all I need, he thought. My main instructing solicitors want to use Bill; a man who hasn't conducted a trial for years, a man who thinks the ten commandments are the only law you need to know and who thinks the only technical aid you need in a court room these days is a quill pen. Whereas I have conducted numerous murder cases for them and secured numerous acquittals for their clients and given them an excellent service in every case!

His taxi drew up outside his flat and he noticed a light was on inside. His mood suddenly changed. He had invited Wendy around tonight for dinner and she had obviously let herself in with a key he had given her. He immediately cheered up. He had a beautiful intelligent girlfriend who loved him. He jumped out of the cab, paying the driver and soon forgot the Jimmy Shorts and Rooney Williams of the legal world. After all, he knew there were plenty more solicitors out there so he had absolutely nothing to worry about.

CHAPTER 9

A NEW MAN

It was Tuesday 1st July and David was making his daily trek into chambers, more out of habit and a sense of duty than any real need. His diary for July, August and September was empty and he had offered to take Wendy on a well-earned holiday abroad. However, she was busy on cases and at the moment could not agree a convenient date. It was no surprise for him as this was a problem he had suffered throughout his career. Cases or returns from other barristers came in suddenly, or trials went on for much longer than expected. Booking a holiday was usually a last minute affair.

David had spent his days catching up on correspondence and enjoying leisurely lunches in and around the Temple. For the most part, he had avoided boozy lunches, mainly due to the influence and watchful eye of Wendy who he was seeing most evenings, much to his delight.

Bill had also been following his usual routine, arriving at chambers at almost exactly 9am, consigning his sandwich to the waste bin, then reading the Times and completing the cross word before going out for his customary undercover lunch. Today turned out differently though. As he was pondering the answer to fourteen down, John walked into his room, carrying two large lever-arch files of papers secured by a pink silk ribbon. He placed the brief on Bill's desk and announced, "Good news, sir, your brief has arrived."

With those few words he left the room before Bill could say anything. Bill put down his newspaper, number fourteen down would have to wait, he had work to do.

He looked at the brief and stared at it for a while as though it was an object from a distant planet. It had been such a long time since he had seen a brief in his own name that he felt a little uncertain what to do with it.

Finally, he untied the tape, carefully storing it in his desk. People were always loosing pink tape in these chambers and he had heard that the cost was now prohibitive. He would keep his safe.

He took the back sheet off the front of the file and looked closely at it to make sure it did have his name on it. Yes, there it was William Bretheridge QC, instructed to represent Paul Morris at the Lewes Crown Court on the charge of murder, leading Graham Martin.

He searched through the papers for the first document he wanted to read. The solicitor's instructions. These would guide him to where he needed to go in the file. He was surprised therefore to find that there were none. He looked closely through the papers to see if they had been placed somewhere else but they had not.

There was an accompanying letter addressed to "The clerk to William Bretheridge QC", but all that was written, "Herewith the instructions to counsel, should counsel have any questions, he should not hesitate to contact James Short of instructing solicitors."

Bill delved further into the file, looking for the client's proof of evidence and comments on the witnesses and exhibits. Again, he could find no work carried out by his instructing solicitors to assist him. All he found was an 'advocate's statement' by Graham Martin advising that legal aid should be extended to cover the instruction of Queen's Counsel and junior counsel. Clearly that had succeeded because there was a legal aid certificate with the papers announcing that legal aid had been extended. Fortunately, the advice provided a brief account of the facts of the case and a draft defence statement. Bill hoped this at least would give him some idea of what the case was all about!

At 10:00am David came into the room. By that stage number fourteen down was a distant memory to Bill and he had delved into the prosecution papers and was thoroughly enjoying an experience he had long forgotten. He looked like a new man. He saw David and cheerfully greeted him, "Hello David, my murder brief has arrived, and I'm just reading through the papers."

David looked at him and tried to hide the jealously he felt. He knew it was a mean thought, after all, Bill had not had a brief for years. He heard himself say, "Good for you Bill, I'm happy you've been instructed in a decent case by a good firm of solicitors."

Bill looked up from the papers and adopted a puzzled frown. "Good firm of solicitors David. I'm not sure about that. Do you know I have no instructions whatsoever from them. I have no idea what the client is saying, I don't even have his preliminary comments. There is an anodyne defence statement that tells me very little and that is it. I've a good mind to phone the solicitors and demand they send me some proper instructions."

David understood the frustration and would himself have liked to complain to Jimmy Short in the past for the same reason, but he knew that it would not help chambers. A number of junior tenants were starting to be instructed by Rooney Williams again and he did not want them deprived of work.

"No, I wouldn't do that yet Bill. I'd have a word with Graham who may have received some instructions that you haven't seen. Also he's probably had a few conferences by now and will be able to tell you what the defence is. I suspect he drafted the defence statement and, as you know, defence barristers see it as their duty to make them 'anodyne' despite the fact the courts try to convince them to add more detail. I'm afraid it's the experience now that a few firms of solicitors do not provide full instructions early on in a case due to legal aid cuts. They're not paid for the work they actually do on a case but are paid a sum based on the number of papers and length of the case, consequently some firms do less work on a case than they used to."

Bill muttered something to himself and continued reading as David seated himself at his own desk and tried to deal with the thorny question of what the answer was to fourteen down in the Times crossword. The solution had been thwarting him since breakfast.

As lunch approached David was somewhat alarmed to see Bill rummaging in his waste paper bin and begin to eat the contents of something he had found in there, whilst continuing to read his brief.

David had more exciting plans for lunch that day. Wendy had said she was likely to finish early at Southwark Crown Court, close to London Bridge and he had offered to take her to a nearby fish restaurant for a decent lunch.

He left the room just after 12:30pm, turning to take a curious quick look back at Bill as he was reading the brief. He could not help but note that Bill had not looked so happy for years. Purpose had returned to his hitherto aimless life. He felt a little embarrassed by his own feelings of jealousy earlier, after all, perhaps it was a good thing for both Bill and for chambers for him to be instructed on this case, even if he questioned Bill's ability to conduct it. No doubt time would tell!

CHAPTER 10

CHAMBERS' POLITICS

Wendy arrived at the restaurant only fifteen minutes late. It was situated just a short walk away from Southwark Crown Court. She was carrying a department store shopping bag with its contents bulging out. Clearly there had been a retail visit along the way.

As usual, the restaurant was busy but David had booked ahead and was sitting at a nice table in the corner drinking a glass of Chablis when she arrived. He was somewhat relieved to note she did not frown as she saw his large glass of wine.

"Hello beautiful", he said warmly, as he rose from the table and gave her a kiss on the lips. She smiled and kissed him back, and sat down as he poured her a glass of wine.

"Thanks," she said, "I need that after the morning I've had. The judge was an absolute pain and the prosecutor was so far up his own backside that I doubt he could see any daylight!"

He noticed a well-dressed, older female on the table opposite squirm as she listened in on the conversation, frowning at Wendy's frustration. David simply smiled as Wendy continued, "So how is my Head of Chambers today?"

David took the opportunity to refill his glass of Chablis, the first had gone down rather well.

"Well, I have another three month gap in my diary so I'm feeling far too relaxed. It's a pity we can't get away for a holiday."

She frowned at him, he had raised this issue a number of times recently and she was annoyed that he did not seem to understand her position. "David, you know it's difficult for me now. I have a lot of cases listed throughout the summer and don't really have a gap. I'm not a silk you know!"

She smiled and he instantly felt disarmed. He realised that he better move on. Pity though, he fancied lazing around on a beach next to her wearing a skimpy bikini. Then he thought to himself, she might look better in it. He smirked at his own humour. He saw her looking puzzled by his expression and he immediately put the thought behind him and decided to change the subject.

"I just left Bill in Chambers. I've known him for years but I don't recall seeing him as happy as he is now. It's surprising the effect a single brief can have on a barrister, even on old silks like me."

Wendy looked surprised, "I think it's shocking that Bill has been instructed on a murder trial. He simply isn't ready or able to conduct one. It's too long since he was last in court and I'm sorry, but I think he's going a bit senile. He keeps forgetting things. He thinks retired judges are still sitting and he has no idea who half the members of chambers are. The other day he asked me who I was and if I was a solicitor visiting chambers!"

David smiled, "Well at least I haven't made that mistake yet."

She looked at him with the same look a mother might give a naughty child, "Really David, it's not a laughing matter. We know that there is a lot less work out there. With legal aid cuts, challenges from in-house advocates and generally less people being charged, it's becoming far more difficult to make a living. We can't afford to have senile old duffers making it worse for the juniors in chambers by annoying our instructing solicitors with negligent advocacy."

David looked surprised. "That's a bit harsh. Bill is certainly no youngster, but he's not a 'senile old duffer.' Yes, he hasn't conducted a case for some years but he has probably conducted more in the past than you and I put together. I think he will probably do a good job. It's like riding a bike, you never forget how to do it."

Wendy raised her eyebrows before dismissing his comment with, "Ok, shall we order?"

A few minutes later they had both ordered and sat in silence sipping their Chablis. David looked at her and placed his hand on hers, "Wendy, we shouldn't argue about this. I didn't get Bill the brief and it's not for me to try to take it away, even if I agree with you and think he's not the right man for the job."

She sipped at her wine before answering, "I know David. It's just so annoying. You should have been given that brief. You would do a superb job and that would be in the best interests of chambers, as well as your own. I won't say more about it now but I am concerned. Graham offered to show Bill some of the papers before legal aid was granted for a silk. Graham told him that these solicitors won't provide any adequate instructions. Bill said he wasn't interested in looking at the papers until there was a silk certificate and then said he won't cross-examine unless he is provided with, I quote, 'typed written instructions'. We all know that Rooney Williams rarely provide adequate instructions but they are a big firm with lots of

68

work and we can't afford to lose them because Bill makes complaints to them."

David nodded, "Graham's an excellent advocate, he will probably have numerous conferences and provide better instructions than Rooney Williams could ever provide. It won't be a problem."

Wendy shook her head and raised her voice slightly, much to the apparent horror of the woman opposite. "You know it's not as easy as all that. Bill is not up to date with the law or procedure. In any event, it's a murder case and not an easy one at that. Graham tells me that from his reading it's likely to be a cut throat defence. Bill will not only be up against the prosecutor, Tim Adams, who we all know is as excellent as he is obnoxious, he will also have to deal with co-defending counsel. I just don't think he will be up to it and you really should do something about it."

David looked round as a waitress approached the table. He gave her a look that probably lingered a little longer than intended and then changed the subject. "Excellent, the oysters have arrived."

Wendy gave him a knowing look in return and decided to drop the subject. She reached out across the table and squeezed his hand lovingly.

David gave her a large grin and they enjoyed their meal together chatting and complaining about judges.

An hour and a half later both returned to chambers after a stroll along the south side of the Thames past the New Tate Gallery and then across the Millennium Bridge.

Wendy went into Chambers first and a few minutes later David followed. Although everyone in chambers knew about their relationship, neither wanted to advertise it.

As David made his way to the silks' room he passed Tim Adams. Tim bore an annoyingly smug grin upon his face. "Hello David, how are you? Busy I trust?"

It was clear that Tim had no interest in the answer to that question but David decided to answer with an equally insincere smile and response. "Yes thanks, I'm fine. How are things with you?"

"Great, thanks. I'm really busy at the moment. I've managed to build up an excellent contact with the CPS down in sunny Brighton and they are starting to send me some great work."

His grin turned into a condescending smirk "I understand that my next murder is against a member of chambers. That's excellent news for me. If I can secure a conviction, I'll be guaranteed lots more CPS work and we all know Brighton is a busy area for crime."

David adopted a serious expression as he answered, "Tim, we both know that we should not seek results in prosecution cases. We should only present the facts and allow the jury to make up their own minds."

Tim's grin slowly sagged as he wondered whether David was being serious. His beaming grin returned as he replied, "Of course David, I know what my duty is. I should re-phrase that. If I provide an excellent service, as opposed to securing a conviction, then I hope to be instructed again. It's an excellent opportunity for chambers and the case is overwhelming. I don't think anyone, especially Bill, would be able to do much with it."

David glanced at him with a look of contempt and went into the silk's room.

He looked over to Bill who was now completely surrounded by papers having removed them from his lever arch files. He was still seated in the same spot, and was buried in the case. However, David noticed there was a change in his demeanour. He looked pale and a lot less happy than he had just a couple of hours before.

CHAPTER 11

THE OLD TENANT

A week had passed and Bill was still reading the papers and bemoaning the lack of any instructions from his client. A package of CDs had arrived containing taped records of the defendants' interviews and a couple of DVDs had been served on him providing compilations of CCTV evidence. Once Bill had opened the packaging he went to see Graham in an adjoining room.

He threw the packages down on Graham's desk. "What am I supposed to do with these?"

Graham shuddered inwardly before replying, "Hi Bill, good to see you."

Bill merely groaned in response. Graham picked up the CDs. "These are the taped recordings of the defendants' interviews. As they both made no comment we don't have to study them in any depth. I just passed them on to you in case you wanted to hear the way the officers put their questions."

Bill looked at him, astonished at the suggestion, so Graham moved on. "The DVDs are a compilation of CCTV evidence from various cameras around the area. They come with a police programme which you can load onto your computer so you can see the various camera angles. They are not very helpful to us, showing as they do, our boy in the area at the right time, but at least they don't show him stabbing anyone, or even carrying a knife."

Bill frowned as he replied. "I do not possess a computer, nor do I want to. They get in the way of good advocacy. All you hear in court these days is someone tapping away on a keyboard. It's really off-putting."

Graham was tempted to ask how he knew this, bearing in mind Bill hadn't been in court for years, but that would be unkind. He decided to move on. "I can show them to you on my computer Bill."

Bill again looked surprised. "Thank you but I don't need to see them. I shall see them in court no doubt. As they don't show the incident and I understand from you that our client owns up to being in the area, I don't need to trouble myself with irrelevant compilations of moving pictures."

Graham couldn't be bothered arguing so he just took the discs back and locked them in his desk drawer. He rather hoped that Bill would go away and let him get on preparing his brief for tomorrow, but Bill had other ideas.

"Do we have any instructions from the solicitors yet? This case will be on us in two months and we do need to know what the issues are."

Graham had tried to explain that detailed instructions would not be forthcoming but that he would put something together from his conference notes. He decided to try a different tack.

"Don't worry Bill they will be coming shortly." Even if I have to create them myself from my own notes, he thought.

"I hope so. I shall need to see the client soon and from what I have seen I shall have to tender a strong advice. It looks to me like he ought to consider pleading to manslaughter or if that is not acceptable to the prosecution, even murder!"

Graham inwardly groaned. He had by now conducted three conferences with the client and with Jimmy Short and the only contribution that Jimmy had made was that the case against the client was a weak one and that it had to be a fight!

"No worries Bill, I'll ensure you have all the instructions you need and then we can arrange a conference with the client. I think you will find the case is far from hopeless when you have had a chance to read all the papers."

74

Bill looked at him with a surprised look. "The point of instructing Queen's Counsel is for him to make this judgment call. In any event as you know, juniors have, 'conferences', Queen's Counsel have, 'consultations'."

He turned quickly and left the room as Graham's jaw dropped. Silly old fool, he thought, he's acting like something out of a Dicken's novel. This isn't the nineteenth century.

He wondered for a moment before having the added thought, God, thinking about it, he was probably called to the Bar then!"

CHAPTER 12

THE CONSULTATION

David strolled into chambers at 10 after another lazy lie-in. It was Thursday 17th July and he had not received a brief and was bored with the lack of work and consequent lack of income.

In the last week he had also seen very little of Wendy, who was involved in a difficult rape trial in the Old Bailey and had to work on the case every evening.

He said his usual 'Hello!' to the clerks, noticing that neither John nor Asif were there, so he spoke to the new first junior, Nick Gobright. "Morning Nick. Where's John today?"

Nick stopped chewing on his breakfast burger that he had purchased on his way in to chambers for long enough to throw his head back in an attempt to contain the half masticated fast food in his mouth while answering, "He's out with a solicitor, sir."

David wanted to grimace at Nick's mouthful but he was more interested in where his senior clerk was.

"Which solicitor?" he asked. "Where have they gone, spot of golf and beer as usual?"

Nick was taken aback. He had never had to answer questions like this in his previous chambers. No one would dare ask where the senior clerk was. He was the boss, he could do as he pleased without being challenged by mere barristers.

"I believe he is with Jimmy Short, sir. Jimmy invited him to a golf day and John has gone to try and drum up some more business. John said something about getting some silk briefs in before he left."

David smiled at the all too transparent answer. He had heard some of the less charitable members of chambers had already made a play on Nick's name and nickname him, 'Gobshite' as a result of his apparent inability to tell the truth. David had no doubt that John had been invited to a golf day by the odious little Jimmy Short, but he doubted very much there was going to be any meaningful discussion about getting a silk brief into chambers let alone more than one!

"Well if he phones in will you ask him to contact me. Thanks."

"Certainly, sir," answered Nick nodding furiously as he wiped the tomato ketchup off his face.

David looked at Asif's empty desk, "Where's Asif?"

Nick hesitated slightly before answering, "He phoned in sick...."

Nick screwed up the burger wrapper and threw it in a bin next to him as he added under his breath, "...again!"

David caught the comment but did not respond as Nick stared innocently back at his computer screen.

David made his way into the silks' room, for a moment toying with the idea of going out for a breakfast burger, but he thought of Wendy's slim hips and disapproving frown and decided to forgo that particular pleasure.

He paused outside the door of his room for a moment. No doubt Bill would be in there, slaving away over his brief, waiting to ask David more questions about recent developments in the law. Oh well I've got to face him sometime he thought as he pushed the door open.

He was surprised to find a vacant room. He walked over to Bill's desk and noticed it was remarkably tidy. No papers strewn around and no sign of Bill. He even checked the waste paper bin to see if there was any sign of Bill's lunch, but the bin was empty. He smiled in relief, and looked forward to having the room to himself for the day with no interruptions.

Two hours later David had finally finished the crossword and countless cups of filter coffee. Slightly wired on caffeine he gazed out of the window at the Temple Gardens, which were bathed in a golden noon sunshine. He thought about his clerk enjoying the beautiful summery day on the golf course, what a job to be a senior clerk he thought almost enviously. As he did so, his mobile phone rang. It was John.

"Hello sir, I understand that you wanted to speak to me?"

David could hear noise in the background including the voice of Jimmy Short shouting, "Same again John? Freddy's buying?"

David quickly responded, "Thank you John. I understand that you are out on a 'golf day' with Jimmy Short. Good of you to call." He had tried not to sound sarcastic but merely friendly, but wasn't sure he had succeeded.

"That's right sir. Jimmy invited me along to meet a few of his firm. I thought it a perfect opportunity to network and see if we can get any more work into chambers."

"Good, any discussion about silk briefs?"

John paused before answering, and wondered what Nick might have said, "Not yet, but don't worry, I'm working on him to send us some more work."

"Good, well keep at it. I shall look forward to hearing what you've achieved later on."

There was silence on the other end of the line. David decided to ask about Bill. "I notice, unusually, Bill's not in chambers today, do you know where he is?"

"I'm afraid I can't help you there. I know he's got a consultation in his murder case today, perhaps he's going straight there from home."

David nodded to the receiver before adding, "Oh well John, have a round on me."

He couldn't help adding the golf pun, knowing full well there would be more drinking than golfing with this lot. John in turn could not resist responding, "Thank you sir, very generous, I shall ensure that everyone here knows you've bought the next round of drinks!"

Damn!

The conversation ended and David returned to the scenic view from his window, making a mental note to curb his sarcastic humour in future!

A couple of hours later, Graham was seated in the canteen in the visitors' centre at Lewes prison. Today was the first client consultation with Bill and frankly Graham was dreading it. He had produced a proof of evidence and comments on the witnesses, based upon his conference notes, but he knew Bill was still unhappy and talking about a plea of guilty. Worse still, Jimmy Short was not going to attend today, something about taking a few clerks out for a boozy golf day.

"You know the sort of thing Graham," Jimmy had boasted earlier to him, "one hour of golf and then five in the bar. I've invited clerks from different chambers so they can all compete to buy me drinks!"

If Bill managed to persuade the client to plead guilty, Jimmy would undoubtedly blame Graham as well and that would be the end to that lucrative source of work. Graham had precious few other sources of work at the moment and he needed to protect this one. He expected trouble ahead with old Bill.

He looked at his watch. It was 1:55pm and the consultation was supposed to start at 2pm! He was getting worried, Bill should have been here well before now. He offered Debbie another coffee. She was conducting work experience with Jimmy's firm. She was only eighteen years old and Graham wondered how appropriate it was for Jimmy to send her to meet a client charged with murder. She was so young, a petite, blonde, girl who was clearly very inexperienced in life. Graham had already discovered that she knew nothing about the case.

He watched the clock as it passed 2 pm. He would have phoned Bill but for the simple fact that Bill did not believe in using mobile phones and, as far as Graham was aware, had never been seen to touch one, let alone use one. He did not even have a number for Bill so he sat and waited and tried to make small talk with Debbie to spare any embarrassment.

It was soon 2:20pm when Graham decided he had no choice but to phone the clerks in chambers. They too were unable to discover what had happened to Bill. Finally, he decided that he had no choice but to go and see the client alone, with Debbie tagging along for the ride. If he left it any longer, the prison would not let him in.

Within twenty minutes they had made their way through security, walked through the prison grounds and arrived at the interview room. Ten minutes later, Paul Morris was ushered into the room and Graham made the introductions.

"Hello, Paul, this is Debbie from the solicitors' office…"

Paul immediately interrupted, "Where's my silk then?" he demanded. "I was told my silk would be here today. My cell mate, Gary, is charged with murder and he's got a trial after mine in October and he's seen his silk four times already!"

Graham hesitated before answering thinking, four times, must be another silk without much work.

"Paul, as you know, you were supposed to see Mr Bretheridge today. Unfortunately he hasn't been able to make it. I don't know why as he hasn't been able to get a message through to me, but I assure you, we will arrange another consultation next week and you will see him then."

Paul ignored him and turned towards Debbie. He looked her up and down with a look that made her feel distinctly uncomfortable. He licked his lips and then gave her a wink and a grin before asking, "Where's Jimmy then. He should be here, he told me he was going to give me my proof of evidence to read through."

Graham saw his task as placatory today and tried to reassure the client, "That's no problem, I've got copies here for you to keep."

He passed the documents over and Paul gave them a quick look before returning his attention to Debbie. He put his best smile on and asked, "How long have you been working for Jimmy then luv?"

Debbie was old enough to know the meaning of his look and blushed, "I don't work for them, I'm just doing some work experience before going to Uni," she answered shyly.

Paul continued smiling as his gaze moved from her face to her breasts. Then a thought hit him. "Work experience? What, you mean you're not even a fucking solicitor? What's going on here?"

Graham tried to calm him but it was hopeless. Paul was on remand for murder, he had acquired a certain respect among fellow inmates and expected an excellent service from his lawyers, knowing there would be many queuing up to take his case over if he wanted. He rose quickly from his seat. "I'm not saying anymore. You better tell Jimmy that he's got to be here early next week with my silk or I'm changing solicitors. There's already a few who've come to see me in here, offering to do my case. I'll give one of them a chance if I don't see Jimmy next week! And don't bring a fucking work experience girl next time," he ordered, giving Debbie a patronising smile as he got up.

A few minutes later Graham and Debbie left the room. Debbie was clearly embarrassed and a little upset, "Did I say something wrong Mr

Martin? I don't want Jimmy to think I've lost him the case."

Graham patted her gently on the shoulder before quickly removing his hand in case the gesture was misunderstood, "Don't worry Debbie, I've seen this type of behaviour many times. He was looking for a reason to get rid of us. It wouldn't have mattered what you said."

Two hours later, Graham arrived back in chambers. After a quick 'Hello' to the clerks he went to David's room and found David behind his desk reading a work of fiction.

"Hello David, have you got a moment?"

David looked up from his book, "Of course, delighted to be of assistance."

"It's about Bill. He never turned up at the consultation, at prison today, the murder case he is leading me on. No one knows what's happened to him. It's very strange! It might cost us the case! The client was furious."

David was genuinely surprised. "I know he's been working hard on this case so I'm surprised he didn't turn up. Have you spoken to John?"

"There's no point, he's with Jimmy Short and a bunch of clerks at a 'golfing day'. There's no point in disturbing him."

"A bunch of clerks? I thought he was out with a firm of solicitors?"

Graham didn't respond. He was in danger of losing a murder brief through no fault of his own, what did it matter who John was playing golf with?

He was just about to say something along those lines when Nick Gobright knocked on the door and came in. David turned towards him and noted the serious expression on Nick's face.

"What is it Nick?"

Nick cleared his throat, "It's Mr Bretheridge sir, we've just heard, he had a heart attack this morning. His wife has just phoned up from the hospital in tears, they don't think he's going to make it!"

David and Graham fell silent for a few seconds, staring at Nick. David was the first to break the silence. "That's terrible news Nick. Can you contact his wife and ask her if there is anything we can do."

Nick nodded silently and left the room. Graham hit the table with his fist. "Damn it, well that's the end of that case for me. The client was on the verge of sacking us today. He will definitely do so now."

David looked at him a little shocked. Graham saw the look and quickly changed his demeanour, "I'm sorry, that was selfish. Of course I'm just as concerned as you are for Bill, it's just I haven't had a decent case in months and now it looks like I'm going to lose this one."

He thought for a moment. "Unless you can lead me? Both Bill and I have discussed the case a few times with you. It won't take long for you to read into it. I've always said you should have been instructed on the case in the first place. Morris will certainly not be able to complain once you're on board."

David smiled, "Thanks for the compliment, but you're forgetting one thing. Jimmy Short has refused to use me in a case as he thinks I'm not a 'fighter'. I'm afraid you're going to have to find another leader and, by the sounds of it, pretty quickly. Now let's focus on Bill and see if there is anything we can do for him."

CHAPTER 13

NEGOTIATION

It was 9am and John was nursing a hangover after his golf day. He wondered for a moment why he had even gone there when he did not like Jimmy Short. The answer was simple of course, Jimmy Short was potentially a good source of work and as he had told John that clerks from rival sets were going, he had gone along to protect chambers' and his own interests.

Of course, a great deal of alcohol was consumed by all and today he was suffering the consequences. It had not helped that after Jimmy left, John carried on drinking with the other clerks, most of who were friends, even if he did not trust a single one of them. He only ever told them things he wanted spread around the Temple, it saved him having to do it himself!

John heard about William Bretheridge's heart attack when he was still at the golf club and after Jimmy had left. He had tried to contact Jimmy but could not get through. Now he was in the clerks' room waiting for an irate phone call from Jimmy. He did not have to wait long, at 9:10am Nick passed the phone to him.

"Jimmy Short on the line, Boss."

John nodded and reluctantly took the phone, "Hello Jimmy, good to hear back from you mate."

Jimmy immediately interrupted him. "What the fuck, what's wrong with the fucking silks in your Chambers? They'll all dropping down dead."

"Jimmy, Mr Bretheridge is not dead. He is in intensive care and I'm sure you'll appreciate he's a valued member of chambers and everyone here is very concerned about him."

"Yeah, well I'm concerned about losing a client. That stupid girl I sent along to the conference told him she was only a work experience girl. She should have told him she was a solicitor! Anyway, I've sent her packing and told her not to ask for any references from my firm."

John felt sorry for the girl, whose only mistake had been to answer the client honestly. He knew how unreasonable Jimmy Short could be. He really should not have sent a work experience girl to see a murder client instead of attending himself, and John also knew it would have been a criminal offence for her to tell a client she was a qualified solicitor! Still, needs must and he now had to try and keep two murder briefs in chambers.

"I understand Jimmy, it was a bit naïve of her to volunteer she was just a work experience girl, but now we have to see what we can do to keep the client happy."

"Well, you tell me what "we" can you do? You told me you didn't have any other silks, that's why you gave me that old fool."

John grimaced at the reference to Bill, but said nothing about it. "Well I do have another silk available who would be excellent for your case."

"Oh yeah, who's that?"

"My Head of Chambers, David Brant QC."

"Fuck off! Over my dead body. I'm never going to use that bastard again."

John was quiet for a few moments before he replied. "I understand your feelings Jimmy. I tell you what. You told me yesterday that you're at your London office today. What are you doing for lunch? I can book us a table at that pub you like, "The Feathers" in Fetter Lane. I can book a table for us, say around 1pm?"

Jimmy was silent for a few seconds before replying, "Let's make it earlier, say 12:30, I may have to ring round a few chambers this afternoon, to find homes for TWO murder briefs, a silk's and a junior's!"

John agreed and put the phone down. He turned to Nick, "I've got to meet Jimmy Short for lunch.

It might take a while. I'll leave the chambers in your hands. I'm sorry its two days running, particularly as Asif is away again."

Nick just smiled before adding, "No problem Boss, I'm used to it."

At 12:25 John was seated at a table upstairs in 'The Feathers'. It was an old pub but had recently been tastefully renovated and was rapidly becoming a favourite haunt of clerks entertaining solicitors. He looked around the oak panelled walls at the various pieces of art, and started thinking about his forthcoming lunch. I ought to get paid double for wining and dining Jimmy Short two days running!

At 12:45 Jimmy arrived suitably late, and was shown by the waitress to John's table.

"Alright John? Started without me then?"

He looked towards a pint of bitter that John had ordered and then turned to the waitress, "Bring me one of those would you luv," He ordered, creasing his face at her in what could only be described as a sleazy smile.

John took a large gulp of his beer, trying to mitigate the effects of yesterday's binge. "Good day out yesterday," he said trying to break the ice.

Jimmy frowned and replied, "Before you say anything else, I've made my mind up, I told you, I'm not using Brant ever again, so don't waste your breath. The only thing to discuss is whether I continue to use that junior of yours or appoint a whole new team from a different chambers."

John smiled, inwardly cringing as he realised it would take a lot longer to persuade Jimmy to use David. My poor liver he thought, and tried to recall briefly where he had last seen his pack of indigestion tablets. Was it in his desk at chambers or his bedside table? He would have to send Nick out for some later.

"Of course, Jimmy, I understand. Shall we order some food before we talk about that?"

David arrived in Chambers at 1pm. He had travelled to St. Gregory's hospital that morning to see Bill. He had not been allowed into his room to see him but he had seen Bill's wife, Jane. He did not stay long as the whole affair was terribly depressing and there was really nothing he could do. He had known Bill for years and had always expected him to be around for ever. It seemed so unfair that Bill got his first decent brief in years and then keeled over with a heart attack. The two were obviously related and he regretted that he had not done something when he first heard that the Bill was instructed.

Of course, in reality, he realised there was nothing he could have done. He could hardly have taken the brief from him or suggested it was too much for him without appearing condescending or worse, jealous. Nevertheless, he could not help but feel partly responsible for Bill's condition.

He passed by the clerks' room and noticed that John was not there. He spoke to Nick. "Where's John today then? Another boozy lunch? Another crucial touting expedition?" he asked sarcastically.

Nick looked up from his computer screen. It was masked from David and fortunately he could not see that Nick was writing inappropriate comments on a social media page.

"John's taken Jimmy Short to lunch."

David looked surprised, "What? Again? Are those two joined at the hip?"

Nick knew where his loyalty lay.

"He's discussing Mr Bretheridge's brief. Apparently Jimmy wants to pull both briefs from chambers now, John is trying to prevent him. He said he was going to do his best to get you the silk brief."

David could hardly argue with that even though he doubted it. "Ok, well could you tell him I would like to see him when he comes in?"

David noticed Asif's empty chair. "Where's Asif? Ill again?"

"Afraid so sir. He phoned in and promised he would be here next week ... with a sick note."

David just frowned and nodded, and made his way to his room.

John looked down at his watch. It was just past 4pm and Jimmy had consumed his eighth pint of bitter. John had tried to match him but moved onto shorts after six pints. Both had enjoyed steak and ale pies with the bitter and John had started to feel a little better for it. Hair of the dog, he supposed.

Jimmy was his usual self, full of banter and boasts about the amount of work his firm had and how excellent members of rival sets were. They had discussed the legal aid cuts and other political aspects of the criminal legal business. He had made various rude comments about members of John's chambers which John had just smiled dismissively at. But with a few drinks in him, Jimmy now looked as if he might be more approachable.

"Look Jimmy, I've known you for years and I've worked with your firm for longer than I can remember. I'm grateful you've given a lot of my juniors an opportunity to build a practice at the Bar. I'd like to repay that. I don't want to see you lose out on this case."

Jimmy looked at him quizzically through slightly glazed eyes.

"It's like this Jimmy. I'm afraid I don't know where Mr Bretheridge keeps his briefs, I suspect it's at his home and I'm sure you understand, I don't want to disturb his wife at a time like this. By the time I've got it back and then sent it on to another silk in another chambers, it's going to be the middle of next week before they even start to look at it. There won't be time to organise a consultation with the client until the following week at the earliest and I understand from Mr Martin that your client has already made threats to instruct another firm if he doesn't see his silk next week."

Jimmy glared at him. "I've told you I don't want Brant. He doesn't fight cases. I need a fighter."

John nodded, "Jimmy, I know you value our friendship and as a friend I have to speak bluntly."

He hesitated to see the effect on Jimmy who tried to raise an eyebrow.

"You know that Mr Brant didn't do anything wrong in that wine fraud. The client wanted to plead guilty and there was nothing Mr Brant could do once he did. David is a good silk. He's got some great results for your firm and he is a fighter. He already knows a lot about the case because both Mr Martin and Mr Bretheridge have asked his advice. It won't take him long to read into it and he'll be ready to have a conference next week."

Jimmy still looked perplexed as he announced, "I've got to go to the loo," he said, curling one side of his face up at John in a smirk.

John watched him as he staggered away, wondering whether he had broached the subject a little too early. Should I have waited till he had another pint in him, he thought?

Five minutes later Jimmy returned.

"What's wrong with your leg mate?" asked John, "Not got the gout have you?"

"No, a football injury, last Sunday. My son can outplay me now. I'm gutted. Anyway, I've been doing some thinking."

He smiled secretly at a personal thought, "Funny how I always think best when my todger is in my hand. Brings me down to earth."

96

He let out a guffaw as John nodded and offered a polite laugh, whilst trying desperately to put the image out of his mind.

Jimmy put out a hand onto the table to steady himself, "All right, I'll use Brant and you can keep the junior brief as well. He better fucking fight it this time or I'll withdraw all my firm's work from your chambers and you'll never see another brief from me or anyone from my firm ever again."

John gave him a reassuring smile, momentarily thinking how nice it would be not to deal with the Jimmy Shorts of the world, but he soon thought of the success he had just achieved. After all, times were difficult at the criminal bar. He couldn't afford to get rid of Jimmy's work, however odious the man was.

At 5pm, John staggered into chambers thinking that after another hard week pulling in the briefs, he really did deserve a pay rise.

Nick smiled as he watched him stagger through the door again. He won't last long if he carries on like this, he thought. It won't be long before I have his job.

John misunderstood Nick's smile.

"That's the way to do it Nick", he preached. "Not only have I kept Mr Martin's junior brief in chambers, I've got Jimmy Short to brief David Brant again!"

Nick nodded as the smile fell from his face. Damn, he thought. Maybe some other chambers will need a senior clerk soon? "Great news Boss. You're the best in the business. By the way, Mr Brant asked to see you as soon as you return."

"Excellent. I need to see him too!"

John made his way carefully to the silks' room. He did not want his Head of Chambers to realise how much he had been drinking. He knocked on the door and entered as David shouted to come in.

David saw John almost stagger into the room smelling strongly of alcohol. This would not do, what example did this set to the other clerks and what would the tenants think if David allowed this?

"John have you been drinking again?"

John tried to assume a look of utter sobriety, "I've had a few. Had to, I was with Jimmy trying to build bridges. You know how much he puts back. The beer hardly touches the sides of the glass!"

"John, you look like you've had more than a few to me. Obviously I expect you to go out and entertain solicitors, but I expect you not to get drunk, especially if you are coming back into chambers!"

John slurred his words, "I've got you the murther brief."

"What?" asked David, truly shocked. John took a deep breath before continuing slowly, "I have got you the murder brief," he repeated slowly. "I spent the afternoon with Shimmy Jort..,"

He paused, and closed his eyes for a second before continuing, "... sorry, I mean, Jimmy Short. He wanted to pull Mr Martin's brief. I persuaded him to keep Mr Martin and then I persuaded him to brief you as the leader."

David was lost for words. He could hardly reprimand his senior clerk in those circumstances. "Well done John! However, I suggest it is in everybody's interest that you go home now. We'll discuss this on Monday."

"OK, the brief should be there on Mr Bretheridge's shelf. He never takes his papers home. You can read it this weekend."

David nodded and got up and went to Bill's shelf as John left the room.

There it was. Bill's last and only brief in years. How sad, he thought. It lay, in almost pristine condition, neatly tied in pink ribbon with Bill's tiny writing on the back sheet. The writing just referred to the time that Bill had so far worked on the case.

David sighed but knew deep down this was the right result. He would take it home and read it over the weekend. He had hoped to see Wendy but she was meeting an old friend on Saturday and had to work on a case on Sunday. It was a perfect opportunity to get to grips with this case and be prepared for a consultation early next week. Although the circumstances were sad, for Bill, things were beginning to look up again for him.

It occurred to him in that moment that the only cases he had recently had were both returns from silks taken ill. In fact, he thought, the only reason I became Head of Chambers was because my Head of Chambers, also a silk, became ill. Maybe it was time he went for a check-up?

CHAPTER 14

WEEKEND OF MURDER

It was Saturday morning and David was looking forward to reading into his new brief.

It was amusing to him that things happened in reverse at the Bar. Most people would be enjoying a weekend not working, but he was looking through the papers in the Paul Morris case after spending the preceding week doing nothing at all!

He pulled the knot out of the traditional pink ribbon which secured the papers, and spread the various sections of the brief across his desk. He did not bother to look for the solicitors instructions, he knew Rooney Williams only too well. He did look through Graham's notes though, which gave him significant details about the case and a useful chronology of events.

It appeared on the face of it to be a straight forward case. Graham's notes dealt with the background. Paul Morris was 19. He lived in Moulsecoomb, near Brighton and had lived in that area all his life. Most of the time he had lived with his parents, although it appeared that when he was seventeen he had been thrown out by his father and lived in a hostel for a few months.

He returned home when he was 18 and got involved in petty crime until a serious incident with his father led to him being thrown out on Saturday, 25th January 2014.

The prosecution were seeking to rely on the incident as evidence in the case against Paul because on 12th June 2014, he was convicted at Lewes Crown Court of causing wounding contrary to section 20 of the Offences Against the Person Act 1861. The prosecution supplied a copy of the conviction and a brief prosecution summary. It alleged that on Saturday, 25th January 2014, there was an altercation with his father in the home and the father had told him to get out. Paul had a knife in his hands and had lunged at his father and cut three knuckles on the back of his father's right hand. It was a minor injury and no hospital treatment was required. David noted that there was no reference to what the defence to the charge had been, nor any comment by Paul about the incident in the papers.

The prosecution note went on to say that Paul had been arrested on Monday, 27th January, and had simply denied the offence without further explanation. On Tuesday, 28th January, he had been granted bail by a Magistrates Court, with one condition that he reside at his Uncle Daniel's address. It was a specific condition of his bail that he was not to return to his parent's home before his trial.

According to Graham's note, on Thursday, 6th March, there was an incident with his Uncle and Paul was thrown out of the address. The police were not informed and Paul was in breach of his bail conditions when he returned to his parents' home.

When he was 17, Paul had become friendly with Michael Ward. They had both been living at the same hostel at the time. They had kept in regular contact since. Michael Ward is a young black male, with a large afro hairdo. He had, it seemed, been disowned by his parents and lived in hostels from when he was 15.

According to Paul, Michael made a living by selling cannabis wraps worth £10-20 a time, and this was how they met Danny Williams who dealt cannabis in the same area. There was some friction between the two as a result.

At about 10:50pm on Saturday, 3rd May 2014, Danny Williams had followed Paul and Michael to Paul's address, and that was when Danny had thrown two bottles through Paul's windows, causing some minor cuts to Paul from the flying glass. Michael was unhurt, though, according to Paul, a bottle almost hit him.

David read how police were called to the scene by neighbours and how Paul told them who had thrown the bottles. He then took the police to Danny Williams' address. Whilst reading this, David took particular note of the fact that the police had told Paul that they would return to Danny's address in the next few days.

However, he noted that the police did not apparently return until the early hours of 6th May. By that time Danny was dead.

Danny had been seen by social workers on the day before his death. Two of them, Lisa Thomson and Jenny Wright, had visited his address on the afternoon of 5th May. Both had known Danny for some time. Both described their roles as 'Leaving Care Personal Advisors', whose function it was, 'to help people to integrate into general public life after they have spent many years in care'.

Danny had not lived there for that long. He had moved in on Friday, 18th April 2014, after spending years in care in the same area. They both described him as potentially having some mental health issues due to long term heavy use of cannabis, although he had never been hospitalised or been advised to see a psychiatrist.

They described seeing him twice a week since he moved into the flat. They had noticed deterioration in his condition in that time. From initial euphoria at having his own place, he rapidly became depressed. The flat was always a mess when they visited, with dirty pots, plates and cutlery, as well as half eaten, maggot-infested takeaways strewn across the floor.

Both of them had noticed how depressed he appeared on 5th May, and both claimed in their statements that they decided to recommend that he be seen by a psychiatrist because of his state. They also noticed that two of Danny's windows were smashed and had been boarded up to keep out the elements. When they asked Danny what had happened, Lisa claimed that he had told them a white boy and a black boy he knew had caused the damage. Jenny specifically recalled him referring to the black boy as "Afro".

David moved on to read through the statements of a number of neighbours who lived near to Danny's address.

He read Richard Brooks' account of previous incidents he had witnessed as well as what he witnessed on the fatal night. He noted that Richard believed the first incident on that night occurred at 12:45am.

He read Shereena and Lloyd Bennett's accounts of that night, noticing the conflict in their descriptions.

He noted that all had attended video identification parades and all had picked out Michael Ward as someone they recognised from that night, but no-one had picked out Paul Morris.

David read through the expert evidence quickly. The pathologist was the highly experienced Dr Herbert Rogers. David had come across him in previous cases he had conducted in London and Lewes. He was about fifty and had been a pathologist for the best part of twenty years. He was very good at his job, although in David's opinion, he was a little too dogmatic at times. He would tend to be adamant that his opinion about the cause and manner of death was an accurate one and rarely accept any other possibility even if it was suggested by an eminent colleague.

Herbert Rogers had seen the body on 6th May and given the cause of death as a stab wound to the heart. He concluded that death would have occurred quickly and that severe force would have been used to inflict this particular wound, which was consistent with an intention to kill.

Louise Harley, a forensic scientist specialising in blood and urine analysis had examined the deceased's blood and urine. There were no traces of alcohol in either sample, so she had concluded that obviously he was not under the influence of alcohol at the time of his death. However, there were traces of tetrahydrocannabinol (THC) suggesting he had either been smoking cannabis shortly before his death and/or was a heavy user which would be the other reason to account for why it was still be in his system.

David went to the kitchen to refresh his mug of coffee before returning to a desk in his bedroom to read the witness statements from the police officers.

Police Constable John Foster and Police Constable Stephen Richards had both given statements about the earlier incident and Police Constable Foster had made a further statement about recognising Morris, Ward and Dickson on the CCTV video had been shown to him.

Detective Constable Barry Nicholas arrested Paul Morris at 4:55am on 9th May 2014, at his father's home. Paul's alleged reply to being arrested on suspicion of murder was, 'Fuck off pig, I ain't done no murder. I don't even know the kid.'

David looked at the statement again. Although it was not an admission, it had all the hallmarks of an old-style 'police verbal' which he had seen so many times when he had just started off in this career, before the "PACE" legislation came into being. This was an acronym for the Police and

Criminal Evidence Act 1984, which was introduced to impose safeguards when suspects were arrested and interviewed by the police. In the days, before "PACE", some police officers would invent comments made by suspects on arrest, to give the jury a bad impression of the defendant before he gave evidence in court.

David questioned whether a young man would really call the police 'pigs' in this day and age? He made a note on the page to check this allegation with the client when he saw him at their consultation next week.

David read on, noticing that it was already past 5pm. He wondered whether to phone Wendy but decided not to. She was seeing her friend tonight and he did not want to give the impression that he was checking up on her. He continued working on the brief and was making good progress getting to grips with the relevant facts.

The next statement he came across was the evidence of the interviewing officer, Detective Sergeant Mark Crook. Clearly Jimmy Short had done his job properly (something David could only reluctantly admit), as Paul had made no comments in interview. Neither had Michael Ward, so it was not possible to discover what the co-defendant would claim happened that night.

The remaining evidence he looked at was the CCTV evidence and phone evidence. Noticeably,

Paul had not been seen on CCTV before the incident, but could be seen immediately after, when Dickson joined him in the street. The phone evidence added little to the case. It just showed that Paul and Michael had been in communication on the days before the incident and after it. David noted that Paul had phoned Michael from his home phone at 12:48am on the day of the murder, just twenty to twenty five minutes before the murder took place.

Although Charlie Dickson had not been traced, the police had interrogated Michael Ward's mobile phone and found the same mobile number listed twice, once under 'Charlie', the second time under 'Dickson'. Clearly that was Dickson's phone and at 11:56pm there was a call from Ward to Dickson and at 01:08am there was a call from Dickson to Ward. The phone evidence showed they were in regular contact before the murder about two or three times a week.

There were also a number of other calls referred to, between Paul and Michael, over the days before the incident and a large number of calls between them after the incident up until the time of their arrests, but there were no excessive numbers of calls just before the incident, no 'spikes' in the call record, to suggest any real evidence of pre-planning.

The final evidence was a statement from DS Crook, stating he was present when Paul Morris was charged with murder on 11th May. The officer stated that the suspect replied to the caution by simply saying, "I didn't do it."

Noticeably, there was no forensic evidence of any of Danny Williams' blood, DNA or clothing fibres on any clothing seized from Paul, nor indeed any of Paul's on Danny's clothing.

David read through the proof of evidence in detail, which purported to set out the client's version and a document headed, 'client's comments on witnesses'. He knew both had been prepared by Graham. Ideally, he would have preferred more detail in both documents.

Paul's version of events was that there had been an incident where Danny had followed Ward and himself home and thrown a few bottles through his window. He assumed that this had something to do with Ward and Danny arguing but the statement did not give a reason.

In the early hours of the 6th May, he claimed he had phoned Ward from his parent's phone and asked him if he wanted to meet up. He had been bored at home and decided to go out. He came across Ward selling cannabis to Dickson. Almost immediately, Danny Williams appeared on the scene and a fight started. He did not want to get involved so had walked away quickly. A few minutes later Dickson had run up to him to ask if he knew what it was all about. He stated that he had told Dickson that Ward and Williams had a history of disputes over whose 'turf' it was to sell cannabis from.

David sat back and looked at the clock again. It was now 7:45pm. He wondered what Wendy was doing. Probably knocking a cocktail or two back, chatting endlessly with her girlfriend. He wondered what she was saying about their relationship. Was she revealing any secrets? Telling her friend more than he himself knew perhaps? Well, no matter he thought. He knew Wendy cared for him and it was probably time for him to open a bottle of his favourite 2006 Rioja Gran Reserva. He had been keeping it for a special occasion and now seemed as special as any.

He was content with his efforts that day. He had managed to read the bulk of the papers. He would spend tomorrow going through the 'unused' material, the evidence which the Crown were not relying on but which could assist the defence and which they were therefore obliged to serve.

Before looking at the unused material he had already formed an impression of the case. On the face of it Paul Morris had a good run at trial.

CHAPTER 15

RENEWING AN OLD ACQUAINTANCE AND MAKING A NEW ONE

David looked at his watch, it was 1:50pm and both he and Graham Martin were in the public canteen in the visitors centre at Lewes Prison. Jimmy Short had arranged to meet them there at 1:30pm but had not shown up yet. David had managed to read all the papers and had formed his own opinion of the merits of the case, which he now discussed with Graham as they waited.

"I note that Bill made a lot of notes throughout the papers with frequent references to 'plea'. However, having read everything, it strikes me that with the current evidence, it's quite a weak prosecution case. There are a number of eye witnesses to the scene, but no-one picked Paul out at the identity parades as being present. He made no comment in interview and the CCTV evidence only shows that he was in the vicinity of the killing, not that he was the murderer. Of course we don't know what the co-defendant will say, but at the moment he has a run on a not guilty plea."

Graham nodded as he added, "I agree David. I'm not sure why Bill was so pessimistic about his chances. Clearly there is evidence of bad blood between Paul and the victim, but that's a long way from proving he's guilty of murder. If one person disliked him, who is to say there were not others that bore a grudge! After all, he was a drug-dealer."

Both looked towards the door as they heard a shout from a familiar voice. It was Jimmy Short, nonchalantly walking into the canteen.

"Hello David! Great to see you, it's been too long!"

David acknowledged him with equal insincerity, "Jimmy it's great to see you to, I agree it's been far too long."

Jimmy turned to Graham and slapping him on the back, said, "Hi Graham, it's always good to see you too mate."

Graham grunted an inaudible reply. He had never been able to master insincerity, which he acknowledged probably explained the poor state of his practice.

Jimmy seemed in no rush and ordered a coffee. He took a sip and sat down before saying, "I'm glad we could get you on board, David. This is just your kind of case - a definite winner. There's no evidence against young Paul."

David nodded, how he hated the words, 'a definite winner.' In his experience there was no such thing. Also it put enormous pressure on an advocate, no doubt exactly what Jimmy wanted to achieve. After all, if the defendant was acquitted, it had always been a forgone conclusion and nothing to do with the advocate's skills. If he was convicted, the solicitor and client would assume it was the advocate's fault, whatever the reality actually was.

Thirty minutes later, the three of them were sitting in an interview room with Paul Morris. After initial introductions Paul asked the only question that was important to him. "So what's my chances, Mr Brant?"

David paused to give him time to phrase the answer properly. "All right Paul, I've read all the papers and discussed the case with your solicitor and Mr Martin. To date the evidence is not compelling. Yes you knew the victim, yes you knew Ward. You had some previous altercation with the victim but no one identifies you as being present when the murder took place even though the CCTV puts you in the vicinity. So far the evidence against you is weak and you have a good case."

Paul smirked, so before he got too confident, David added, "Of course, we don't know if the prosecution will serve any further evidence and we don't know what Ward will say. It's likely he will try to blame you to detract the jury from the strength of the evidence against him. We have to be prepared to deal with that."

David paused before continuing, "I understand he has been remanded here as well. Have you spoken to him? Do you know what he is going to say?"

Paul shook his head as he answered, "No he won't talk to me. He's in the same wing as me but he keeps avoiding me."

David nodded, "Then it's fair to assume that is on his lawyer's advice and he will blame you for the murder."

"I'm not guilty Mr Brant. I didn't do no stabbing."

David nodded ignoring the double negative and was about to speak when Jimmy interrupted and added, "Don't worry Paul, the jury won't believe him. They'll think he's trying to protect himself."

David gave a weak smile before continuing, "Very well, this is our first meeting and I intend to see you a few times before the trial, but there are a number of matters I'd like to cover today."

Paul shrugged his shoulders. "OK, I've got nothing to hide."

"Good. Now I see that you were arrested by a Detective Constable Nicholas."

"I don't know the police officers' names."

"I understand that. He was the officer who arrested you and he says when you were arrested on suspicion of murder, you replied, 'Fuck off pig, I ain't done no murder. I don't even know the kid.'

Did you really say that? I didn't think your generation called the police 'pigs' anymore?"

"Yeah I did".

David raised his eyebrows slightly before continuing,

"You said you didn't 'know the kid'?"

"Yeah I did."

"But you'd taken the police to his address just a couple of days before?"

"Yeah, but I didn't know his full name, did I?"

"They say you gave them the name Danny Williams."

"That's a lie, I never told them that. I said I knew him as 'Danny', I never knew his last name."

"Alright, now the prosecution are making an application to put your previous convictions before the jury as evidence of 'bad character'. I need to take you through those."

"What's 'bad character'?"

David paused before continuing, "In certain circumstances, the prosecution can put your previous convictions before the jury to demonstrate what is called 'propensity'."

David could see Paul's blank expression.

"To show that your convictions are relevant to the present charge because they are of a similar nature."

"I ain't murdered anyone."

"No, but they say your recent conviction where you used a knife to injure your father is relevant because it shows you are willing to use a knife to injure."

"That's shit, I didn't have no knife and he was only scratched and it was an accident."

Jimmy interrupted, "I can help you there. One of our firm picked up Paul's case as duty solicitor. We represented him at trial. One of our in house barristers represented him, Charlotte Williams. We weren't happy with the result, we thought Paul should have been acquitted. We've let her go since."

David remembered Charlotte from when he represented Damian Clarke at the Bailey. She was quite capable of being lazy as a junior to a silk but by all accounts when she conducted a case as the sole advocate she was very able. He suspected that Rooney Williams had 'let her go' for financial reasons not because of the result in one case.

He turned to Jimmy, "Tell me what happened in that case?"

Jimmy shrugged, "It should be in your brief."

"I have the prosecution application for bad character, a copy of the convictions and the prosecution's statement of facts, but I would like to know a little more."

Jimmy frowned before continuing. "Paul had an argument with his father. The father asked him to leave the house and Paul hit him. His dad claimed he had a knife in his hand and it cut him across the knuckles of his right hand. Paul said he had no knife and his dad hit out at him and damaged his knuckles when he hit the sharp edge of a kitchen door. In the end Paul's dad didn't want to support the prosecution but they forced him to come to court and give evidence. He said he couldn't remember what happened so the prosecution treated him as a hostile witness and put his witness statement to him which he then claimed was true. Paul was convicted by the jury of section 20 wounding. The sentence has been put back until after this case."

David turned towards Paul, "Is that what you remember of the case?"

"Yeah, I never had no knife. My dad made that up because he was embarrassed that he'd punched a door and hurt himself and he was annoyed with me for answering him back."

The consultation continued in the same vein for the next hour and a half with David asking various questions and Paul giving various answers. Eventually at 4pm they were told by the prison staff they had to leave.

Jimmy left them at the prison and David and Graham walked back to Lewes railway station popping into a local public house for a pint and post consultation meeting.

After they were served with two pints of the local bitter, Graham asked David, "So what did you make of Paul?"

David put his pint down, thinking before answering, "He's a young man probably with a mental age of someone a few years younger than his real age. He presumably had a poor relationship with his family and has now got into something very serious which he doesn't know how to handle."

"Did you believe him when he answered your questions?"

David paused again whilst he thought of an answer. "Sometimes, but frequently he was evasive or taking time to think of something to make up. If we are forced to call him as a witness and he acts like that in court, he'll be hopeless and he won't have a chance!"

CHAPTER 16

THE PHONE CALL

It was 5:10pm on Friday, 25 July and David was still in chambers. He had not seen Wendy for a whole week. She had been out with her friend on Saturday and then away in Leeds conducting a possession with intent to supply heroin case for the last five days. They had spoken a few times but it had been snatched conversations for short periods and had felt a little strained to him. Tonight she was due to come back from Leeds and he was hoping to spend the weekend with her.

He had been wondering whether he should try to advance the relationship to the next level. After all, they had been together for over eighteen months now.

Yes, perhaps it was time to ask her if she would like to live with him in the Barbican. The place was big enough for two and they spent most of their time there anyway when they were not appearing at a distant court.

He was warming to the idea. Perhaps he should take her out for a romantic meal and pop the question over a glass or two of champagne?

He did not realise he had a big beaming grin on his face as John walked into the room.

"Hello sir," John wondered what David was grinning about but thought better of asking and continued with his news, "I just wanted to tell you personally. I've had a call from Jane Bretheridge. It looks like Mr Bretheridge is going to pull through although obviously he won't be able to work again. Mrs Bretheridge says that the Doctors have told her that he will need to retire and rest."

"That is excellent news. Can you get one of the junior clerks to organise a card and some flowers from chambers?"

"Already done sir, I got Asif to do it."

"Excellent, well done."

For a moment David thought how efficient the clerks were, before quickly dismissing the idea. He then remembered that Asif had not been in chambers until today. "So Asif's recovered from his mysterious illness has he?"

John was quiet for a moment before replying, "It appears so and he has promised to bring in a Doctor's note next week."

"Good." John nodded as he left the room.

At 5:25pm David decided to call Wendy and suggest that romantic meal.

He phoned three times but there was no answer, just voicemail. He found this surprising, as she had finished in Leeds at lunch time with another acquittal and he expected her back in London by now.

Perhaps she went for a drink with the solicitor?

By 5:55pm he had left three answerphone messages and four texts but had still not received a response.

He could not believe that he could not get in touch with her. He was planning to invite her to live with him in an expensive flat in the Barbican, and make a life together and she could not be bothered to pick up the phone!

He sat in his room wondering if he should just pop to Briefs and wait for her to call. At least he could enjoy a glass or two of wine. However, his mobile then rang and he saw with a mixture of relief and delight that it was Wendy. For a moment he wondered whether he should ignore it but then realised how foolish that thought was.

"Hello, and how is sunny Leeds?"

Wendy paused before answering. "Leeds has been fine. We were acquitted and then I went for a quick drink with the solicitor."

Good, he thought, that explained why he could not get through to her.

"Are you back in London now? I thought it would be nice to have a meal together. It's been a while since we have seen each other."

Again there was a pause from the other end of the line.

"David, perhaps we should meet for a drink instead?"

David was surprised. "Why is anything wrong?"

"I can explain over a drink."

David gave a shrug to indicate he was not bothered, ignoring the fact that it could not be seen by Wendy. He then asked, "Shall we meet at Briefs?"

"No, I think it would be better if we met a little further away from chambers."

"Why?"

"Let's discuss it over a drink."

"Alright, but why all the mystery?"

"Let's meet at London Bridge. There's a nice wine bar there called 'Claret Smile', shall we say 7pm?"

"What kind of name is 'Claret Smile', it sounds like the name of a horror film." David was trying to make light of their somewhat serious conversation.

"I'll see you there, got to go now," she said. Shall we meet there at seven or not?"

David recognised the tone. Now was not the time to make facetious comments. "Ok, shall I wear a red carnation?"

He immediately regretted the comment.

"I'll see you at seven."

With that the phone went dead and David's cheery countenance changed to a puzzled frown as he looked at his phone. A moment ago, he had been thinking about asking Wendy to live with him! In time he would propose to her, in somewhere romantic like Venice and, finally, he would marry her and they would honeymoon in Rome and see his favourite sites again, this time, with the woman he loved instead of alone like the last few times. Only minutes on from these warm comforting thoughts, it sounded like she was going to dump him in some unpleasant little wine bar. What had gone wrong, he wondered helplessly?

CHAPTER 17

AN EVENING DRINK

At 7pm promptly, David walked through the door of the 'Claret Smile'. He noticed the place was packed with local office workers and doubted very much that he would find a table at this time of night but, to his surprise, he saw Wendy, seated at a table for two, with a bottle of Rioja Reserva open and a half empty glass of wine in front of her.

He looked at her from a distance. She was dressed in the same cocktail dress he had seen her in at that chambers party so long ago. She looked absolutely stunning.

He thought for a moment, why do women have to look so incredibly attractive when they are about to dump you? It brought back memories of his wife Sarah who got dressed up and put on her makeup before telling him to leave the house!

He approached the table slowly as Wendy looked up and gave him a pleasant smile.

Perhaps I'm being silly, he thought. She's not dumping me after all.

"Hello David, it's nice to see you."

Perhaps things are not so bad, he thought, and lent towards her to kiss her on the lips. She moved her head to the side and it landed on her cheek instead.

He frowned wondering if his suspicions may have been right after all.

"It's nice to see you as well." Was all he could manage to say before sitting down, feeling uneasy.

She looked at him and raised her eyebrows slightly. He had always found that quite attractive in the past but now found it distinctly unsettling. He decided to say something quickly, ignoring his concerns, "So, why are we meeting here?"

He groaned inwardly, he had not meant to say that yet!

"I thought it would be better to meet away from chambers. There are a few things I would like to talk about."

David helped himself to a large glass of Rioja, replenishing Wendy's glass too, before responding, "OK. What do you want to discuss?"

He assumed a purely defensive posture which Wendy immediately observed. "I would like this to be pleasant, if at all possible, David."

He let out an audible grunt before taking a long sip of the wine.

Wendy ignored him and continued, "I've been thinking a lot in Leeds."

He wanted to make some sarcastic comment but wisely decided against it and carried on listening.

"I have enjoyed our time together."

Here it comes, thought David.

"I just felt I ought to tell you that I met an old friend last weekend."

He looked puzzled, he already knew that.

"I haven't seen him for several years now."

David could not help the frown that appeared on his face as he repeated to himself the word, 'him'.

Wendy ignored it and continued, "We had a relationship when I was a solicitor that went on for a year, we even lived together for a few months, but it didn't work out then and we went our separate ways. I haven't seen Michael since then."

She had never mentioned living with anyone when they had discussed past relationships. In fact, she had said very little about previous boyfriends in all the time he had known her.

"Who is Michael?"

"Michael Summers, he worked at my firm, Thatcher and Cook, but he became bored with the job and decided to travel the world. He said he would keep in touch but never did and, quite frankly, I almost completely forgot about him. However, he recently came back and asked if we could meet up."

David gave her a questioning look. How could she forget someone she lived with, he wondered.

"I had forgotten how much I cared for him, and still do," she continued as if she had read his thoughts.

David took a gulp of his wine and refilled his own glass. She had not touched hers.

"Anyway, on Saturday he invited me back to his flat and I went."

She paused before adding, "I stayed overnight."

David's eyes widened behind his half empty glass, which he put down before asking, "You did what?"

"Nothing happened," she answered with a sigh.

"You stayed the night with an ex-boyfriend, in his flat, and I am supposed to believe nothing happened!"

"If I tell you nothing happened you should believe me!"

David grunted again, before taking another swig of fortifying Rioja. He noted that it was actually quite a good wine, but he could not enjoy it properly at the moment.

"Anyway, he asked if he could see me again tomorrow night and I agreed."

David's eyes were wide open now. He finished his wine quickly and got up.

"Well, I trust the two of you enjoy yourselves."

She took his arm as he began to turn and walk away.

"David I was telling you this because I care about you. I've been torn about what to do. I've had a few sleepless nights in Leeds and I decided I had to tell you the whole story because…"

He did not let her finish but shrugged off her hand and announced "Goodbye Wendy, it was nice getting to know you."

He marched out of the wine bar, ignoring the heads that turned around to witness his raised voice and dramatic exit. He decided to leave with all the dignity he could muster, which was slightly hampered by the fact he walked into the door hoping to push it open and missing the sign that said pull.

Once he had properly negotiated the exit, he walked quickly to London Bridge station, ignoring his phone when he saw that Wendy was calling him. There was a queue of people waiting for taxis, but he soon managed to get one. "Barbican, please!" he ordered.

The journey took about twenty minutes but seemed longer to him as he re-played the scene in the bar with Wendy. He regretted losing his temper, but he felt deeply hurt. It had reminded him too much of his meeting with Sarah, when she had dumped him. He thought Wendy was meeting a girlfriend last weekend, not an ex-boyfriend and telling him that she had stayed the night with an ex-lover, a man she had been with for a year and then expecting him to believe that nothing had happened between them was just absurd. No, that was it, that was the end of their relationship, it was nice whilst it lasted.

The cab dropped him off and he paid with a twenty pound note, telling the driver to keep the change without even checking how much the fare was. The driver quickly drove away.

David entered the flat and made his way straight to the fridge. Unceremoniously, he removed one of the three bottles of vintage 2003 Pol Roger champagne that he kept there. Tonight was a night to celebrate. After all, he was a bachelor again!

CHAPTER 18

FURTHER EVIDENCE

David awoke at just after 9am on Monday morning. The weekend had been a bit of a blur. He had finished off two bottles of Pol Roger on Friday night, spent most of Saturday recovering until he had started on the final bottle at around 6pm, followed by a bottle of Rioja Reserva. He had ignored several calls from Wendy and deleted her answer phone messages without even listening to them. As far as he was concerned, he needed a clean break.

He woke late on Sunday and tried to do some more work on his murder case. He found it difficult to concentrate on the case however and a further bottle of Rioja Reserva that evening did not improve his mood. He did not feel drunk, just depressed, tired and generally unwell. He had not drunk that much in a long time and his body was suffering from the abuse.

At 10am, he made his way into chambers, deleting a number of text messages from Wendy, again, without reading them. No doubt she wanted to tell him how wonderful her weekend had been with 'Michael' and commiserating with him. Well, he had no time for that nonsense. He had work to do.

By 10:30, he was seated at his desk staring at a cup of black filter coffee and the unopened brief of R v Paul Morris. He was awoken from his day dreaming by the ringing of his desk phone. It was Jimmy Short on the line.

He closed his eyes temporarily as he thought that Jimmy Short was probably the last person in the world he wanted to speak to today.

"Hello Jimmy, how are you?" he asked cheerfully.

"Fine, David. I've just opened some papers that were sent by the CPS on Friday. It's a Notice of Additional Evidence in the Paul Morris case. There are three further statements. Apparently they arrested that Dickson chap on suspicion of murder on Wednesday 4th June and never told us! He was interviewed and initially made no comment but then during a second set of interviews he claimed Paul was the murderer. The case was then sent to the CPS who took over a month to decide what to do. They then decided not to charge Dickson with murder but use him as a prosecution witness! He made a statement on 15th July 2014, and the CPS has only just served it today. It changes nothing, it's still a fight."

David paused for a few seconds before asking, "You mentioned three statements, what about the other two? Who made them?"

"One's a statement from his girlfriend, Tracey Andrews, also made on 15th July. She just says he came home that night and told her he had seen the fight. The other is from the pathologist but it adds nothing. None of this changes anything David."

David would have liked to tell him exactly what it changed and potentially how serious this development was, but he decided against it. Jimmy Short was unlikely to listen and would just get wound up and David was not in a mood to deal with that today. "Alright Jimmy, can you send the statements to chambers by email so I can have a look at them."

It was past 11am when the statements arrived on David's desk and he began to read through them. He started with the statement of Charlie Dickson.

Charlie Dickson was nineteen, unemployed and a drug user. He stated that he lived with his twenty-one year old girlfriend Tracey Andrews and her three year old son, Jimmy, who she had from a previous relationship with someone he knew only as 'Terry'.

Tracey was paid her benefits money into her bank account every other Mondays and it cleared just after midnight. He had become accustomed to collecting it from the same cashpoint machine at around 1am, every other

Tuesday morning. He would then seek out a dealer and purchase a £10 wrap of cannabis which he would enjoy smoking before returning to Tracey with the remaining money.

He knew Michael Ward was a drug dealer and regularly purchased his drugs from him. He was not a friend, just his dealer.

On the night of the murder he had phoned Ward and arranged to meet to buy the cannabis. He had just purchased it when Danny Williams appeared. He knew Danny because he had purchased some cannabis from him once.

Danny started arguing with Ward about Ward dealing on his 'turf' asking Ward what the hell he had been doing outside his flat that night. Ward told him to fuck off and Danny became quite aggressive. There was a struggle and Ward knocked Danny to the ground. Suddenly, from nowhere, Paul Morris appeared, raised his hands above his head, and brought them down forcefully on Danny's chest as he lay on the ground. Dickson had not seen a knife, and there had only been one blow before Paul walked away quickly. He saw Danny get up and walk away as well. Michael Ward ran away in a different direction, and Dickson ran after Paul to find out why he had attacked Danny.

He caught up with Paul and walked with him. He claimed that Paul told him that he had attacked Danny because, the other day, Danny threw some bottles through his parent's window and almost 'brained' him. Paul had then said, 'Danny had it coming.'

Charlie Dickson claimed that he thought nothing more about the incident until he saw the news on the television the following Friday night that Morris and Ward had been arrested on suspicion of murder. He then panicked, he was scared that he might be arrested so he threw away the jacket and jeans he had been wearing that night and went to stay with his Aunt in Brighton. He returned after three weeks and went back to Tracey's flat, where he was arrested a few days later.

David put the statement down and took a sip of coffee. This changed things a great deal. Finally, the prosecution had a witness who not only put Paul at the scene, but had him delivering the fatal blow. Obviously, Charlie Dickson had a reason to lie and the statement read like he had been given an inducement along the lines of, 'If you give evidence we won't charge you with murder.' Nevertheless, it was also a believable account!

David turned next to the statement of the girlfriend, to see if that supported or helped Paul's case in any way.

Tracey Andrews' statement was only a few pages long. She was twenty one years of age, and she confirmed that Charlie lived with her and had become a father-figure to young Jimmy. She had not seen Jimmy's father, Terry, since she had first told him she was pregnant.

She knew Charlie smoked cannabis and did not like it. She would not let him smoke in the house or in front of Jimmy, but she let him take £10 a fortnight from her benefits to buy 'a draw', because it seemed to relax him.

She said she did not know Paul Morris or Danny Williams and had not heard Charlie talk about them until after the murder. She knew he bought his cannabis from a lad called "Afro" but she had never met him.

She remembered that sometime around midnight on 6th May, Charlie had gone out to collect her benefits money from an ATM that was no more than five minutes' walk from their flat. At the request of the police she had obtained a statement from her bank that showed the money was withdrawn at 1:07am.

She had fallen asleep and been woken when Charlie returned, just before 2am, when he had told her he had witnessed a fight. He said that he had just bought a 'draw' off his friend Afro when this other lad appeared, another drugs dealer, called Danny. Danny started arguing with his friend and a few blows were exchanged between them. Then, within a few seconds, another man had come out of nowhere and struck Danny to the ground. Afro and the other youth then made off quickly in different directions. He had seen Danny get up and walk away, so had thought there was nothing wrong. He then ran off and caught up with the man who he said was called Paul. Paul had told him he had a problem with Danny and Danny 'had got what he deserved'.

Tracey stated that Charlie had learnt about the death the following day when she had seen a 'memorial account' for Danny set up on a social media page, by one of his sisters. She had pointed it out to Charlie. He left her address the following day and had not come back for a few weeks. When he returned, he told her he had gone to London. A few days after he came back the police came round and arrested him.

David moved onto the further statement of Herbert Rogers. He had been asked whether it would be possible for Danny Williams to get up and walk away after receiving the wound to his heart. He stated that Danny would have died soon after he received the injury but, 'nevertheless, even having sustained this wound the deceased would have been capable of purposeful activity for a short period afterwards, measured in seconds rather than minutes.'

David put Rogers' statement aside and thought about Dickson's statement and that of Tracey Andrews. Clearly there were discrepancies between what Dickson had told her and what he told the police but were those discrepancies significant enough to make a difference? The clear problem was that her version of what she was told on the night, coupled with Dickson's evidence clearly suggested that Paul Morris was the killer!

CHAPTER 19

A FURTHER CONSULTATION

"You've got nothing to worry about Paul. Just 'man-up'. David will get you off."

David was finding Jimmy Short at his most irritating, using his stock phrases in order to ensure the trial went ahead.

A consultation at Lewes Prison had been arranged at relatively short notice and David, Graham and Jimmy had met at 2pm. Jimmy had continued to say there was nothing to worry about, despite David pointing out the difficulties Paul now faced as a result of the additional evidence. Jimmy was obviously trying to get his opinion in quickly, before David had a chance to speak.

David waited until Jimmy had finished before adding, "Well Paul, I'm afraid it's not as simple as that."

He could see across the table that Jimmy's smile rapidly fell into a frown.

"Jimmy of course makes some valid points. Charlie Dickson of course has a reason to lie. The law of joint enterprise in this country is very strict and no doubt he has been advised about that and fears that, if he does not give evidence, he might be charged as an accessory."

Paul looked at him blankly before asking, "What's joint enterprise?"

David paused before answering, "I'm sorry I thought that someone on your wing in the prison might have told you about that concept by now. A lot of young men are convicted in this country because of the law of joint enterprise. The law states that you can be liable for a crime even though you did not commit the criminal act yourself. For example, one defendant could stab a man and kill him and be guilty of murder but so could another defendant who might have supplied the knife or encouraged him to use it or even agreed that some other crime be carried out such as a burglary, but also be aware that the other man might use the knife to kill or cause serious injury in the course of the burglary."

David smiled believing that he had managed to explain the difficult concept of joint enterprise so that Paul could understand it.

Paul nodded, though he still wondered what a 'concept' was and had no idea what an 'accessory' was.

"As I was saying, Charlie Dickson undoubtedly has a reason to lie, namely to protect himself from prosecution, but the problem is that his version does fit the prosecution case and we can have no doubt that Michael Ward, having had a chance to read the statement, will say the same thing. It does make the case stronger against you."

Jimmy's frown grew bigger.

Paul hammered his fist down onto the table in frustration.

"I didn't do it. I had nothing to do with that killing. I saw Danny and I walked away. I didn't want to get into any trouble. I'm not stupid. I knew I'd taken the police to that address just the day before. I'd have to be a complete idiot to go there and kill him."

Jimmy's frown changed into a smile.

David looked closely at Paul, thinking that he easily met that description of a 'complete idiot,' He decided to say something else, "I will be honest with you Paul, this evidence does cause you difficulties. However, if you say that you are not guilty, then there is no question we will fight this case. However, it is right to tell you, no one can guarantee you an acquittal."

David glanced at Jimmy as he said the last sentence, Jimmy just kept on smiling.

After a further hour and a half of taking instructions and answering questions David,

Martin and Jimmy left the prison. As Jimmy left, he could not help but add, "I think Paul's got no worries, no one's going to believe Dickson. Paul will definitely walk."

David looked at him for a brief second and just stared at him in response.

CHAPTER 20

THE DOCTOR'S NOTE

David was seated at the head of the conference table in chambers. It was 6:30pm on Friday night and he had called an emergency chambers meeting. The room had been re-arranged so that most of the tenants in chambers could be seated, although a lack of chairs meant that some were standing at the back, and one or two had to peer in through the open doors at the back of the room.

Wendy had managed to get a seat relatively close to David's. As usual, she was looking really attractive, wearing a flattering knee length black dress, with her rich brown hair worn down around her shoulders with her eyes made up with subtle make-up. So far he had managed to avoid eye contact but he knew that would not be possible for the whole evening.

After everyone had settled down he began addressing them, "Thank you all for coming at such short notice. I know it has not been easy for all of you to get here and I also know how inconvenient it is to get everyone together on a Friday evening. However, I thought it essential to call this meeting because a serious issue had arisen in chambers."

He looked around the room. He had already discussed the matter with some tenants and he expected most had heard what the issue was by now.

He continued, "As you know, Asif has been taking a great deal of time off sick recently. He was asked by John to produce a Doctor's note, and he finally produced this."

David held up a piece of paper which, from a distance, looked like a standard Doctor's sick note.

"John was concerned when he received it and brought it to my attention on Wednesday night. It does not take an expert to realise that this is a photocopy of a genuine Doctor's note and the dates on the original have clearly been altered. John searched through Asif's employment file and discovered an identical sick note with the exact same signature in the same place but with different dates. It is obvious that Asif has forged it to justify his unacceptable absence."

There were a few murmurings around the room before David continued. "As a result, I asked to see Asif in my room yesterday to ask him a few questions. I told him that in accordance with chambers disciplinary procedure, our meeting could be postponed and he could have someone present to represent his interests, but he declined.

Within minutes he admitted that he had forged the certificate. He stated he was under a great deal of stress recently which had nothing to do with chambers."

There was a sigh of relief from a couple of members of chambers who specialised in employment law and knew the potential consequences of an action based on an employee's work-related stress.

"He told me that he was having problems with the police. According to him, his car was broken into and his bank card was stolen along with his PIN code which he, rather surprisingly, kept with it. Apparently, £3,000 was withdrawn from his bank account. This is the limit of his overdraft facility and he claims that it was done without him realising it. He told me that he had not realised the card had been stolen because he had not used it recently. The bank did not accept his explanation and the police became involved. They decided not to press charges but the bank refuses to accept Asif's excuse and are pursuing an action for the £3,000 and interest."

Sean McConnell, a somewhat outspoken barrister at the best of times, could not help himself, "What absolute bollocks David. Our clients come up with better lies than that. Has anyone checked the petty cash?"

Tim Adams, always keen to make a point, responded, "That is a little unfair Sean. No one is suggesting he has taken anything from chambers, otherwise we would have heard about it by now. I think we should hear what David's proposal is."

Sean immediately became quiet. Tim had just suggested him as a junior in the prosecution of Paul Morris in Lewes. It wouldn't help his career to become embroiled in a public argument with his potential leader.

David waited patiently until attention fell upon him again, "Thank you Tim," he continued, "The issue is what do we do with Asif? I have checked with John and there is no suggestion that any petty cash has gone missing. However, Asif has clearly forged a Doctor's certificate and tried to mislead chambers.

Obviously, it is not great for the reputation of chambers if one of its clerks is retained after discovering that he is being investigated by the police for a potential fraud. The issue is do we sack him immediately for gross misconduct, sack him and give him some money in lieu of notice or keep him on and settle simply for a written warning?"

The room almost erupted with different voices crying out in support of the different proposals. It was the reason why David had called the meeting. He knew there would be polarised views as to what to do and it helped for everyone to feel as though they had had their say before he made the final decision himself.

He looked around the room and noticed that Wendy had raised her hand as if she was in a school. He could not ignore her now, so he addressed her, "Yes, Wendy, what do you think?" he asked in his best professional voice.

There were a few smiles around the room. It was popular gossip around chambers that the relationship between them had become distinctly icy recently.

Wendy ignored their expressions and addressed the room with confidence, "We are all advocates and we present our clients' cases daily. We know that a lot of youngsters get into trouble through immaturity and naivety and we see daily that they come before the youth courts, eventually receive some form of custodial sentence and inevitably go on to become career criminals. I often think that if they had been dealt with more constructively earlier on, they might never go on to commit more and more serious crimes."

Sean McConnell could not help himself, "Don't say that Wendy, we'd have no clients! Then where would we all be?" He laughed, finding himself highly amusing as usual.

A few laughs could be heard erupting around the room, even Wendy smiled sweetly before continuing, this time looking directly at David, "Asif has been a good clerk until recently. In fact, he was one of the hardest working clerks and I think he will be a great loss to chambers. It takes a while for a junior clerk to find their feet in chambers and work with such commitment as he has. Clearly he was stressed at the time, and he has made a terrible mistake. Isn't it possible to forgive this one transgression with a formal warning? We should try to understand what he was going through and give him some guidance and assistance in the future. Tell him that if there are any further incidents he will be dismissed, but that we value him and feel he deserves one more chance because of his past loyalty and support."

The room was strangely silent for a few moments. It was David who finally spoke. "Thank you, Wendy. I don't think that this should be a majority decision of chambers and indeed chambers constitution makes it my responsibility, but I would like a show of hands as to who believes we should dismiss him either immediately or with notice and who believes he should be given a written warning."

After putting the three propositions to the vote the members of chambers were overwhelmingly in favour of keeping Asif but issuing him a written warning.

David was a little surprised by the result. He had thought chambers would want to sack Asif, and give him some money in lieu of notice, rather than give him a second chance. He had made his mind up now and was pleased that he had the backing of chambers. He decided that everyone deserves a second chance, and he looked at Wendy and smiled at her.

CHAPTER 21

SUCH A ROMANTIC EVENING

The meeting had only taken one hour which was a record as far as David could recall. A large number of barristers in one room usually meant endless opinions, responses, squabbles, personality conflicts and the exercise of everyone's inalienable right and desire to be heard. Almost inevitably, such meetings went on forever. Perhaps it was because it was Friday night, everyone wanted to go home, or, more likely, continue gossiping in a wine bar or a pub.

David decided to invite everyone along to Briefs, where he spent £220 on four bottles of champagne. He announced that he had decided to give Asif a second chance because of how loyal he had been to chambers in the past. Whilst there were a few objections from one or two, generally everyone was happy and the meeting ended in relative success.

As the night had worn on and more Champagne had been consumed, the number of chamber's members dwindled, until only a few were left and David had found himself sitting next to Wendy. It had not taken long before Wendy had announced that she had not seen Michael again and David responded by telling her he had missed her a great deal. Within a short time, they were involved in a happy conversation and, after some initial expressed reluctance, Wendy agreed to meet David for dinner the following night.

Now, it was Saturday night, and David was sitting opposite Wendy in the Shangri-La restaurant, on the 52nd floor of the Shard in London.

It had taken David some effort to get a table there at short notice but he had managed it, mentioning that they were considering having their chambers party there which would be worth a considerable amount to the restaurant.

The views of London from the window of the restaurant were simply stunning. He was seated opposite the building known as the 'Gherkin' and below, to his right was the Tower of London and Tower Bridge. The Sun was setting and the vast expanse of London was bathed in a red and orange glow. The only view that topped this for David was the view of Wendy, who was now sitting across the table from him, looking ravishing, dressed in a figure-hugging silk multi-coloured summer dress.

As soon as she had sat down opposite him, he had realised how much she meant to him. Two

Bellini cocktails later, and it seemed to him that they had never been apart, even though a day before he had thought their relationship was over. He looked at her and involuntarily uttered, "You look beautiful."

Wendy smiled and replied, "You look pretty good yourself."

The meal was not disappointing. They settled for the four course set menu. Crab followed by Scottish lobster and English caviar and then the organic beef rib eye for him and the Cornish Turbot for Wendy. There was barely room for desert.

He was determined not to mention Michael. After all, it could ruin a wonderful evening. He poured them both a glass of the Chilean Cabernet Sauvignon and asked, "So, what have you being doing the last few weeks?"

Wendy's smile changed to a slight frown. David realised it was a stupid question.

"I mean, have you been done anything nice?"

For God's sake he thought to himself as her frown deepened, stop digging! He had to recover the mood.

"It's so wonderful to be together, just the two of us," he said quickly, hoping to get things back on a romantic track.

Wendy felt forced to answer, "David, please don't ruin a wonderful evening. I'm with you and happy to be with you. I don't want to be with anyone else. If you are asking about Michael in your less than subtle way, I haven't seen him since that first night. I realised straight away that the only person I wanted to be with was you."

David's grin broadened before she added with a smirk, "Although, sometimes I wonder why!"

His smile widened, "Shall I order a bottle of Champers to celebrate?"

"You don't need to get Champagne darling," She said to him softly, taking his hand.

"I know, but I want to. I am so happy to see you again!" And really happy you haven't seen Michael again, he thought to himself.

A bottle of Champagne arrived and they both enjoyed it, laughing over stories from court, and mutual acquaintances they had bumped into and heard gossip about. The evening out was coming to a close and David did not want it to end there.

"Wendy, I don't want to be presumptuous, but I booked a room here tonight. Just as a special treat. Obviously there is no pressure, but I would love you to stay with me."

Wendy smiled at him and winked, "It's a good thing that I brought a night bag with me then isn't it!"

He looked quizzically at her as she had no bag with her.

She smiled, "I checked it in with reception, just in case you didn't invite me."

They were soon making their way in the lift down to the 42nd floor, where their luxurious, Japanese-inspired double room awaited them . David had already checked the room out. It was tastefully decorated with fantastic views of London. The toilet had slightly surprised him though, as, when he flushed it, it responded by shooting warm jets of water into areas he was not expecting!

He was very impressed with the room overall, despite its cost. He also liked the bathroom which had a TV screen built into the mirror, so that one could watch programmes whilst sitting down on the lavatory. The Hotel had thought of every comfort it seemed.

Wendy was also clearly impressed, though slightly surprised when she looked out of the window to see straight into another bedroom because of the design of the building, but the push of a button prompted the electronic shutters to shield them from any possible prying eyes.

Within a few minutes they were cuddled up in the huge soft bed together. David held her closely and felt that everything was right with the world again.

CHAPTER 22

YET MORE EVIDENCE

David strolled into chambers on Monday morning, whistling cheerfully. The weekend had been a great success and Wendy had returned home with him on Sunday. She had agreed to go on holiday with him and they had spent a relaxing Sunday trawling through the internet to find Villas in his favourite resort of Arillas in north-west Corfu. By the end of the evening they had booked a holiday together for two weeks, from 16th - 30th August 2014. Wendy even agreed to return two cases she had in that period. He could not be happier. It would give him time to rest and relax before beginning the Paul Morris case.

At 10am, David was still wearing a grin, when he heard that Jimmy Short was calling him. He continued smiling, even Jimmy Short could not ruin his mood.

"Hello Jimmy! How are you?"

"Fine, David. I've just received further evidence from the CPS. They must wait till late Friday night before putting these bloody things in the post!"

David continued smiling as he asked, "What does it say Jimmy?"

"It's from a prison snitch. No one is going to believe him."

David's smile slowly faded, "What does it say Jimmy?"

"It's a bloke called Joey Talbot, a black man, also known as "Pumpman" because his trademark is to use pump action, sawn-off shotguns during bank robberies. He's currently awaiting sentence for possession of a pump action sawn-off shotgun with ammunition and a wicked eight-inch, serrated hunting knife. He also apparently had camouflage coloured body armour and a ski mask in a holdall in the boot of his car. Your average armed robbers' kit basically."

"Sounds like a nice chap."

"Yeah, well, he was banged up with Paul Morris. He's made a statement to the police. He claims Paul confessed to him that he was the killer. He claims that Paul told him that he went round to the flat because the bottle Danny threw at his Dad's window almost hit him. Paul told Pumpman that he had to "sort Danny out". He told him he went to the flat with Ward but Danny wouldn't let them in. Paul told him Ward left to sell some weed to some other kid, then

Paul saw them together and saw Williams approach them. Paul supposedly told him that he pulled out the knife he always carries.

Pumpman even claims that Paul told him that he had used it to cut his own Dad for "dissing" him. Paul supposedly told him he attacked Williams when he was on the ground. He even says that Paul told him he ran off, threw the knife away down a drain and was joined by 'the kid' who was with Ward."

David's smile was now a frown, "Does he say why he is willing to give this evidence?"

"He claims he came forward because he didn't like the fact that Paul was boasting that there was no evidence against him and there was more against Ward and Ward would probably be convicted and he'd get off.

It's still a fight David. No one is going to believe a prison snitch."

David could not help himself, "Jimmy, we both know that juries don't like prison snitches but they do believe them occasionally, particularly when their story is credible. Sadly, this version of events fits in perfectly with the prosecution case. We had better see Paul this week and see what he has to say."

Jimmy raised his voice at the other end of the line, "It fits in with the prosecution's case because someone has told him what to say. It's still a fight David."

David raised his eyes but remained impassive as he replied, "Let's see what Paul says about this evidence shall we?"

CHAPTER 23

A FURTHER CONSULTATION

"I bet you're beginning to wish you hadn't taken this case on now!"

Graham Martin was munching on a cheese and salad sandwich, seated opposite David in the second class carriage on the 12:47 train from London Victoria to Lewes. They were travelling together from chambers to Lewes prison for a further consultation with Paul.

David had a peek at his own sandwich purchased from a shop outside London's Victoria station. He decided against taking any risk with the greyish off-smelling prawns and discarded it before replying, "I wouldn't say that. It is a murder case after all and, if it was easy, this job wouldn't be half as enjoyable."

Graham laughed, "I'm not sure this job is enjoyable anymore."

"Oh, come on now Graham, what other job could we get where we could wear fancy dress and call people liars all day long without any personal comeback!"

Graham smiled and continued eating his own sandwich, looking at David's discarded prawns. He thought, you just cannot go wrong with cheese, prawns are a different matter though!

He looked out of the window as the train left East Croydon station, "What do you think about this latest evidence? It certainly doesn't help young Paul."

David looked up from the papers in front of him. He was re-reading the statement of Joey Talbot and the notes of a conversation that a Detective Constable Bryant had with him. "There's no doubt that Talbot's statement doesn't help Paul. The only question is, is it fatal to his defence?"

David grinned as he added, "Of course, our 'learned' solicitor, Jimmy Short, doesn't think it will cause any problems."

Graham smirked, "Jimmy Short wouldn't think it caused any problems if the client admitted the offence to the police and to us, and even begged to plead guilty. Jimmy would still say, 'it's a fight'."

Both laughed before returning to look at their papers for some last-minute preparation for the consultation.

Less than an hour later, they pulled into Lewes in the Sussex countryside. It was a beautiful, sunny August day and neither looked forward to being confined in a stuffy old Victorian prison room for the next few hours.

Graham looked wistfully towards the local Lewes brewery, "Pity we can't stop off for a pint of Sussex's finest ale."

David nodded but pointed to a vacant taxi just outside the station, "Sadly, one of the difficulties with this job is that occasionally we have to forgo the pleasure of a pint for a prison visit!"

A ten minute cab ride took them to the bottom of the hill that led to the prison gates. Jimmy Short was waiting to greet them at the top.

"David, Graham, good to see you both. I managed to see Paul briefly this morning. There's no problem, he denies that he said anything to this Talbot-snitch. He still wants to fight the case."

David and Graham exchanged a quick, knowing look, but did not say anything.

Twenty minutes later, they were allowed into a box room upstairs in the prison where Paul was seated, waiting for them.

After some polite greetings, they were all seated, and David produced the statement of Joey Talbot.

"Now, Paul, you've already been told by Jimmy that a prisoner in this prison, Joey Talbot, has made a witness statement to the police. He alleges that you told him you committed this murder."

Paul immediately interjected, "He's no longer in here. He left pretty quickly after he grassed me up."

David nodded, "That's not surprising. He was unlikely to stay in the same prison as you, once he made these allegations. I'm not suggesting that you would do anything but other prisoners don't react kindly to someone who goes to the police and discusses what goes on in here. The real question you have to concentrate on, is whether there is any truth in what he says?"

"It's a load of lies Mr Brant. I have met him a few times. He used to come to my cell to talk to me. We did talk about case, but I never told him I killed Danny."

David looked at Jimmy, who was smiling broadly. He turned back to Paul, "Joey Talbot has given quite a detailed account of what he says you told him. It pretty much follows the prosecution case. I appreciate that you say you didn't give him these details, do you know where he might have got them from?"

Paul looked towards Jimmy who nodded at him.

"I've been fitted up, Mr Brant. They all know I didn't kill Danny. The police have told him and offered him something to say I told him!"

There was silence around the table for a moment, suddenly punctuated by Paul smashing his fist down on the Formica topped table. "It's not fair that the fucking police are allowed to use his lies."

Everyone remained silent for a few seconds. Paul noticed a prison officer looking inquiringly into the room and immediately calmed down, turning towards David, "What are my chances, Mr Brant?"

David was about to answer when Jimmy Short butted in, "You've got a good run son, no one will believe a prison snitch."

Jimmy looked towards David for support. David ignored him and replied to Paul's question, "Of course, Jimmy is right that juries don't like prison snitches. They realise that a prison snitch has every reason to lie and, indeed, we will make the jury aware that he is likely to get a significant reduction in his sentence for helping the prosecution in your case."

Paul looked at him hopefully before David continued, "However, the problem for you is that his account is a pretty detailed one. It is unlikely that the jury will believe the police have 'fitted you up'. After all, if they were going to, why not 'fit-up' Ward at the same time, they have charged you both and yet Talbot says very little about Ward.

The reality is they are more likely to believe that this account came from someone who knows a lot about the case, either because he was there himself or because he was told about it by someone who was. I would be lying to you if I didn't tell you that it does make the case against you much stronger."

Jimmy's face fell in horror and Paul stood up abruptly at this unwelcome news. He tried violently to push his chair back but gave up when he realised it was screwed to the floor.

Feeling stupid and angry he shouted, "I didn't do it Mr Brant. I didn't do it."

He looked down at the table and paused for a few seconds before sighing and looking directly at David.

"Alright, I'll tell you the truth. Joey Talbot was there! He is the person who supplied drugs to both Ward and Williams. Williams hadn't paid him and was boasting that he wouldn't. I was there when Dickson, Ward and Talbot were approached by Williams. I was on the opposite side of the road. It was Talbot who killed Williams. He then gave the knife to Ward, who

168

ran away and got rid of it. That's why I ran. I ran away from them both. I was scared. Dickson ran as well and followed me. He was really scared too. We agreed we wouldn't say anything for fear of what Talbot might do. I can't believe they are all blaming me. It's not fair, and it's not true!" he declared desperately.

After a moment, Paul relaxed again and sat back down at the table as David asked him, "Paul, you've never told us this before. You have always claimed you did not know who killed Danny. You never mentioned Joey Talbot was even present and you certainly did not say anything about him being involved, or being the killer."

Paul nodded, "I know but, Mr Brant, I was too scared. Joey Talbot is a really dangerous man. I didn't want to mention it. I was afraid he'd kill me or get someone in here to."

David looked surprised, "If Joey Talbot killed Williams, why is he getting involved? Why would he give evidence against you? The last place he would want to be is in court being cross-examined by your lawyers and called a murderer."

"I don't know, Mr Brant, all I know is that it's the truth. Joey Talbot was there and he killed Danny Williams."

"So those are your final instructions?"

"It's the truth Mr Brant."

"It's a good job we haven't served the defence statement yet."

He turned to Graham, "Can you amend your draft defence statement to include our latest instructions and serve it on the prosecution?"

Graham made a note and smiled, replying, "Of course."

David questioned Paul about the incident again with Graham asking him the odd question. Jimmy remained silent but wore a massive grin. It was clear to him that whatever the truth was, there was going to be a trial.

After a further half hour of David quizzing Paul, he asked Paul if there were any questions that he had.

Paul looked towards Jimmy and then back to David. "Yeah, what about the phone evidence from the prison, can they really use that?"

Both David and Graham looked towards Jimmy suspiciously. Jimmy looked down at his shoes.

"What phone evidence from the prison?" asked David.

Paul looked puzzled and looked towards Jimmy who was now inspecting his nails.

"The stuff Jimmy showed me this morning!"

Jimmy raised his head and looked in David's direction. "Yeah, sorry about that, the evidence only came in this morning. I forgot to mention it to you."

David could not ignore Graham's eyebrows which had risen to the middle of his forehead, and neither could Jimmy.

"Here let me get it for you, I got my secretary to make copies for you both."

He fumbled through the papers in front of him and produced a large brown envelope containing two copies of statements.

"It's yet another Notice of Additional Evidence. I bet they'll be serving these right up to and throughout the trial. It's disgraceful the way the CPS never gives us proper disclosure of its case in good time."

David just nodded and took the papers from him, handing one set to Graham.

After a few minutes reading, David turned to Paul. "It says here that they are relying on two calls that you made to your family from a prison phone. The first was on Wednesday 4th June, 2014, when you phoned your parents from prison. You spoke to your Dad and said, 'Dad please don't give evidence against me, you know

I didn't mean you to get hurt.' He responded, 'I'll think about it, son. You know I still love you.' You then said 'I love you too Dad.'

The evidence also states that on 19th June, 2014, after you had been convicted of wounding your father, you made a further call to your parent's address. Your father spoke to you and said, 'Sorry son, they made me give evidence against you.' You replied, 'It's alright Dad, I know you didn't have no choice.'

Later, during the same conversation, your father was discussing the murder case with you and you apparently said, 'I'm waiting for the results of the DNA. I'm worried it might come back positive.'

Paul looked down at the table, "I don't remember saying that."

David lent forward over the table, towards his client, "The trouble is Paul, that the prosecution has served a disk of the phone recordings with the transcripts. We will listen to it but it is likely that the transcript is accurate."

Jimmy decided he had been silent long enough, "Maybe you'll be able to get the conversations excluded David, Human Rights, Right to Family Life, that sort of thing."

A little knowledge is a dangerous thing, thought David. Jimmy had no idea what he was talking about.

He turned to Paul, ignoring the comment, "I assume you used an ordinary prison phone?"

"Yes."

"No doubt you used a phone card you had purchased in the prison?"

"Yes."

"And no doubt there was a big sign above the phone saying that all phone calls would be monitored and recorded."

Paul hesitated for a second before reluctantly confirming, "Yes."

"Then the only basis for excluding these calls is their relevance. Do you deny that you injured your father with a knife?"

"Yes, it was an accident as I've always said."

David nodded, "Then the prosecution will be allowed to rely on the evidence about the calls to suggest you were guilty of wounding your father. In relation to the second call, on your case, your DNA would not have been on him that night and his would not have been on you. Therefore the prosecution will say it's important that you were worried about the DNA because, the reality is you would only have been worried about it if you had been a lot closer to him than you have told us. Close enough to have been his killer."

CHAPTER 24

ARILLAS, CORFU

David took a long sip of his Pina Colada, sighed happily and lent back in his reclining chair, watching the huge red Sun disappear over the horizon. The sky was now a mix of colours, a dark red sun surrounded by an orange glow reflecting off a dark blue sea. The waves along the beachfront on the other side of the road lapped constantly against the sandy beach, giving the moment a timeless feel. The view from the Perseus Bar was truly wonderful and marred only by a few tourists standing in front of him clicking away with their cameras trying to catch their 50th shot of the sunset.

David and Wendy were in Arillas on the North-West Coast of Corfu. It was one of his favourite holiday destinations where Sarah and he had enjoyed so many excellent holidays together before the divorce. It still held fond memories for him though, and he had been happy when Wendy agreed to come with him. He imagined that they would enjoy the relaxed atmosphere there of this simple, under-developed, tourist spot, where everything seemed to move at a snail's pace.

They were staying in a villa he had hired in the next village along, called Afionas, an artists' village with German bakeries and eccentric painters and sculptors, as well as the older generations of locals who had managed to cling on to their rustic homes. Afionas was situated right on top of a steep hill side, overlooking the sea and Diapontian Islands, the sunsets were even more staggering from a height where they were set against the vast expanse of shimmering red and orange sea.

Tonight though, David had brought Wendy to his favourite Cocktail Bar in Arillas, right next to the beach. The barman, Stephanos, remembered him well from the many years he had been visiting Corfu and brought across a couple of perfectly mixed Pina Coladas to their table. He had yet to discover the delights of adding coconut cream to the drink, but his mix was nevertheless superb.

They arrived in Corfu a week after David's last conference with Paul in Lewes prison. He had been happy to leave the case, and its mounting problems aside, just as he had been happy to try and put aside the troubling affairs of chambers. Sadly the latter had proved difficult with his clerks telephoning him every other day with some trivial matter which they made sound like a looming catastrophe which only he could defuse.

He looked forward to travelling to one of his favourite restaurants, with its anglicised name, "The Boar Inn". It served a good and remarkably cheap Greek red wine and grilled halloumi cheese, called saganaki, which made David's mouth water whilst ordering it, not to mention his main course a very large, almost cartoon-sized, grilled pork chop. He had no idea where they got the chops from because he had never seen a pig on the island, but they tasted better than any he ever tasted anywhere else. He tried to ignore the looming return journey to England in just two days' time, and the pressures that awaited him as a silk and Head of Chambers.

However, just as he was putting these thoughts out of his mind, his phone rang and he saw that it was Graham Martin. He was tempted to ignore it, after all, he was on holiday and it was almost 8:30pm! Of course, he knew he was two hours ahead of British time, and as it was Graham and not a clerk, it was probably quite important.

"Hello Graham, and what horrible calamity has occurred to disturb my holiday?"

"Hello David, I am sorry to bother you on holiday but they have listed the Paul Morris case tomorrow for a mention. It seems that a High Court Judge is going to try the case and they want to ensure that we are trial ready. He is sitting tomorrow. It's Mr Justice Knight. You know him, his nickname is "To-Knight" because he is so particular about details and, as a result, everything takes so long in front of him.

I wouldn't have bothered you but he is so finicky and will want to check that I've been in touch with you. You see I've just received the defence statement of the Co-Defendant, Michael Ward. Needless to say, he agrees with virtually everything Charlie Dickson and Joey Talbot say. He claims it was Paul who carried out the murder. He also says Paul was with him earlier when they went to visit Danny Williams' flat. He says it was Paul's idea and he just tagged along. He had no intention of doing anything and thought they were going on a social visit to 'cool down' the situation between them after the bottle-throwing incident. He says he was surprised that Paul was so aggressive when he got there. He then left and met Dickson, who he sold some drugs to. Danny then approached them complaining and he says Paul came from out of no-where and stabbed Danny to death. I just wanted to know this, do you want me to go see Paul and take any further instructions from him about this, or do you want me to amend our defence statement as a result of theirs? Also, shall I raise any pre-trial issues at this stage?"

David was brought rapidly back to reality. The tranquillity of a sunset and a soothing Pina Colada in the company of his beautiful girlfriend, was replaced with an image of Lewes Crown Court and a crotchety High Court Judge.

He sighed and directed his junior on the next steps in preparation for what had rapidly become an overwhelming case against their client.

CHAPTER 25

BACK TO REALITY

David and Wendy returned to London on Saturday, 30th August, sporting tans, plus a few extra pounds. On Sunday, Wendy had returned to her flat after lunch and David had begun looking at the Paul Morris papers again, hoping to find something that he might have missed. He was also reading Graham's note of Friday's hearing.

Graham had sent him an email, which had surprised David a little as Graham rarely used emails. Apparently, the hearing had been listed at 10am in Court 3, but had not been called on before the Judge until just after 12. It had finished just before 1pm, with the Judge making a number of directions that the parties observe before the trial. Many were steps any competent counsel would undertake anyway before a trial, so he ignored these.

After a few hours of refreshing his memory on a few matters, and making further notes, David gave up hope of finding anything new or helpful in his papers, and opened a bottle of Greek red wine which he had brought back with him. It was one of the most expensive he had bought out there. It was strange that they never tasted the same when he brought them back to England.

He decided not to go to chambers on Monday, feeling that he deserved an extra day off, but on Tuesday, he knew he had no choice as head of chambers, and went in to face any new dramas in the clerks' room.

He arrived at 10am and noticed that the clerks' room was its usual hive of activity. In particular, Asif, the first junior clerk, looked busy, and a quick look at his computer screen confirmed to David he was working on chamber's matters and not looking up the exploits of some footballer or communicating by social media with his "friends". He was pleased with his decision not to dismiss him and that he had given him a second chance as he was working harder these days and had not taken a further day off ill.

John was away on holiday and David noticed that Nick was seated at his desk. Behind him, was a new picture on the wall. David moved closer to have a look. It was a picture of John with a few friends lounging by a pool, all drinking bottles of Spanish beer. John was facing the camera and holding his bottle of beer in the air as if he was toasting something.

Underneath was a caption in bright red, "Working hard for you all."

He turned to Nick and raised his eyebrows, "What's this all about?"

Nick smiled and turned round, "I saw it on John's personal website, and I couldn't resist downloading it and adding my own caption."

David smiled, he now had the measure of Nick and knew exactly what the purpose of this photograph was. "I'm sure John will enjoy the joke when he gets back."

With that, he left the clerks room, not doubting for one moment that the picture would be consigned to the bin by Nick the day before John returned to work. Devious chap that, he thought, but useful. Might make John work a little harder to keep his job.

Within a few minutes, David was seated alone in his own room. He was grateful for the peace, but it was not long before the phone rang and Asif announced it was Jimmy Short on the line.

As David picked up the phone and heard Jimmy's gruff voice, his mind wondered back to a small sandy cove in Corfu. He imagined retiring there and putting the Jimmy Shorts of the world behind him – for good.

"Hello David, I heard you were back. Nice holiday? Quite a jet-setter aren't you!" Jimmy did not sound sincere, just sarcastic.

"I went to Corfu Jimmy, less than a three hour flight, I have hardly been jetting around the world!"

Jimmy laughed. At least he's in good humour, thought David.

"Anyway David, I was just ringing to discuss Paul's case. You heard what happened on Friday, 'Judge ToKnight' making loads of unnecessary orders."

"Yes I did, don't worry, Graham and I will deal with all the necessary ones before trial."

"I don't doubt it David, that's why I'm glad you two are there to represent young Paul. Anyway, I wanted to talk about Ward's defence statement. No surprises there then. We all expected that, it changes nothing of course. No one's going to believe this lot, they're clearly setting Paul up."

David immediately thought, God help us, I wish he would stop going on, we all know he wants a trial simply because he gets paid more.

However, he kept it polite and replied, "It doesn't help Paul though does it. It's a definite cut-throat defence and we know what usually happens in those.

They all go down for murder because the jury don't believe anyone!"

CHAPTER 26

THE FIRST DAY OF THE TRIAL

At 8:17 on 8th September 2014, David and Graham caught the train from Victoria to Lewes, carrying cups of steaming coffee and Emmental cheese pastries. After all, it was a long journey and David felt they deserved the treats.

As they boarded the train, they noticed their opponents in the case, Tim Adams QC and Sean McConnell were seated by a window in the same carriage. David saw them first and was in the process of turning around, trying to make a tactical withdrawal to the carriage behind when Tim saw him.

"Hello David, hello Graham. Good to see you both. It's a lovely day to pop down to the Sussex countryside. Though I'm assuming we won't have the benefit of your company for long. Presumably your chap is going to see sense and plead?"

David adopted a carefree smile, "Tim, Sean, good to see you both. Sorry to disappoint you, but I suspect we will see a lot more of each other over the next couple of weeks ... unless of course, you see sense and drop the case. In those circumstances I might even be able to persuade my client not to seek costs against the CPS."

Tim gave a half-hearted laugh, "Good one David. Seriously though, the evidence has rather been mounting up against your chap hasn't it? Have you seen Joey Talbot's most recent statement? Won't you be able to make your man see sense, even at this late stage?"

David grinned at Tim before adding, "Anyway gentlemen, Graham and I have a few matters to discuss about the case, so to avoid any potential embarrassment, we'll move to a different compartment. See you later in Lewes."

David and Graham found a couple of spare seats and seated themselves in the next carriage.

"So what do we have to discuss?" asked Graham innocently "I thought we had covered everything?"

David nodded, "We have, it's just the thought of an hour's journey in the company of Tim! Not something my stomach can stand on a Monday morning!"

Graham smiled, sat back and opened his newspaper.

Just over an hour later they arrived at Lewes station and walked up the steep hill from the station to the Court. Tim and Sean insisted on joining them but there was no more banter about the case and they made small talk about the local judges.

They arrived outside Lewes Crown Court just as a small queue was forming at the doors, waiting to go through security.

David noticed an older woman and a younger one directly in front of him. The younger was heavily made up with a large curler in her hair at the front. David presumed that was what passed for fashion these days.

The older woman appeared to David to be a little nervous and he heard her say to her young companion, "I never like to go through these things, I'm always scared I'm going to set the bloody alarms off and I don't like the idea of them giving me a body search."

"Don't worry," the younger girl had replied, "They only search your bags, not you. Though last time I came here I was really embarrassed. I'd forgotten that I had a screwdriver, a knife and a razor in my bag!"

Her older companion expressed no surprise at this but the young girl turned around noticing David giving her a look of real concern. He immediately looked at his watch, appearing to study the time impatiently. He didn't want to offend her, after all he thought, she might be one of his jurors!

After a coffee in the Women's Royal Voluntary Service canteen, and a quick visit to the cells to see that Paul had been produced from custody, and was ready for the trial to start, David and Graham returned to the advocates' robing room. There Tim was discussing the prosecution case with William Smythe QC and Jason Herd, the counsel instructed to defend the co-defendant, Ward.

Tim gave David his usual beaming smile, "David, I think you know everyone."

David nodded in acknowledgment. He knew William Smythe from years ago when they were both junior barristers. He was an amusing chap without any apparent side to him, so David quite liked him. Jason Herd was different. He was from a mainly prosecution set of chambers. He occasionally defended and he had developed a certain arrogance that comes only from those of limited ability, who fervently believe they have been treated badly in their careers at the Bar.

Tim continued without noticing any change in David's demeanour, "I was just discussing the case with Ward's team. I told them if they pleaded to manslaughter and offered to give evidence against your bloke, I might be able to avoid prosecuting their chap for murder. I'm afraid I can't make a similar offer to you, the only plea I could accept in your client's case, is a plea to murder."

Jason gave a big smirk which David ignored, although he returned Tim's smile with equal insincerity, "Tim, it never ceases to amaze me what steps you will take to avoid a trial. You must be concerned about the state of your evidence if you need to have the likes of Ward as a prosecution witness! I rather hope he does plead and give evidence, it will make my task that much easier."

Tim's smile grew even bigger as he continued the typical robing room banter that could be heard before many a trial, "Not at all David, Not at all."

After a brief discussion about preliminary matters, George, the usher for Court 3, entered the robing room and announced that the Judge wanted to see all counsel in his chambers.

Ten minutes later, they all filed into Mr Justice Knight's rooms.

Mr Justice Knight was of the "old-school", friendly, polite and frank. He rose to greet them all, "Gentlemen, good to see you, please take a seat. I'm just about to order what passes for a coffee around here, do join me."

All accepted gratefully of course and engaged in idle chit-chat until the coffee was delivered. Once they were all comfortable Knight directed the discussion towards the trial in hand. "Is this really a trial?" he asked raising his eyebrows at the two defence teams.

All around the room stared at him. It was Tim who spoke first. "It certainly appears to be Judge," he said in an equally disapproving tone.

Knight sipped at his coffee muttering between sips, "Dear, oh dear."

He looked out of the window and noticed it was unusually sunny for September.

"Gentlemen, having read the papers and, in particular, the Defence Statements, I can see that this case involves a cut-throat defence. Ward is definitely saying that Morris committed the murder. I have also seen the Defence Statement of Morris, where he states that the prosecution witness, Joey Talbot, committed the murder and that Ward is therefore lying about this.

Now as you may know, before I came to the High Court Bench, I spent most of my practice on planning enquiries. Indeed, I spent all of my time in silk on planning enquiries. I regret that the only criminal cases I conducted were a few road traffic matters, and that was a long time ago. Longer than I care to remember, in fact! However, one thing I did learn from colleagues at the criminal bar is that in a case of cut-throat defences, everyone tends to get convicted!"

David felt the comments were directed towards him, so he replied, "Judge, it has been known, but one can always hope that the truth will come out during the trial process."

Knight's smile left his face as he adopted a more serious expression and replied, "One can only hope David, one can only hope."

CHAPTER 27

THE PROSECUTION OPENING

Half an hour later, Mr Justice Knight was sitting on the bench facing the advocates, fully robed in his red and white gown and wearing a wig. Although Court 3 had a spacious public gallery, the advocates' seats were quite cramped with the juniors seated behind the silks who always took the front row. There had been no preliminary legal issues to argue before the judge at the start of the trial. The only legal issue that had arisen at this stage was the relevance of Paul Morris's previous conviction. All parties had agreed that the admissibility of this evidence would be determined after most of the Prosecution's evidence had been heard.

The first task was to swear the jury in and this had been quickly done, each member either swearing on the bible or affirming that they would try the case on the basis of the evidence alone.

Once the remaining jurors, who had not been selected, had left court, Mr Justice Knight gave the jury the usual warnings about ignoring what they had heard about the case in the media, if anything, and not to play detective during the trial. He warned them against doing any of their own research on the internet or anywhere else, reminding them that there would be dire consequences for anyone who breached his orders and telling the jury that, sadly, in some cases, it had been necessary to hold jurors in contempt of court and even imprison one or two for failing to observe these rules.

Once these formalities were out of the way, Tim Adams rose to his feet and turned to the jury. He gave them his best smile and David noticed how a few of the female jurors returned it. This did not surprise him, Tim always tried to charm his jurors. He was amused to see though that one or two of the male jurors seemed to warm to him immediately as well. It was not unusual, jurors tended to favour prosecutors at the beginning of a trial. They were in a strange environment with a new and unusual task to perform and here was a person who was, on the face of it, trying to help them.

Tim introduced the advocates to the jury and then the smile left his face as he continued, "Ladies and gentlemen, this is a serious case. The defendants are charged with the most serious crime there is. Murder!"

He paused to let the word sink in.

"The facts are simple. In the early hours of Tuesday 6th May of this year, a young man, named Danny Williams, was found in Saunders Road in Moulsecoomb. He had been stabbed in the heart. Despite the most determined efforts of police officers and paramedics, his life could not be saved.

He was found a short distance away from his home, a flat he had moved into only two weeks before, on Friday 18th April, 2014. A murder investigation began at once and police discovered that within the previous couple of weeks, Danny Williams' flat had been visited by a large number of youths, including both of these defendants.

You will hear, and it is right that you do, that Danny Williams dealt in cannabis around the immediate area of the flat, to feed his own habit and probably for financial gain. It is also clear that Michael Ward, the defendant who sits nearest you in the dock, with an afro hairdo, also dealt drugs in the same area."

The jury all looked towards Ward and noticed his hairstyle. David wondered why it had not been changed. He had represented many 'skinheads' in his time at the Bar who had grown a full head of hair by the time their trial had come around. It could also work in reverse and

Ward would have been wise to lose the memorable 70's disco look for this trial.

Tim Adams continued, "The police discovered that there had recently been some friction between these defendants and young Danny Williams. On Thursday, 1st May 2014, some of the windows in Danny's flat were broken. It is clear he suspected these defendants had something to do with it, because a couple days later, on Saturday, 3rd May, he went to Morris' address. Both Morris and Ward were at the address and Williams threw some bottles through the front window. It is important to note that Morris was injured by flying glass. To use words that you will hear in this case, "he was almost brained."

It is noteworthy that neither Morris, nor Ward, for reasons best known to them, contacted the police, but a neighbour did. The police attended Morris' home in the early hours of Sunday morning, on the 4th May. After some time, they were allowed access and they noticed the damage. Ward refused to speak to the police other than to give them his name, but Morris did. He pointed to his injury and he stated he knew who had thrown the bottles. He then took the police to Danny's address. Danny was not there at the time so the police took Mr Morris back to his own address.

The next important date is Monday 5th May, when two social workers, Lisa Thomson and Jenny Wright, attended Danny's flat. They place young homeless men in accommodation and part of their jobs is to check how it is maintained. They noticed Danny's flat was in a mess and there was a distinct smell of cannabis wafting throughout. They also noted the broken windows and they asked Danny about this. Danny told them that the damage had been caused by two local lads, one was white and the other one black with an Afro hairdo.

In the small hours of Tuesday, 6th May, Richard Brook, a neighbour of young Danny's, was awake. Now, he will tell you that he was not particularly fond of Mr Williams because of the type of people who would visit Danny's house at all times of the night, making loud disturbances in the neighbourhood.

On this occasion Mr Brook was awoken by loud noises outside his bedroom window. It sounded to him like someone kicking at a door. He looked at his clock and noted that it was 12:45am. He did not look out of his window at that stage for fear of being seen by whoever was causing this noise. He did not want them to direct their attention towards him. He did however hear someone say words to the effect, 'You almost brained me the other night, let me in or I'll fucking kill you.'

You may think that was an important comment considering that only the 'other night', Mr Morris was injured by flying glass as a result of bottles thrown through his window by Danny Williams and may have felt that if he had sat any nearer to the window that he might have been 'brained' by a flying bottle.

Mr Brook also heard one of the youths shout words to the effect, "You owe me, you little shit!" This was probably a reference to the damage that was caused to Mr Morris's windows.

Eventually, Mr Brook did look out, and what he saw was three men leaving the area, from the direction of the deceased's house. Two were white and one was black with an Afro haircut. He later identified Ward at an identification parade as being this black youth.

As the three youths left the area they were seen by other neighbours, Shereena Bennett and her son Lloyd. Possibly because of the darkness, Shereena thought they were all black youths, but Lloyd is sure they were two white youths and a black youth. Both Shereena and Lloyd later identified Ward at a police identification parade as being one of the youths seen that night. They both placed this sighting at about 1am.

Shereena will tell you that she noticed that Ward received a phone call as he was leaving the flat.

Mr Charlie Dickson takes up the story from here. He is in a relationship with a young mother, Tracey Andrews. She receives benefits which are paid into her bank account just after midnight every other Monday night. Mr Dickson collects the money for her from a local cashpoint.

Mr Dickson uses cannabis and every time he collects the money, he uses £10 of it to buy a 'draw', as he puts it. He buys his cannabis from Ward and on this occasion we have records to show that he drew the money out of the bank at 1:07am and then phoned Ward at 1:08am.

They arranged to meet and at about 1:15am they did so, in roughly the same area as Danny's body was later found. Mr Dickson will tell you that he bought some cannabis off Ward and immediately afterwards Danny approached them complaining that Ward was dealing on his patch.

You will hear from Shereena and Lloyd that at about this time, they heard someone shouting outside, 'I will fucking kill you.' They looked out and saw four youths. Three of them faced the fourth and then all of them disappeared out of sight into the nearby alleyway.

There was a struggle between Ward and Danny and Danny got knocked to the ground. You will hear from Dickson that Morris then came from nowhere. He will tell you that Morris launched himself at the prone Williams and, raising his hands together over his head, he brought them down forcefully onto Danny's chest. Dickson will tell you that he did not see a knife, probably because of the dark, but it is clear from the injuries that Danny sustained, that Morris had a large sharp knife, which he plunged downwards with all his force into Danny's heart."

Tim demonstrated the gesture to the jury with such force that a couple of jurors flinched and backed away from him in their seats. Satisfied with the effect of his words, he continued, "Mr Dickson states that everyone moved quickly away from the scene and you will hear that this was clearly seen by both Shereena and Lloyd Bennett. Shereena Bennett immediately called the police and that call was logged at 01:23. You will hear that Lloyd actually left his flat to try and give assistance to the mortally wounded Danny.

Mr Dickson will tell you that he was shocked by what had happened and he ran after Morris to ask him what the attack was all about. Morris told him about the earlier incident, when Danny had thrown something through his parents' windows and as he had put it, 'Almost brained him'. Morris then made the telling comment that 'He had it coming.'

You will hear that police obtained CCTV from the area and although little of interest was recorded, Mr Morris can be seen walking quickly away from the incident and Mr Dickson can be seen running up to him. They are both then seen talking to each other. Other CCTV catches Ward running away in the opposite direction.

Both Ward and Morris were arrested on the same day and Mr Dickson was arrested later. However, no charges were brought against Mr Dickson as there was no evidence that he participated in this murder.

Murder charges were brought against both Ward and Morris. Morris on the basis that he was the one who plunged the knife into young Danny's heart, killing him, and Ward on the basis of what is called joint enterprise. He had gone to the home of Danny with Morris, either intending to cause serious harm to Danny or knowing that Morris had that intention, and he was there to assist him and did assist him shortly afterwards and never, at any stage, tried to withdraw from this wicked plan.

However, the evidence does not stop there. Both Ward and Morris were remanded in custody to Lewes prison. There is nothing strange in that, you would expect those charged with murder to be remanded in custody and certainly you should not hold it against these defendants that they were."

Tim was giving the jury his biggest most reassuring smile at this stage. David found this pretence of fairness to be the most annoying and, quite probably, the most effective part of the prosecution opening.

Tim continued smiling, then he paused, and dropped his smile as he continued, "It was whilst in prison, members of the jury, that Morris met a prisoner named Joey Talbot. Joey Talbot is a man of violence, a man with previous convictions and a man who himself is held on remand, facing serious charges. You will no doubt be asked to consider all of that when you consider his evidence and it is right that you do so.

The prosecution accept the many faults of Mr Talbot, however, they say that his evidence can be believed in this case because it 'corroborates', in other words, it 'supports', the rest of the prosecution case. He confirms that he spoke to both Ward and Morris whilst in custody. Importantly Morris took the opportunity to tell Mr Talbot what had happened, something he did not do when he was interviewed by the police!

Both Morris and Ward have told him effectively the same story. That they had gone round to Danny's address that night to 'sort him out' but that they could not gain entrance. Ward went off to do a drugs deal with Dickson and then Danny appeared. Morris told Joey Talbot exactly the same story as Mr Dickson had told the police. He murdered young Danny because 'Danny had it coming' for throwing objects through his parents' windows."

Tim paused for a second before continuing, "There you are members of the jury. That is the case against the defendants. Let me just add one thing. The opening is not the evidence. You will hear that shortly. The opening is there to assist you when you consider the evidence and sets out the prosecution's case.

Please also bear in mind, his lordship is the judge of law and you will take the law from him, not from any of the advocates in this case. Although there is one matter of law I will bring to your attention, out of all fairness, and that is that the prosecution has brought this charge, and it is the responsibility of the prosecution to prove its case, which it must do to a very high standard of proof. As his lordship will direct you in due course, you cannot convict either defendant unless you are satisfied so that you are sure that particular Defendant is guilty.

Now, with his lordships' leave, I will call the first witness."

David noticed how the jury were already eating out of Tim's hands. They had smiled at him and nodded through parts of the opening. He had succeeded in making the case simple and clear for them. It was not a great start for his client Paul Morris. The evidence sounded overwhelming and the jury were already accepting everything Tim had said without David even saying a word yet. He looked down at the papers in front of him and thought that he would not mind so much if it was not for the fact that the evidence was in fact overwhelming and would probably get even stronger as the trial unfolded!

CHAPTER 28

THE FIRST WITNESS

Tim turned around to look at his junior, Sean, who smiled back with a gentle nod, the sign of his approval of the opening speech. Content with this, Tim turned back to face the jury and announced that his first witness was Police Constable Foster.

Starting with the motive, thought David.

Police Constable Foster walked into court and took a quick look around at his surroundings before making his way to the witness box. He adopted an unconvincing air of confidence, making it obvious to the judge and advocates that he was not used to being in the Crown Court. He was no doubt more comfortable making short appearances in the Magistrates Court, dealing with the drunk and disorderlies and public order offences.

The officer took the oath and answered a few preliminary questions from Tim about his duties, training and experience, before he moved onto the main evidence.

"Officer, I want to ask you about a visit you made to a property in Moulsecoomb in the early hours of Sunday, 4th May, of this year. Do you recall making such a visit?

"Yes I do, sir."

Tim gave his biggest beaming smile to the jury as he moved on. "No doubt you took a note of the circumstances of your visit?"

"Yes I did, sir."

"When did you make your notes?"

"When I got back to the police station, about an hour and a half after the event."

"Was that the first opportunity you had to make those notes officer?"

"Yes it was, sir."

"Were the matters fresher in your mind then when you made the notes, than they are today?"

"Yes, sir."

Tim turned to Mr Justice Knight, "My Lord, might the officer have your leave to refer to his notes, in order to refresh his memory?"

The Judge turned to the defence advocates, "I assume there is no objection."

Both defence leaders did not even rise as they both said, almost in unison, "None whatsoever."

Both tried to suggest that they welcomed the officer relying on his notes, when in reality, there was no possible objection to him using them.

The Judge nodded and his gaze fell on the witness, saying, "Officer, you may refresh your memory from your notes. Please do not read them out slavishly, but only rely upon them when you need to refresh your memory."

PC Foster nodded obediently at the judge and then opened his notebook and began reading out verbatim, what appeared there. No one bothered to stop him.

"On Sunday, 4th May, at approximately 12:20am", he recited, "I was in company with Police Constable Stephen Richards in a marked police car when we received a call to attend an address in Moulsecoomb. It was reported that someone had caused criminal damage to the windows of a dwelling house. We arrived at 24 Neville Street, Moulsecoomb at approximately 12:30am and noticed that the front window of the property was smashed and there were some glass fragments on the pavement outside the house. We noticed upon entering the property that most of the broken glass was actually inside the property.

On first approaching the building, I knocked on the door and called out, "Police, please open the door!"

I immediately heard sounds of people rushing around in the house, and we heard the flushing of toilets. We assumed ...."

The Judge stopped him, "Don't tell us what you 'assumed' officer, just tell us what happened."

"Certainly, sir."

The Judge winced inwardly at the officer's improper use of his judicial title. He thought how annoying it was that police officers did not seem to know how to address him properly. Nevertheless, he resisted the urge to say anything.

Tim, noticing the Judge's reaction tried to smooth things over for his witness, "Just tell his LORDSHIP, and the jury, what happened next please."

PC Foster looked at the Judge, "Certainly, sir", he repeated, as Tim sighed helplessly. "It was at least five minutes before the door was opened by a young man with an Afro hairstyle. He gave his name as Michael Ward, one of the Defendants in this case."

He looked towards the dock and pointed out Ward. It was what the lawyers would call a 'Dock Identification' and totally impermissible, but no one could be bothered stopping him as Ward did not dispute this evidence and accepted that police visited him as described so far.

Tim decided to take control of his witness now, "Officer, did you have any conversation with Mr Ward?"

"Not really, he gave me his name but would not answer any other questions."

"Were there any other people in the house?"

"Yes, the Defendant, Paul Morris ..." Again he pointed at the dock, ".... came to the door almost immediately and started talking to us."

Foster was becoming more confident in the witness box, and visibly breathed in and stood up straighter as he answered Tim's questions.

"I told Mr Morris we had been called by a neighbour because of a complaint that someone had been smashing windows. Mr Morris told us to come in and 'see for ourselves.' We went into the living room where we both noticed that there was glass over the floor in front of the main window. Some of the broken glass was clearly from brown coloured bottles.

I asked him what had happened and Mr Morris told us that a couple of bottles had been thrown through the window. He said he had been hit in the head by some broken glass. He showed us a couple of minor cuts on his forehead."

"Did he tell you who had thrown them?"

"Yes, he said that they had been thrown by someone they both knew."

He looked down at his notebook, "A Mr Danny Williams."

"Did he say why Mr Williams had thrown the bottles through the window?"

"He said he didn't know."

"Did you have any further conversation with either of them?"

"I asked both men if they knew where Mr Williams lived. Mr Ward refused to answer but Mr Morris told me he knew and could take us there."

"Did he?"

"Yes sir, he came in our police car with us and pointed out Mr Ward's address …" He looked down at his notes again, "… number 4A Saunders Road."

"Did you gain entrance to that property?"

"No sir, we knocked on the door but no one answered. I told Mr Morris we would get police to visit the address over the next few days and arrest Mr Williams. We then took Mr Morris back to his home address."

David made a visible sign, busily underlining this part of the evidence and was happy to note that a couple of members of the jury were watching him.

Tim just ignored him and carried on, "Did you notice anything in particular about number 4A Saunders Road?

"I noticed that two of the windows must have been broken because they had been boarded up."

"Did you ever visit either address again?"

"No sir. That was my only involvement in the matter and I don't believe that Police Constable Richards had any further dealings either."

Tim smiled and told the officer to remain in the witness box, as there may be one or two questions from the defence.

David rose slowly from counsel's wooden bench. Lewes Crown Court had been designed a long time ago and the benches were a little restrictive. He put it down to the fact that barristers must have been smaller in the past and definitely not because he had been putting weight on from wining and dining Wendy. He moved his notes from the bench so he could rest them on his lectern as he cross-examined the witness.

"Officer, you have told us that you visited this address as a result of a call from a neighbour?"

"Yes, sir."

"Someone had clearly thrown a couple of bottles through Mr Morris' window. As you've told us the main distribution of the broken glass was on the inside of the window and that was where the broken bottles were found?"

"Yes sir."

"Clearly Mr Morris and it appears Mr Ward, were the victims of a crime?"

"Yes sir."

"As you have told us, Mr Ward would only give you his name. He was not very cooperative?"

"No, he wasn't, sir."

"On the other hand, Mr Morris told you about the incident, told you who had committed the offence, gave you his address and even took you there. He was very cooperative with police wasn't he?"

"Yes sir, he appeared to be."

"There is no 'appearance' about it, officer, he was totally cooperative."

"Yes, sir."

"We know that Mr Williams was either not at home when Mr Morris took you there or he was not answering the door?"

"Yes, sir."

"I just want to suggest one thing to you about this officer. You had access to a police computer to conduct checks on addresses that night didn't you?"

"Yes, sir."

"No doubt you checked who the registered occupant was at the address?"

"I would have done, yes, sir."

"I suggest that Mr Morris said he knew the occupant as "Danny" but did not know his surname?"

The officer looked at his notebook. "No sir, I am sure he gave me the name Danny Williams."

"After finding that Mr Williams was not at home that night, you informed Mr Morris that the police would be attending the address again, sometime over the next few days?"

"Yes sir."

"Clearly the police could have attended at any time of the day or night?"

"Yes sir."

"So you left Mr Morris with the impression that police would be attending Mr Williams' address in the next few days at any time of the day or night?"

Foster looked surprised at the question, after all, to his mind he had answered this several times. "Yes sir, as I've already said."

David smiled, "So Mr Morris was left with the impression that if he attended Mr Williams' address in the next few days at any time of the night or day, the police might be there to greet him?

Foster still seemed confused, "I suppose so, sir."

David looked at the jury hoping the point was made, "Thank you officer, I have no further questions."

William Smythe rose from the bench. He had not intended to ask any questions of this witness but he felt duty bound to ask one or two, just to keep the client happy.

"Police Constable Foster, I represent Mr Ward who sits behind me."

Foster and the jury all looked at his client who was staring into space, apparently oblivious to his unenviable circumstances. Smythe had thought it might be sensible to identify who he represented to the jury but one look at Ward's vacant expression and he quickly decided not to do it again.

"You have told us, as a result of my learned friend's questioning ..."

He pointed to David before continuing, "That Mr Ward was uncooperative?"

"Yes sir."

"Let us just examine that for a moment shall we. As you have accepted from my learned friend, Mr Ward was the victim of a crime. Namely having bottles thrown through the window of the room he was sitting in?"

"Yes sir."

"No doubt this had been a frightening event for him?"

"I imagine so."

"You have no doubt come across cases similar to this where the victims of crime are still in a state of shock and not always able to easily communicate so soon after an incident?"

"I have sir."

"I suggest to you that Mr Ward gave you his name, but was in a state of shock and unable to supply any other information. Are you able to dispute that?"

"No sir."

William sat down again, content with his few questions.

Tim immediately stood up to re-examine his witness after his unhelpful answers to the defence.

"Police Constable Foster, you were asked some questions by Mr Brant, Queen's Counsel on behalf of Paul Morris. You have told us he was 'totally cooperative.' Did he tell you anything about his previous dealings with Mr Williams?"

"No, he didn't."

"Did he tell you that Mr Williams had his own windows smashed a few days before?"

"No he didn't."

"Did he tell you what his feelings were towards Mr Williams?"

"No sir."

"He told you that he did not know why Mr Williams had thrown a bottle through his window?"

"That is correct sir."

"He gave you no idea?"

"No, sir."

"You have told us that you left him with the impression that police would visit Mr Williams' address again?"

"Yes sir."

"Did you leave him with the impression that police would be outside Mr Williams' address every hour of the day or night?"

"No sir."

"In your experience, considering police resources, how often would police have visited this address over the next few days in relation to this matter?

"Probably once or twice at most."

"In fact, have you since discovered that the police did not go around to that address again until after Mr Williams was murdered?"

"I am aware of that now."

"Thank you. You were also asked questions by Mr Smythe, Queen's Counsel on behalf of Mr Ward. He asked you whether Mr Ward was in a state of shock. Can you assist us with this?"

"Not really sir, I asked him a number of questions and he simply shrugged and wouldn't answer."

Tim smiled, "Thank you, officer." He turned to the Judge, "Unless your Lordship has any questions for Police Constable Foster, I shall call my next witness."

CHAPTER 29

THE EXPERIENCED WITNESS

Police Constable Richards entered the court room and without looking around made his way straight to the witness box on the right hand side of the court. It was clear to all the lawyers in court that he was no stranger to this courtroom or indeed the witness stand. Although still only a Police Constable, he was about five years older and obviously more experienced than his colleague who had just given evidence.

No one in court knew it, but PC Richards had just passed his sergeant's exams and was hopeful that a position would be found for him in a local police station soon. He was adamant he was not going to be verbally trapped by the defence barristers and determined not to give anything away in cross-examination that could assist them.

Tim took him through the same questions that Police Constable Foster had just been asked, and of course the same answers were given. He then focussed on the issues that David and William had cross-examined Police Constable Foster about.

"Officer, did Mr Morris say who threw the bottles through his parent's windows?

"Yes sir, he did."

"What name did he give you?"

The officer looked at his notebook as if he could not recall, "He gave the name Danny Williams."

"Thank you. Did he tell you why he thought Mr Williams had thrown bottles through his father's window?"

No sir, he told us who he thought had thrown the bottles, he took us to where he lived, but other than that he did not assist us with why he had damaged the property."

"Thank you, officer. Now, in relation to Mr Ward, can you tell us what state he was in when you saw him?"

Richards looked puzzled. "He seemed to be normal, sir."

"How long did you have him under your observation?"

"Probably no more than ten minutes."

"Did he appear shocked to you during that period?"

"No sir, I don't believe that he was."

"Why do you say that?"

"He looked normal to me sir. He looked a little angry, but not in a state of shock. I've seen many people in a state of shock and he did not seem shocked to me."

Tim appeared very satisfied with the answers as he casually said, "Would you remain there please officer," before sitting down.

David decided not to question him as there was little he could improve upon from Police Constable Foster's evidence. He smiled as he thought to himself that the secret of good advocacy is not necessarily what questions you ask, it's also knowing when not to ask questions.

He watched as William Smythe got to his feet, pulling the sides of his gown into place, and looking at this smooth, confident, officer as he prepared to cross-examine him.

David shook his head slowly from side to side, it was clearly not a lesson that Smythe had learnt over the years Perhaps he thought the art of cross examination was to examine crossly!

Smythe had actually considered not asking any questions either, however, he decided that with his experience, he could get the better of a simple police constable, and impress his client and the jury with his forensic skills.

"Officer, may I ask what your degree is in?"

The police officer seemed surprised at the question, "I don't have a degree sir."

"Well what courses have you taken in psychology or psychiatry?"

"I haven't sir."

"Really, well are you able to tell us what the clinical signs are for nervous shock say, or post-traumatic stress?"

"I can't sir."

"So, you are not suggesting to the jury that you are an expert on the effects of shock on a victim of crime?"

"No, I am not sir." He paused, "However, I worked in road traffic for eight years and, sadly, I have witnessed the aftermath of many hundreds of accidents where victims were in a state of shock. I can state quite clearly that it appeared to me that your client did not fall into that category, but was simply refusing to answer any questions other than his name. I felt he had an uncooperative, anti-police, attitude."

Smythe raised an eyebrow at the witness as he responded, "Officer, are you really trying to assist this jury with your evidence?"

"I'm simply trying to answer your questions."

Williams' junior, Jason Herd, put his head down as if to make a note, but David heard him whisper to his leader, "Move on Bill." He knew William was just sparring with the witness needlessly and such games were always dangerous in cross-examination.

William Smythe turned around and threw a cold look at Jason before turning back to the witness.

"Officer, I suggest that although you may well have witnessed numerous road traffic accidents and seen and questioned numerous victims, you are not an expert on the effects of shock and you are not in a position to assess whether Mr Ward was in a state of shock or not?"

The officer paused whilst he considered the question before replying, "I'm not suggesting I am an expert sir. I have been asked what I witnessed and from what I saw, it appeared to me that your client was simply refusing to answer questions and exhibiting an anti-police attitude."

William sat down without a further word. He had at least learnt the lesson that when you have been forced to dig a hole for yourself, there comes a time to stop digging.

Tim rose to his feet and stated with a beaming smile directed towards the jury, "I have no re-examination in the circumstances, unless Your Lordship has any questions, can this witness be released please."

David looked at him whilst thinking that at least a member of his chambers knows when not to ask any more questions, what a pity he happens to be the prosecutor in this case!

CHAPTER 30

THE 'LEAVING CARE PERSONAL ADVISOR'

After a light lunch in the hotel restaurant across the road from the court building, David and Graham returned to deal with the afternoon's witnesses. Tim had decided to call Lisa Thomson, one of the social workers who had had dealings with Danny Williams just before he died.

Lisa Thomson walked slowly into court and stood in the witness box, putting on a pair of reading glasses to read the oath. David presumed, she was about forty and unmarried as she was not wearing a ring on her wedding finger. Other than that, he found it difficult to read anything about her upon first impression.

Tim began with a little background information, "Ms Thomson, I understand that you are a social worker who had contact with Danny Williams before he was killed?"

"My correct title is 'Leaving Care Personal Advisor'," she replied, looking at him over the rim of her reading glasses.

Tim smiled at her in as friendly a manner as possible, "Thank you. I stand corrected. Can you tell the jury what the duties of a 'Leaving Care Personal Advisor' are please Ms Thomson?"

"My function is to help people, usually young men, to integrate into society after they have spent many years in local authority care."

Tim smiled, "The same sort of duties as a social worker then!"

There were a few smiles from members of the jury and before Lisa could respond, Tim immediately asked, "Can you tell the court a little about Danny Williams?"

Lisa looked at him coldly over the top of her glasses before taking them off and answering, "Yes, he was put into care when he was twelve. His family said they could not 'handle' him." She replied curtly with a degree of censure in her tone.

There was a loud noise of clear disapproval from a group of people in the public gallery. Mr Justice Knight looked up and gave them a stern look and they immediately quietened. David looked around and noticed the noise had come from people who had earlier been pointed out as members of Danny's family. It was not the first time he had seen a deceased's family attend court to watch a trial with seeming concern, when they had shown little interest in the deceased when he was alive.

Lisa clearly felt the same as she just ignored the noise and continued, "Danny was placed with potential foster parents on a number of occasions but the placements were never really successful and he rarely stayed with any one family for more than three or four months.

I came across him when he was 17 and he was assigned to me. He seemed very depressed at the time and I worked with him to try and build up his confidence."

"From your knowledge of Danny, how would you describe him?"

"Danny was vulnerable and very child-like. I found him reasonably polite and easy to deal with most of the time but his general lifestyle was chaotic and this often lead to him becoming frustrated and excitable.

Some of the team dealing with him had concerns for his mental health on occasion, but he was never referred to see a psychologist or psychiatrist because he always became rational again after a short time. It was thought his problems were more behavioural than mental."

Tim nodded before continuing, "We have heard that he moved to 4A Saunders Road,

Moulsecoomb, on Friday 18th April, 2014. Why was he moved there?"

"He had been living in a hostel for a year before the move and we felt he was under the influence of others and suffering as a result. Despite it being in breach of the rules of the hostel, it was known he was smoking cannabis and it was also suspected that he was selling it.

It was decided he might benefit from being moved into the community to get him away from these negative influences in the hostel. However, this may have actually aggravated the situation because when he died he was living on his own and clearly not coping well with it."

"Why was that?"

"Soon after he moved in, we had complaints from the residents that lived in the area where Danny's flat was. He was having lots of visitors, at all times of the day and night. There were complaints of drug taking, rubbish was left all over the streets and there were complaints that families were being kept up at night because of these visitors being loud and disruptive."

"When did you last see him?"

"I arranged to meet him at the flat on 5th May of this year, with Jenny Wright from my department, and I saw him then."

"What was the condition of the flat like at that stage?"

"I remember that before we entered the flat, I could see that the windows had been smashed and boarded up. When we walked into the flat, it was in an horrendous state. The place was filthy, there were stains and debris all over the floor, surfaces and bed linen. There were large pieces of broken glass on the inside of the property from the broken windows. The air was thick with the smell of cannabis. It looked like it had been used for wild parties and drug-taking not as a home for a young, vulnerable man."

"How would you describe his condition?"

"He seemed quieter than usual. He looked very depressed. This is when I thought we should refer him to a psychiatrist, just to check on his mental health. When I got back to the office I contacted the Mental Health Unit of our local hospital, to get Danny an appointment."

Tim nodded, "Of course he was never able to keep it was he."

Lisa could not help but look towards the dock as she answered with obvious contempt, "No, he was not."

Tim smiled as he noted the jury following her gaze, and then asked, "You have mentioned that there were broken windows and broken glass in the property. Did Danny say how that had occurred?"

She again looked towards the dock, "He said the window was broken on Thursday, 1st May. He said a white boy and a black boy had caused the damage."

"Did he give you any names?"

"He did not tell me their proper names although he said the black boy was known in the area as "Afro" because of his hairstyle."

Some members of the jury followed her gaze again, this time towards Michael Ward, who had shrunk down into his seat ever so slightly, suddenly very aware of his conspicuous hair-do.

Satisfied that he had managed to give as favourable a description of the victim as he could in the circumstances, Tim thanked his witness and sat down.

David rose to his feet and looked at Lisa, waiting until she had had enough of staring dangerously at the Defendants and had turned her gaze back towards him.

"Ms Thomson, you have given us some of the history relating to Mr Williams."

He was not going to call him 'Danny' as it made him sound like he was referring to a youth rather than the adult he had been. He continued, "Perhaps you can help me with a few other matters that you touched upon."

He smiled at her, which was immediately met with a steely frown. He adopted a more neutral expression before continuing. "From what you say, Mr Williams had a few problems in the hostel he was living in?"

"Yes."

"He did not get on with other residents?"

"The problem was he got on a little too well with other residents!"

"Yes, so you have told us. It was suspected that not only was he taking cannabis, he was dealing in it, presumably for a profit?"

"I don't know if it was for a profit."

"Have you ever come across a drugs dealer who deals to make a loss?"

"No, though it could be to finance his own cannabis taking."

"It would certainly be for a profit then, but let's move on. He was moved into his own accommodation, as you have told us."

"Yes."

"Unfortunately that did not work out either."

"No."

"You visited him regularly?"

"Yes, with other members of my team."

"You have told us about the smell of cannabis in the flat?"

"Yes."

"And the fact it was clearly being used for parties?"

"Yes."

"Presumably it was obvious to you that he was not only selling cannabis for a profit, he was using council accommodation, paid for by the ratepayers of Moulsecoomb, to allow people to smoke cannabis in a relatively safe place?"

"Yes."

"I want to turn to 5th May. You have told us that he told you that a white boy and a black boy had smashed his windows?"

"Yes."

"He never gave any indication who the white boy might be?"

"No."

"So it could have been any white boy in the area?"

"Yes."

"In relation to the black boy he was a little more specific. He referred to him as Afro because of his haircut?"

"Yes."

"In your experience are there many black boys with Afro hairdos in the Moulsecoomb area?"

"No."

William Smythe looked closely at David and was about to intervene when David said, "Thank you, let's move on. Mr Williams told you that these boys had smashed his windows. Did he say that he had done anything about it?"

"No, he never said anything else about it."

"He never told you that he had thrown bottles through someone's windows?"

She looked surprised, "Certainly not!"

David thanked her and sat down. William Smythe got up from the bench and pulled his court gown over his shoulders.

"Ms Thomas…"

"It's Thomson."

William looked at her as if this was an irrelevant difference but added politely, "I am so sorry, Ms Thomson. Did you make any notes of the conversation you had with Mr Williams on 5th May?"

"I made a brief note in my diary when I returned to the office."

"Do you have that with you?"

"Yes, I do."

"Please do look at it."

Lisa got the diary from her bag, copies had already been served on the Defence as unused material. David knew what was coming as William continued, "You will see the entry for 5th May. The jury do not have this but does your note of the conversation say this, 'Danny said his windows had been broken after he had been visited by some boys. I think he said the windows were broken by a white boy and a black boy was with him as well.' There is then a full stop and it continues, 'The black boy with him he knows as Afro.' Is that what it says?"

Lisa read through the note. "Yes, it does."

"So your note taken on the day suggests that the white boy..," He looked towards the dock, "...whoever that was, was the one who broke the window. The black boy, Afro, was present, but there was nothing to suggest that he had taken any part in breaking the windows?"

Lisa looked up from her notes, "I suppose so."

"There is no suppose about it, that is what appears in your notes isn't it?"

"Yes."

William smiled at the jury as he sat down. David noticed that a young man on the front row smiled back.

David's expression did not change, but he knew the trial was going to play out just as he thought, with any good point he managed to draw from a witness being easily contradicted by his co-defending counsel, Smythe. He realised he would have to try something a little more subtle, and began planning his cross-examination of the next witness.

CHAPTER 31

ALL ABOUT THE TIMING

The case was adjourned early on Monday afternoon as no other prosecution witnesses were available to give evidence until the following day. Even though all counsel caught the same train back to London, David and Graham sat in a different compartment to 'discuss the case'.

On Tuesday morning all counsel again got on the same train from London Victoria and exchanged pleasantries and as usual David did his best to avoid talking to Tim.

Just over an hour and half later they were all seated in their respective places in court as the jury was brought in. Tim Adams QC called his next witness, Richard Brook.

After he was sworn Tim asked, "Mr Brook, at the time of this incident, you lived in Saunders Road in Moulsecoomb and were a neighbour of the deceased in this case, young Danny Williams?"

Richard Brook reacted slightly upon hearing the Danny's name, before replying, "Yes, that's right."

"May I ask, did you live alone at the time?"

Richard's shoulders sagged a little at the question, it was clearly a sore subject. He had been married when a short-lived affair with Michael, a male colleague at work, had put an end to that union, and had forced him to move into this cheaper, rundown area of Moulsecoomb. He had lived alone now for over two years and presently saw no possibility of his situation changing. He did not like to be reminded of the fact.

"I live alone and did so at the time," he replied softly, hoping that would be the end to the personal questions.

Tim noticed his demeanour and decided to move quickly on, he did not want to alienate one of his important independent eyewitnesses.

"Did you know young Danny Williams?"

"I had seen him in the street, but we never spoke."

"No doubt you witnessed a number of comings and goings at that property before his death in the early hours of 6th May?"

"I certainly did. From the moment he moved in there seemed to be constant parties and loud noises coming from that flat at all times of the day and night. It was dreadful for all of his neighbours. I couldn't sleep most nights without using some earplugs that a friend had bought me as a joke."

"As a joke?"

"Yes. A friend at work called Michael bought them." He paused for a second before carrying on, "He said I never listened to anything that was said to me, so I might as well have these earplugs, then at least I'd have an excuse."

There were a few smiles around the court. Tim smiled as well and continued, "Yes, quite. Now, I want to ask you about the early hours of 6th May of this year. Do you recall that day?"

"I most certainly do. It was a Tuesday morning and I had to go to work early that day."

"Tell us what you can remember."

"I had gone to bed at about 10:00 pm and I was woken at just before 1am by loud noises coming from that man's flat."

"You mean Danny Williams' flat?"

"Yes."

"How do you know it was just before 1am?"

"When I woke up, I looked at my digital clock which stands on my bed-side table. I recall it was 12:45am."

David made a point of deliberately and loudly underlining the time which resulted in a quizzical expression forming on Tim's face. He dismissed the gesture as irrelevant and continued, "What did you hear?"

"I heard very loud banging and shouting. I went to my window to open the curtain and then I heard a loud voice say, 'You almost brained me the other night, let me in or I'll fucking kill you.' It was a very loud and aggressive voice."

"Did you recognise the voice?"

"No."

"Can you tell the jury, did the person have a local accent or an accent from somewhere else?"

"I couldn't really tell."

"Did you look out from behind the curtain?"

"No, as I said, the voice sounded very aggressive and I didn't want to draw attention to myself."

"Did you hear anything else?"

"Yes, after a short time I heard someone say, 'You owe me, you little shit!', also in a loud voice."

"Could you tell whether it was the same person as the previous voice?"

"No, it might have been, I can't really say."

"What happened next?"

"I heard very loud banging on Mr Williams' door, as if someone was trying to smash their way in."

"What did you do?"

"I wondered whether I should phone the police, but, after a few minutes, the noise stopped and the visitors went away. I did look out then and saw three men. One was a black boy with an Afro haircut and the others looked like white boys, but I couldn't be sure. They were wearing hoodies with the hoods up. I waited until they had gone and I went back to bed, using my earplugs this time."

Tim turned to the jury, "Ladies and gentlemen, there is no dispute that Mr Brook later identified the defendant Michael Ward at an Identification Parade, as the black boy he had seen and just described as the one with the Afro hairdo."

The judge looked at William Smythe seeking confirmation. Smythe rose to his feet and said, "That is correct, my Lord, there is no dispute about that fact."

Tim turned to him and said, "Thank you", and then turned back to Mr Brook. He asked him to remain in the witness box, as there may be one or two more questions.

David rose to his feet and smiled at the witness. Richard Brook just looked at him curiously, wondering what he was going to be asked.

"Mr Brook, as you have told us the neighbourhood became very noisy after Mr Williams moved in?"

"Yes that's right."

"Large numbers of people visited him there?"

"Yes."

"You presumably saw many youths visiting the address?"

"Yes I did."

"No doubt you saw older people visiting as well?"

"Yes."

"No doubt you were kept awake by the parties and the noise?"

"I was."

"Did you ever form the impression that Mr Williams was dealing in drugs?"

Richard looked at him sternly, "Yes, I did, I saw him sometimes handing little packages over and taking money."

"Did this happen frequently?"

"Very frequently, almost every day I'd say."

"Did you ever see Mr Williams getting his drugs from anyone?"

Richard paused before answering, "I don't think so."

"From a black man, in his mid-thirties?"

"No, as I said, I don't think so."

"In the early hours of the 6th May you were awoken again by a loud noise?"

"Yes."

"You have told us that you looked at your clock and noted that it was 12:45am?"

"Yes."

"This was a digital clock and presumably was accurate?"

"Yes, it's set by radio signals that come from Rugby I believe, so it's never out by more than a few seconds or so."

"So we can assume from that that it must have been almost exactly 12-45am when you heard this loud noise?"

"Yes."

"Thank you Mr Brook that is very helpful."

Again Tim looked at him quizzically. David smiled at the jury and then turned back to Mr Brook.

"You have told us that there was only one person you recognised outside Mr Williams' flat that night and as we have heard that was Mr Ward?"

"I didn't know his name."

"No, of course not, but the fact is you did not recognise the other two. You could not even say if you had seen them before."

"No I couldn't."

"Nor could you say which one of these three made the comment, "You almost brained me the other night, let me in or I'll fucking kill you"?"

"No I couldn't."

"Nor could you say whether it was the same person who said, 'you owe me, you little shit!'?"

"That's correct."

"These other two, you thought they might be white?"

"Yes."

"But your witness statement states that you were unsure?"

"That's right, they were both wearing hoodies with the hoods up."

"So one or both of them could have been black?"

"They could have been but I don't think so."

"But you cannot be certain?"

"No."

"In view of them wearing hoodies I assume that you could not tell their ages?"

"No, I didn't really see very much of them, I was concentrating on the youth I did recognise."

"So it follows, one of them could have been, for example, a black man in his mid-thirties?"

"I suppose so, I don't know."

David thanked the witness and sat down as William Smythe got to his feet.

"There is no dispute that it was my client, Michael Ward, who was the black boy with an Afro hairdo who was there that night. However, he does dispute that it was him who said any of the words you have referred to. You are not able to help us in this matter. You cannot say it was him who said those words?"

"No, I can't."

"So it could have been one of the white boys you have referred to?"

"It could have been any of them."

William Smythe sat down and Tim re-examined the witness. He was not completely sure where David's cross examination was going but he knew that Paul Morris's defence statement stated that Joey Talbot was the killer, so he needed to remove him from the scene outside Danny's flat.

"Mr Brook, when first questioned by the police you referred to three people outside Mr Williams' flat?"

"Yes, I did."

"You have fairly said that you cannot be certain who, and in answer to my learned friend, Mr Brant's questioning, you said that one or both of them may have been black?"

"Yes, I did."

"Now, thinking back to the night, you recognised Mr Ward as we know. What colour do you believe the other two men were?"

"I believe they were both white".

CHAPTER 32

THE NOSEY NEIGHBOUR

Richard Brook left the courtroom at speed, trying to put as much distance between himself and that place as quickly as possible. He feared that he might be called back and asked more personal questions. As he was leaving through the door of the court, he heard the prosecutor announce that his next witness was Shereena Bennett and he felt an immediate sense of relief.

A few minutes later, Shereena Bennett, appeared. She was a heavy-set black lady who clearly had respect for the court system as she was dressed in a fine navy and white skirt suit and climbed as elegantly as she could into the witness box. She took the oath in a serious and sombre tone and turned to look respectfully at the barrister who was standing and addressing her.

Tim gave her a beaming smile before asking her, "Ms Bennett, you live in Saunders Road, in Moulsecoomb, close to an address where Danny Williams lived?"

"Yes, I live at number 4, in the ground floor flat next door to his flat."

Tim looked at her statement, "Now, please don't take this the wrong way, as I don't mean this disrespectfully, but are you the sort of person who takes an interest in what is going on in her own street? A healthy concern if I can put it like that?"

She looked a little surprised before answering, "I used to be."

There were again a few smiles from the jury. David smiled as well, wondering about the unusual approach that Tim was taking with this witness. He was effectively asking his witness if she was a busy-body, in front of the jury! Still, he thought, everyone has their own style at the Bar.

Tim just continued smiling at the witness and continued, "Were you aware, for example, when it was that Danny Williams moved into number 4A Saunders Road?"

"I became aware within a day or so of him arriving."

"Why was that?"

"Well, the whole area became a lot noisier with people visiting his flat every day."

"During the day or at night?"

"Both."

"Did he have a lot of visitors?"

"Yes, he did."

"Did you recognise any of them?"

She immediately looked at the dock and saw Michael Ward.

"I saw a few people who came quite a lot. Especially the boy with the Afro haircut," She answered, nodding in Mr Ward's direction.

Tim looked down at her witness statement again, "From what you saw, did you ever think Danny Williams was involved in drug dealing?"

She nodded, "Yes, I suspected that something like that was going on. People would turn up and shout his name and he would appear. There were so many youngsters wearing hoodies constantly going in and out. They were black and white, males and females, of all ages."

"All ages?"

"Well, teenagers, and twenty and thirty year-olds."

"Did you see any drug dealing?"

"Yes, I saw things being passed between hands. I thought that it must be drugs."

"Did you see Danny pass or receive anything?"

"Yes, he was the one selling the drugs. He would pass little packages and receive money in return."

I want to ask you about the early hours of 6th May of this year. The day Danny Williams was killed. Can you recall that day?"

"Oh yes, I remember that poor lad dying."

"Can you describe to us in your own words what you saw and heard that night?"

"Yes, it was about 1am when I was woken by a loud noise. My bedroom is at the front of the property, next to my son Lloyd's bedroom. I looked out of the window and saw three men at Danny's door...."

Tim intervened, "Now, presumably it was dark in the area at that time?"

"Yes it was."

"Was there any street lighting?"

"There was some, but it wasn't very good."

"Did you notice what the men were wearing?"

"Jeans and hoodies."

"Did they wear their hoodies up or down?"

Again she looked at Ward, "The one with the Afro had his hood down. The others had theirs up."

"We know that you recognised the boy with an Afro later, when you attended an identity parade and picked out Mr Ward, who sits in the dock. I understand there is no dispute that he was present. However, from what you tell us, did you get a good look at the other men?"

"Not really."

"I think it's correct that in your witness statement you thought these men were both black men. Do you still think that is the case?"

"I know that Lloyd thought they were white but I am sure they were black."

"Even in the poor light whilst their heads were covered and..."

David stood to his feet, "My learned Friend appears to be in danger of trying to cross examine his own witness. This lady has said she was sure the men were both black, he should really leave it at that."

Mr Justice Knight looked up from his notebook, "I am sure Mr Adams was just trying to assist the jury, but I'm sure we all have the point. Mr Adams, can we move on."

Tim gave the judge a polite bow which the judge completely ignored, "Of course my Lord, I was just trying to assist."

He turned to Ms Bennett again, "Very well, tell us what you saw?"

"When I looked out, the men were all walking away from Mr Williams' door. I noticed the boy with the Afro haircut make a phone call although I didn't hear what he said. He then seemed to look up at me so I moved behind the curtains."

"What happened then?"

"Lloyd had woken up as well. He came to see if I was alright. We then discussed whether we should call the police. I had a sip of water from a glass I have by the bed and discussed it with him. A few minutes later, we heard another loud noise."

Tim looked at her witness statement and noted the reference to her drinking rum from a bottle she kept in her room. He decided to ignore it.

"Tell us what you heard?"

"Well, it was swearing and I don't like to repeat it."

Tim smiled at her, "Do not worry Ms Bennett, we have heard it all before in these courts and we have to know from you what you heard."

"Well, someone said something like, 'I'll eff'ing kill you.' I went over to my curtains and saw the same three men confronting Danny Williams, who was backing up into an alleyway. I called out to Lloyd and he saw it as well.

I decided to close the curtains because I was scared. It was then I heard a terrible scream, it sounded like a woman's voice. I went to the curtain again and saw two of the men running away. Both had their hoodies up. I then saw Danny staggering out of the alleyway. He walked for a few yards and then collapsed."

"Did you see what had happened to the man with the Afro hairstyle?" asked Tim.

"No."

"What did you do?"

"I called the police. Lloyd went out to see if he could help Danny."

Tim turned to the jury, "Ladies and gentlemen, it is an agreed fact between the prosecution and the defendants that Ms Bennett's 999 call was logged at 01:23 in the morning of Tuesday 6th May 2014."

He then turned back to Shereena, "Thank you Ms Bennett, will you stay there, there may be some further questions from the other barristers in this case."

Shereena looked at David suspiciously as he stood to ask her questions and she did not feel any more comfortable when he tried to give her his most reassuring smile.

"Ms Bennett, I only have a few questions so I won't keep you very long."

Her expression did not change as she looked at him stony-faced. Hr healthy respect for the court was becoming strained as she wondered what else she was going to be asked.

"As we have heard, Mr Williams had only lived in the street for a short period of time?

"Yes, just a few weeks."

"Nevertheless, you noticed a deterioration in the area from the moment he first arrived?"

She looked puzzled as she replied, "What do you mean?"

"Sorry, as you have told us from the moment he first came, lots of people attended his address at all times of the day and night?"

"Yes."

"It was often very noisy?"

"Yes."

"And no doubt the area was littered with discarded takeaways and the like?"

"Yes."

"Further, as you have told us, you learnt that he was dealing in drugs?"

"Yes, I saw him selling drugs."

David tried another smile but gave up when he saw it had no effect on this witness, "Yes, thank you. Now clearly Mr Williams was supplying drugs, and we know it was cannabis."

She nodded carefully at David.

"Of course, he had to first receive his supplies in order to sell them. Did you ever see anyone supply him with drugs?"

She thought for moment before replying, "No, I don't think so."

"You have mentioned different people attending the flat of different colours and ages?"

"Yes. Do you recall a black man ever attending his flat, aged in his mid-thirties?"

"I saw many people visiting his flat. I do recall one large black man who was about that age, once coming to his flat in an expensive black Mercedes car."

"Does the name Joey Talbot mean anything to you?"

She looked puzzled again, "No it doesn't."

David never expected it to, he just wanted to mention the name in front of the jury and hopefully couple it in their minds with an expensive black Mercedes car.

"Very well, you have told us what you saw in the early hours of 6th May. You place the events at about 1am. Could it have been slightly earlier at, say, 12:45am?

She hesitated before answering, "I suppose so, I didn't check the exact time."

"You told us that three men came to Mr Williams' flat. We know that Mr Ward was one of them as he has admitted this since you picked him out at an identity parade."

William Smythe looked up from his own notes and almost rose to his feet because of David's emphasis on the word 'since' but he decided to leave the point and not emphasise this unhelpful evidence by causing a fuss.

David quickly continued, "You recall Mr Ward was on the phone at one stage, can you say whether he had received a call or made one?"

"No, not really."

"You have told us, as you told the police at the time, that you are sure that the other two men were black."

"Yes."

"Is it possible only one of them was black and the other was white?"

"I thought they were both black men."

"Very well, we know you did not get a good view but was one of those black men about mid-thirties?"

"I couldn't tell their ages."

"May one of the men have been the same man you saw arrive on a previous day in the black Mercedes?"

"It may have been but I thought the men I saw were not as large."

"But, as you have told us, you did not get a good view. After all, it was dark, the street lighting was poor and the whole incident was over very quickly?"

"Yes, that's true."

"So, it may have been the same man or it may not have been?"

"I suppose so."

"Now, there were effectively two incidents, the first which had woken you up, when you saw the men outside Mr Williams' flat, and the second, where you saw the same three men confronting Mr Williams?"

"Yes, that right."

"You mentioned that between these two incidents, you discussed what you had seen with your son, Lloyd, and you took a sip of water. You then said a few minutes later that you heard another noise outside?"

"Yes."

"I suggest that more than a few minutes had passed between the incidents?"

"What do you mean?"

"Well, I suggest the first incident occurred at 12:45am, and lasted no more than a few minutes. We know that just after you heard the scream and the men ran away it was 01:23 because that is the time you phoned the police."

"Yes."

"Well there must have been more than just a few minutes between the two incidents?"

"It only seemed a few to me."

"I appreciate that it is some time ago now and you may have forgotten?"

"I thought it was only a few minutes."

"Well, let us just go through what happened after the first incident. You and Lloyd discussed what you had seen."

"Yes."

"And you poured yourself a drink of rum from a bottle you keep in your room?"

Shereena looked distinctly embarrassed now so David added, "Ms Bennett, believe me there is no criticism intended, it must have been a frightening incident. No doubt a stiff drink was required?"

"Yes."

"Presumably you sipped at the drink as you discussed what you had seen with Lloyd?"

"Yes."

David looked down at her witness statement and picked it up so she and the jury could see he was reading from it, "Then you poured yourself another rum and it was whilst you were drinking this that you heard the further noise?"

Shereena looked down at her feet as she answered quietly, "Yes."

"All I am suggesting, and believe me there is no criticism of you, is that this must have all taken more than a few minutes?"

"I suppose so."

David thanked her and sat down. William Smythe now stood up to cross-examine her.

"Ms Bennett, I represent Mr Ward..."

He turned to the jury, "... who admits being there that night."

She nodded at him as he tried to gain eye contact with her but she was still looking down at her feet.

"I am going to suggest that you are wrong and that he was not with two black men that night, but with two white men. Isn't that right?"

Now that the subject of her drinking rum in her room was not being referred to, she looked up.

"I am sure they were black."

"But you accept you may have been wrong?"

"I may have been, but I don't think I am."

"Now, you were awoken by a loud noise?"

"Yes."

"At about 1am?"

"Yes."

"Can you tell us what it was?"

"It sounded like shouting."

"Did you hear what was said?"

"No, I didn't."

"Or who was shouting?"

"No."

"Later on, you heard someone say something that sounded like, "I'll fucking kill you", is that right?"

"Yes."

"Again, you cannot say who said this?"

"No."

"Now, you refer to three men advancing towards Mr Williams, so he was backing into an alleyway?"

"Yes."

"You had not seen what happened immediately before this?"

"No."

"You had not seen what Mr Williams had done?"

"No."

"Nor heard what he had said?"

"No."

"You could not tell whether he had acted aggressively or not to one or more of the group?"

"No."

"Presumably, from what you saw, you saw Mr Williams backing into an alleyway and the three men following him?"

"Yes."

"Presumably, from what little you saw, you cannot say whether the three men were advancing aggressively towards him or not?"

"Well, I heard the scream."

"Yes, but that was when they were out of sight. You did not see if one of the men came from nowhere and suddenly attacked him whilst the others merely watched in shock?"

"No, I suppose not."

"Yes thank you, I have no further questions."

William sat down as Tim announced that he had no re-examination. As it was approaching lunchtime, Mr Justice Knight told the jury that they should take an early lunch and be back by 2:05pm.

David watched as Shereena left the court, completely bemused by what had just happened. Again he felt his own questioning had gone well before William had done his best to limit its effect. It was, on the papers, an overwhelming case against his client, but he did have a defence if only David could develop it. The problem was that every time he advanced Paul's case, William got up and pushed it back to the start. David had to see if he could do something about that with the next witness.

CHAPTER 33

THE NEIGHBOUR'S SON

David and Graham lunched in the restaurant next door to the court and avoided discussing the morning's evidence just in case any jurors were present. As they were seated, Tim and Sean entered.

"Watch out the smiling assassin has just walked in," Graham warned.

David acknowledged them both as Tim approached and said "You were a bit harsh with Ms Bennett weren't you David. Was it necessary to mention her nocturnal rum habit in front of the jury?"

"Enjoy your lunch, Tim," David replied, making it abundantly clear to Tim that he was not interested in his jibes.

Back in Court 3 at a few minutes past 2pm, the next witness, Lloyd Bennett, strolled in and was directed to the witness box. He was wearing an embroidered shirt and a tie, it was clear that he had inherited his mother's pride in his appearance.

David also noticed that Lloyd's shoes had been shined for court and he instinctively looked down at his own shabby pair before quickly looking away in case anyone else noticed this neglect.

Despite making an effort with his appearance, Lloyd gave the air of someone who clearly had better things to do. He worked part-time so he could attend college to complete his A Levels. He had to take time off work to attend court and was conscious that he was losing money as a result, which he clearly resented.

Tim started his examination taking his witness through the usual background details; where he lived, who he lived with, the fact he lived next door to the deceased, before he moved on to the events of 6th May.

"Mr Bennett, can you tell us what time you went to bed on the evening of 5th May?"

"It was probably around 11pm, I had to go to bed early as I had an early start the next day. I work every Tuesday." He emphasised the word 'Tuesday' to demonstrate that he was missing work today. Tim just ignored this irrelevant fact.

"Did you manage to get to sleep?"

"Yes, fairly quickly."

"When did you wake?"

"I didn't notice the time, it was probably around 1am."

"What woke you?"

"It was loud shouting coming from outside of next door."

"Did you hear what was said?"

"No, but the voices sounded angry."

"What did you do?"

"I looked out of my window and saw three men outside the next door flat."

"Can you describe what they looked like?"

Lloyd looked at the dock as he replied, "One was a black boy with an Afro style haircut. The other two were white."

"Are you sure the other two were white?"

"Yes, I'm positive."

"Did you recognise either of them?"

"No."

"Thank you. Now it is an agreed fact between the parties to the case that the boy with the Afro hairstyle was Michael Ward, one of the defendants in this case. You later picked him out at an identity parade?"

"Yes."

"Having seen the men outside, what did you do?"

"I went to my mother's bedroom as I knew she would be worried. There had been a lot of these incidents recently with people making loud noises outside and in the flat next door. I know she was worried about it."

"What happened next?"

"My mum poured herself a rum from a bottle she keeps in her room. She only started keeping it there since Danny Williams moved in. We discussed whether to call the police but decided not to, as we hadn't heard that much by then. About fifteen to twenty minutes later, we heard someone outside shout something like, "I'll fucking kill you".

My mum immediately went over to her curtains to see what was happening and then called me over. I went across to the window and saw the same three men forcing Danny into an alleyway."

"Where is the alleyway in relation to your property?"

"About 20-25 metres away."

"How were they forcing him?"

"They were advancing towards him and he was backing away."

"What happened next?"

"We discussed what to do and as we were talking we both heard a terrible scream. It was really loud and blood-curdling"

Tim looked closely at Lloyd who now seemed to be enjoying the attention he was receiving.

"What did you do?"

"We went back to the window to see what was happening and saw two men running from out of the alleyway. We then saw Danny stagger out, walk for a few yards, and then collapse. I ran out of the flat to see if I could help him but, when I got to him, he was covered in blood and was unconscious. I tried to stop the bleeding but wasn't able to and a few minutes later, an ambulance arrived and they took over."

"Thank you, will you wait there," Tim instructed.

David took a quick look at his notes before turning to Lloyd. "Mr Bennett, I note from your witness statement that you were either at work or college during the day, so, presumably, you did not see who came and went from Mr Williams' address?"

"No, I didn't, but I saw enough people coming and going when I got home."

"He had many visitors?"

"Yes, almost every night."

"Did you witness him drug dealing?"

"I saw things happening that looked like he was dealing."

"Did you ever see him receiving supplies of drugs?"

"I saw lots of people coming round but I don't know who supplied him with his drugs."

"Did you ever see a large black man, mid-thirties, driving a black Mercedes, come to his address?"

"I don't remember seeing anyone like that."

"Do you know someone named, 'Joey Talbot'?"

"No." David noticed that Lloyd was very adamant in his 'no', perhaps a little too adamant. He decided to move on anyway. "Let's move on to the early hours of Tuesday 6th May. You were woken by a loud noise?"

"Yes."

"You thought this was at around 1am but you did not have a clock, could it have been earlier at 12:45?"

"It could have been."

"Your bedroom is further away from Mr Williams' address than your mother's is?"

"By a couple of metres, it's the next room along."

"So your view of Mr Williams' door would have been slightly more obscured?"

"Only slightly."

"You looked out and saw three males. One we know is Mr Ward, the other two you did not know?"

"No, I did not."

"Presumably you only had them in your view for seconds at most?"

"Yes, as soon as I saw them I went to my mother's room as I knew she would be worried."

"Were they both wearing hoodies?"

"I think so."

"With the hoodies pulled up over their heads?"

"Their heads were covered."

"Did they have their backs to you or did you see their faces?"

"When I first saw them, they had their backs to me. Later on, I caught a quick glimpse of their faces."

"You believed from the quick glimpse you got, in poor lighting and at a restricted angle, that they were both white?"

"I'm sure they were."

"To be fair, you did not see them for long?"

"No, I didn't."

"You did not have them under observation as long as your mother did?"

"Probably not, she spends more time looking out of her curtains than I do!"

There were a few laughs from some members of the jury.

"Could it be that you made a mistake and one or both of these men were black like your mother has said in evidence before this jury?"

"I don't think so."

"The sodium light shining on them and a fleeting glimpse may have played tricks on your eyes?"

"I don't think so."

"You saw them a second time. Again, for less time than your mother?"

"Yes."

"Were their backs to you then too?"

"Yes."

"You then saw two men leaving the alleyway, followed shortly after by Mr Williams?"

"Yes."

"Was one of those men Mr Ward, the man you described with the Afro hairdo?"

"Yes."

"The other man you believe was white?"

"Yes."

"Did he go off in a different direction to Mr Ward?"

"Yes they went off in opposite directions."

David thanked him and sat down.

William Smythe got up slowly from his seat and after exchanging a brief comment with his junior who showed him his notes of the evidence, he asked, "Mr Bennett, I want to ask you about the early hours of 6th May. You are in no doubt that you saw my client, Mr Ward and two white men together outside Mr Williams' flat?"

"That's right."

"It was about 1am when you first saw them?"

"Yes."

"Then you later saw the three men with Mr Williams?"

"Yes."

"You caught only a glimpse of what was happening before all four men moved into the alleyway out of sight?"

"Yes."

"You had not seen what had happened immediately before?"

"No."

"You had not seen what Danny Williams had done?"

"No."

"You did not hear what, if anything, Mr Williams said?"

"No."

"In giving evidence earlier you stated, 'Mum immediately went over to her curtains to see what was happening and then called me over. I went over and saw the same three men forcing Danny into an alleyway'?"

"Yes, that's right."

"Now, I don't doubt that was your perception and belief, but what I am suggesting to you is that all you actually saw, was Mr Williams backing into the alleyway and the three men going into the alleyway. You did not see anyone physically forcing him into the alleyway?"

"No, I suppose not."

"It may well be that what you saw in a fleeting moment was just one of the group of three, threatening Mr Williams, but the others simply observing what was happening and following?"

"They all seemed involved to me."

"Yes, but you only saw them for a split second?"

"Yes."

With that, William thanked him and sat down.

Tim rose to his feet swiftly to re-examine his witness, "Mr Bennett, you accept that you only saw things from a restricted angle and for a split second?"

"Yes."

"However, what were the words you heard before seeing these men advancing towards Mr Williams as he retreated into the alleyway?"

"I'll fucking kill you."

"From your position, and from what you saw, did you have any doubts whether these men were acting together or not?"

"None whatsoever, they all seemed to be acting together to me."

CHAPTER 34

THE PATHOLOGIST

Tim announced that his next witness was Herbert Rogers, the pathologist who had conducted the post mortem. He explained to the jury that he would have preferred to call other witnesses first but, due his busy schedule, Herbert Rogers would have to give evidence that day.

A few minutes later, the pathologist entered the court room, making his way straight to the witness box. He was no stranger to Lewes Crown Court, having given evidence there regularly over the previous twenty years, often in that very courtroom. He was much in demand in other parts of the country as well, and had given evidence in most major court centres in the United Kingdom during his career.

He took the affirmation. He felt he had seen too many dead bodies and human tragedies in his time as a pathologist in his work, and had long ago rejected the idea of a God, a matter that caused his devout Catholic wife, considerable consternation.

Tim took him through his impressive list of qualifications. He was a Bachelor of Medicine,

Bachelor of Surgery (M.B.ChB.), Fellow of the Royal College of Pathologists (F.R.C.Path). He held a Diploma in Medical Jurisprudence in Pathology (D.M.J.Path) was a registered medical practitioner and an Honorary Lecturer in Forensic Pathology at the University of Kent and had been for the last twelve years.

There was no doubt to everyone in court that he was clearly an expert in his field.

Tim took him carefully through the medical evidence in the case. Herbert Rogers explained all the injuries he found on the body of Danny Williams. There were a number of old small scars and bruises and some fresh cuts and grazes which probably occurred shortly before death but had no direct connection with it. There were also injuries caused by medical intervention when the paramedics had tried to keep him alive. Having explained and eliminated these, Tim then moved on to questions establishing the cause of his demise.

"Mr Rogers, can you tell us what the cause of death was?"

"Certainly, death was caused by a single stab wound to the heart."

"Can you describe that injury?"

"Yes. Having examined the body fully, I came across one large stab wound in the upper left side of his chest. The deceased was 1.78 metres tall, which is about 5 feet 10 inches. There was a stab wound to the midline anterior chest, that is the front of the chest, located 139cm above the heel. It measured 2.5cm by 1.2cm gaping, that is when viewed without manipulation, when the edges of the wound were closed it measured 2.7cm. It had a 'fish tail ending' which suggests that the knife used might have had a serrated edge.

The wound penetrated slightly downwards and from the left hand side of the body to the right, through the chest muscle and then continued between the 4th and 5th ribs on the left hand side of the body. The wound extended into the body, and there was an injury to the sternum, the breast bone, and then it continued internally causing an injury to the pericardium, the sac protecting the heart. The pericardium had 150 mls of blood and blood clots when I examined it. It then penetrated the left hand side of the heart where it came to a stop. The track of the wound was about 6.5 cms in length."

David noted that a young man on the jury was looking almost white in colour. Tim did not seem to notice, and proceeded with his questioning as if they might have been discussing the weather.

"Were you able to estimate the size of the knife from these injuries?"

"Not an exact size but I would expect the width of the blade to be somewhere between 2.5cm and 3 cm and the length of the blade to be in excess of 6cm."

"You say in excess of 6cm but you have told us that the wound depth was 6.5cm?"

"Yes but skin and organs can compress when pierced in this fashion and hence a wound tract can be deeper than the length of a blade. In this case I would not expect there to be much compression hence the blade is likely to be over 6cm in length, probably much larger in view of the width of the blade."

"Yes, thank you Doctor. Can you assist as to what degree of force was needed to cause this injury?

"Generally not much force is required for a sharp knife to penetrate the skin. The only real resistance is the skin itself and then the knife continues through muscle relatively easily. Obviously there is some resistance as anyone who carves a joint of meat on a Sunday can confirm."

The young man on the jury was now very white indeed. Herbert Rogers noticed the colour drain from his face, but was not concerned, and carried on, "However, here the knife hit bone in the ribs and sternum and then continued. In my opinion it would have taken severe force to cause the damage I saw and for the knife to then continue and cause damage to the heart. In view of the area of the injury and the force used, I concluded that it was consistent with an intent to kill."

Tim nodded, "I see. Now, Doctor, we will hear from a witness in this case that, after receiving the injury, Mr Williams was seen to get up and stagger for a few yards before dropping to the ground. Is that a possibility after receiving a stab wound to the heart?"

"Oh yes, the stab wound penetrated the chest cavity causing some damage to the 4th and 5th ribs and then the sternum before it damaged the heart. There would definitely have been some blood loss as is evidenced by the fact blood was found in the pericardium and the left chest cavity. This blood loss would have caused a degree of cardiac tamponade, this is where the blood accumulating in the pericardial space around the heart, begins to constrict and exert pressure on the heart thereby stopping it from functioning properly. However, this would not happen immediately and the victim would have been capable of a short period of purposeful activity after the wound was inflicted."

"In this case we know that Mr Williams was stabbed in an alleyway and then collapsed about 20-30 meters away near to his home address. Would 'purposeful activity' have included him travelling this distance?"

"Oh yes, I have come across cases in the past where persons have been stabbed in the heart and then performed quite remarkable levels of activity, for example running for 100 metres. However, this activity could be estimated in tens of seconds of activity rather than minutes. They would very rapidly collapse."

Tim thanked him and sat down as David rose to his feet. In reality he had no real questions to ask but he wanted to say something as the evidence had clearly had an impact on the jury. He thought it was probably worth trying a bit of Locard.

"Dr Rogers, the angle of the fatal injury was downwards and from the left hand side of the body to the right. Can you tell from those angles whether the injury was caused when Mr Williams was standing or whether he would have been laid out prone at the time?"

Herbert Rogers thought for a few seconds before answering, "The injuries would have been consistent with him standing, but I cannot rule out the possibility he was prone and the assailant was standing over him."

"Can you assist whether the injuries indicate that the assailant was right or left-handed?"

"No I can't assist on that. These situations are dynamic and peoples' positions can change a great deal. I would just be guessing if I said right or left-handed."

"You told us the possible dimensions of the knife and the fact it might have a serrated edge?"

"Yes."

"Presumably the blade could have been much longer than 6 cm?"

"I've already said that."

"It could presumably have a 20cm blade?"

"It's possible."

"It could have been for example, a hunting knife?"

"It could have been."

David smiled, now it was time to rely on Locard.

"Doctor, have you heard of Locard's Exchange Principle?"

The pathologist, sighed before answering, "Yes, I am familiar with Locard's Principle. It's a principle created by a French criminologist, not a pathologist though."

"Can you explain it to us?"

"Basically it states that where two bodies meet they leave a trace on each other."

"In other words 'every contact leaves a trace'?"

"Yes, that's probably a better way of putting it."

"So, "put simply", in a case like this, Locard's Exchange Principle states that if Mr Morris was in close proximity to Mr Williams when he was stabbed and came into contact with him, you would expect a trace of that contact to be left on both Mr Williams and Mr Morris?"

"Yes that's what the principle states."

"That trace could be DNA from blood, saliva, sweat or a fibre of from either's clothing, or some other trace such as a fingerprint or palm print on something susceptible to retaining such prints?"

"Yes."

David thanked him and sat down, satisfied that as there were no such traces, he had secured a valuable piece of evidence in favour of his client.

William Smythe quickly stood up and quickly glanced at David before turning back to the pathologist. "Mr Rogers, in your experience is it possible for two persons to come into contact and not leave any identifiable trace?"

"Depending on the circumstances, yes."

"For example, if an assailant stabs once with a knife and immediately withdraws the knife and moves away, it is possible that none of the victim's blood would end up on the assailant?"

"Yes, that is possible, particularly if the assailant withdraws the knife before the victim bleeds freely."

"Indeed, it is possible that no blood would be left on the knife that was used by the assailant. Blood could be wiped off the knife, from the skin and also the clothing, as it is withdrawn?"

"Yes that is possible."

William looked at David and smirked as he sat down. David smiled back but could not help thinking how he was beginning to dislike this co-defending counsel.

CHAPTER 35

EYEWITNESS TO MURDER,

It was now Wednesday morning and Charlie Dickson walked slowly into court and headed towards the witness box. He knew that he could just as easily have been making this walk from the dock, where he could see Michael Ward and Paul Morris now sitting. He caught Michael Ward's eye and began to nod at him, before thinking better of it.

He was sworn by the court usher and gave his name to the court before Tim began his questioning, "Mr Dickson, I understand that you live in the Moulsecoomb area and did so in May of this year."

Charlie looked down at his feet and mumbled quietly almost to himself, "Yes."

"Mr Dickson, you will have to do better than that. The jury needs to hear your every word. Please look up and speak up."

Charlie looked towards the jury and then immediately away again and nodded.

"I understand that, in May this year, you lived with your girlfriend, Tracey Andrews, and her three year old son, Jimmy."

Again he mumbled in reply, "Yeah."

"Please do speak up Mr Dickson." Tim reminded him impatiently. "Now it's right isn't it that you are a drug user and a regular smoker of cannabis?"

Mr Justice Knight immediately intervened, "Should I give a warning to this witness that he need not answer that question for fear of incriminating himself."

Tim gave a large grin as he addressed the Judge, "I see no need my lord, Mr Dickson is not going to be charged for smoking cannabis."

"Nor for murder!" Graham said in a sotto voce voice behind David. David smiled, although the smile quickly faded when he spotted a male in the front row of the jury who had clearly caught the remark and was now frowning at Graham.

Tim had not heard the comment and carried on with his questioning, "Please answer the question Mr Dickson?"

"I'm not a regular user. I smoke a little now and then, and only when I can afford it."

"Now I understand that you do not work. Do you claim benefits?"

"No."

"How do you live then?"

"Tracey claims benefits and we live off that and off money her parents give her."

"How are Tracey's benefits paid?"

"Into her bank account."

"Is it right that you collect the benefits for her."

"Yeah, they clear in her account just after midnight on Mondays. I go and draw the money out and give it to her."

"Do you give all of the money to her?"

"No, she lets me keep £10 so I can buy a draw of cannabis."

"Who do you buy from?"

He pointed to the dock, "Usually from Afro, but if he hasn't got any I buy it from anyone who sells it."

"We know him as Michael Ward. Did you ever buy any off Danny Williams, the victim in this case?"

"Yeah, once, about two weeks before he died, when I last collected Tracey's benefits."

"Tell the jury what happened on the night Danny died?"

"I went out just after 1am and went to pick up Tracey's money from the cash-point nearest her flat. As soon as I got it I phoned Afro, sorry, Michael Ward, and arranged to meet him to buy a draw."

"We have a record from the bank showing that money was drawn out of the account at 1:07am. Was that you?"

"Yeah."

"We also have phone records showing you called Mr Ward at 1:08am, would that be the call you've mentioned?"

"Yeah."

"Did you meet up?"

"Yeah, a few minutes later we met up in Saunders Road."

"Why Saunders Road?"

"That's where he said he was."

"What happened when you got there?"

"I bought the draw."

"Then what happened?"

"Danny Williams appeared and started shouting at Michael."

"Can you recall what he said?"

"Yeah something to do with this being his turf and asking what Michael was doing outside his flat that night."

"Did you know what he was talking about?"

"No."

"Had you been outside Mr Williams' flat that night?"

"No, I didn't even know where it was."

"What did Michael Ward do in response?"

"He just told him to fuck off'."

"Then what happened?"

"Danny went for Michael and there was a fight between them."

"How did that end?"

"Michael Ward knocked him to the floor and then he ..." the witness pointed at Paul Morris in the dock but Tim interrupted him before he finished his sentence, "Sorry, Mr Dickson, we have certain rules in court about identifying suspects. Are you able to use a name?"

"Yeah, Paul Morris. He came from nowhere and stabbed Danny."

Tim was silent for a moment before asking, "Did you see a knife?"

"No, I only heard later it was a knife."

"Well, tell us what you saw, not what you learnt later."

"I saw Paul Morris attack him when he was on the ground. I didn't see a knife. I thought he hit him. I saw him put his hands together and bring them down hard on Danny's chest. Then he got up and ran away."

"Did you hear anything said by anyone?"

"No, I think everyone was just shocked. Michael Ward ran off, Danny himself got up and walked away, and I ran after Morris to ask him what that was all about."

"Did you catch up with him?"

"Yeah."

"Did you speak to him?"

"Yeah, I asked him what it was all about. He told me Danny had thrown bottles through his parents' windows and they had almost hit him. He then said Danny 'had it coming',"

"What did you do then?"

"After a few minutes, I went back to Tracey and told her I had seen a fight. I didn't think any more about it until I saw the news on the TV on Friday night that Danny was dead and those two had been arrested," he said nodding towards the dock.

"What did you do then?"

"I panicked. I thought the police might be after me as well even though I hadn't done anything. I packed a bag and went to stay with my Aunt in Brighton. I returned after three weeks, expecting that things would have quietened down, and went back to live with Tracey. A few days later, I was arrested."

"You were arrested, gave your account to the police and, as the jury has heard, you were not charged."

"No."

"Yes thank you, I have no further questions for now, will you stay there as defence counsel may have some questions for you."

CHAPTER 36

CROSS EXAMINATION OF THE EYEWITNESS

David got up slowly from the bench and faced the witness. He knew how important it was to discredit his evidence. He needed an in-road to attack his character. He picked up a copy of Charlies Dickson's first interview. "Mr Dickson, what were you arrested for?"

"Suspicion of murder," answered Charlie as if he were almost amused by the charge.

"So the police tracked you down at your girlfriend's address and arrested you on suspicion of being a party to the murder of Mr Williams?"

"Yeah, but they were wrong, obviously" he answered with contempt.

"That must have been a frightening experience?"

"It was, I was terrified at the time."

"However, according to you, you had done nothing wrong?"

"That's right, nothing at all!"

"You had just been buying some recreational drugs when it happened and you were merely a witness to the killing?"

"That's right. I didn't even realise he had been killed at the time!"

"After your arrest, you were taken to a police station, and there you had the advantage of seeing a solicitor. I don't want to know what he advised you, such communication is privileged, but, suffice it to say, as a result of his advice, you made no comment in response to each question the officers put to you in interview?"

"That's right."

"I have a copy of that interview here. You can see it if you wish. The police were putting questions to you along the following lines, 'We know you were there?', 'We know you were in a group confronting Danny Williams', 'We know you were a party to the murder?' Questions like that?"

"Yeah, that's right."

"It must have seemed to you that the police thought you were involved in the murder?"

"It did."

"They even put it to you that you were one of the lads who went to Mr Williams' address that night and banged on his door demanding to be let in?"

"Yeah, they did."

"Had you gone to his door that night with others and demanded to be let in?"

"No."

"They put to you what an eye-witness had said. They suggested that you were one of three people who confronted Mr Williams forcing him into an alleyway?"

"Yeah, something like that."

"Of course, according to you, that never happened?"

"What do you mean?"

"Well, according to you, you were not in a group confronting Mr Williams. You say that he approached your group and started fighting with Mr Ward?"

"That's right."

"Those independent eye-witnesses must have got that wrong?"

"Yeah."

"Or, you are lying!"

"I'm not lying. I've no reason to lie."

"Really? Well that is a matter for the jury to decide. I suggest that you have lied to this jury and that Paul Morris never attacked Mr Williams. You have made that up to protect yourself, to protect Michael Ward and to protect the real killer?"

Charlie looked distinctly uncomfortable as he replied, "That's not true."

"When do you say you first heard that Mr Williams was dead?"

"On the Friday afterwards. I saw it on the news."

"Are you sure it wasn't on the Wednesday?"

"No, it was the Friday. I remember, I was shocked by it, I remember!"

"Didn't your girlfriend, Tracey, point out there was an internet memorial page for Mr Williams?"

Charlie hesitated before answering, "No, I'm sure I heard about it on the TV, on the news. That's why I left on Friday night."

"You told the police that once you learnt he was dead, you threw away the top and jeans you had been wearing that night. Is that right?"

"Yeah."

"Why?"

"I just panicked. I thought they might have blood or something on them."

"Why? According to you, you weren't close-by when Mr Williams was stabbed. How could you have got blood on your clothing, unless you were a lot closer to him than you have told us?"

"I just panicked. I wasn't thinking straight was I? Anyway, the clothes were old."

"You didn't throw the clothes away because they were old though did you. You've just told us you threw them away because they might have blood or presumably DNA on them from Mr Williams, or fibres from Mr Williams' clothes."

"I just panicked."

"You told the police that you went to stay with an Aunt in Brighton?"

"Yeah, I did."

"Why did you run away?"

"I was scared."

"Or is it because you were involved in this murder and have not told us everything? Are you hiding something?"

"No. I'm not hiding anything," he answered defensively.

"Did you stay with an Aunt in Brighton, or is that a lie? Did you actually stay in London?"

Charlie looked suspiciously at David, "No, I went to stay with my Aunt in Brighton."

"You told Tracey you went to stay in London?"

Charlie looked surprised, "No, I told her I went to stay with my Aunt who lives in London Road, in Brighton."

David smiled and decided to move on, "You have told us you were arrested for murder. You at first made no comment and then you gave the police this story about Mr Morris being the killer?"

"It's not a story, it's the truth."

"By the time you provided that story, the police had alleged that you were a party to the murder of Mr Williams?"

"Yeah."

"It was in your interests to divert them, to turn their attention from you?"

"I just told the truth."

"I suggest you told them a series of lies, blaming an innocent man for the murder."

"No, I told the truth."

"You were in custody, being detained by the police, and it was alleged that you were guilty of murder so you decided to blame someone else?"

"No, I never."

David could see that Charlie was gripping the edge of the witness box, his knuckles were white.

"Did you know Paul Morris before that night?"

"No."

"He wasn't a friend then?"

"No."

"So you had no reason to lie to protect him?"

"No."

"Michael Ward was a friend?"

"Not really. I just bought weed off him now and again."

"But you had each other's phone numbers and were in regular contact with each other?"

"Only so I could contact him about buying weed."

David picked up a bundle of spreadsheets listing the phone data. "Mr Dickson, you told us you purchased weed every two weeks when you collected your girlfriend's benefits?"

"Yeah."

"As you told us, you didn't always purchase from Mr Ward, you purchased from other dealers as well. You even purchased drugs from Mr Williams on one occasion didn't you?"

"Yeah..." Charlie looked puzzled at the questioning.

"On that basis, you would only need to contact Mr Ward every two weeks or so in order to buy drugs?"

Charlie looked anxiously at the spreadsheets in David's hands before answering, "Maybe a bit more than that."

"We have the telephone records here, which demonstrate that you phoned Mr Ward or he phoned you, on average two or three times a week. Clearly that was to discuss more than just a fortnightly drugs deal?"

"Well, I probably discussed other things as well."

"And you met up as friends?"

"Occasionally we met, but not that often."

"You met up as friends?"

"Occasionally, not often."

"When you were at the police station being questioned on suspicion of murder, you had to divert police interest in you. You obviously didn't want to blame a friend so you picked on the innocent Mr Morris didn't you?"

"That's not true."

"You say you left your girlfriend's flat at 1am on the night of 6th May?"

"Yeah."

"We know you got your girlfriend's benefit money out of the bank at 1:07am and immediately after you phoned Mr Ward, at 1:08am?"

"Yeah."

"You say you then went and met him in Saunders Road where you witnessed this killing?"

"Yeah."

"Was that the first time you had met Mr Ward that night?"

Charlie was again looking uncomfortable as he answered, "Yes."

"You left Tracey's flat much earlier than 1am didn't you?"

"No, I didn't."

"We know from the telephone records that, at 11:56pm on 5th May, Mr Ward phoned you. I suggest you left your flat just after that call in order to meet him, and that meeting was just after midnight?"

"No, it was after 1am."

"Your girlfriend, Tracey, says you left the flat just after 12 midnight."

"I didn't, it was later."

"You went and met up with Michael Ward just after midnight didn't you?"

"No."

"There was a third man there as well?"

"No, there wasn't."

"Do you know a man called Joey Talbot?"

Charlie gripped the witness box even more tightly. "I don't know him," he said nervously.

"Maybe you know him by his street name, 'Pumpman'? He is so called because of his use of a pump-action sawn-off shotgun whilst he commits armed robberies."

Charlie looked very uncomfortable now.

"I know of him. He's not a friend though."

"How do you know him?"

"He lives in the area."

"He was there that night when you joined Michael Ward wasn't he?"

Charlie looked afraid now as he answered, "No."

"Are you afraid of the "Pumpman"?" asked David, feigning concern for the witness.

"No."

"Are you scared of him because you know he was the one who committed this murder?"

"No," he answered looking towards the public gallery at the back of the court where there was a slight movement by a member of the public.

"The three of you went to Mr Williams' flat that night and started banging on the door?"

"That weren't me." he insisted.

"Did 'Pumpman' tell you Mr Williams owed him money?"

"No, he didn't."

"Money for drugs he had supplied to Mr Williams?"

"No!"

"I suggest the three of you were outside Mr Williams' flat at approximately 12:45am that night. Mr Ward was shouting words along the following lines, 'You almost brained me the other night, let me in or I'll fucking kill you'?"

"No."

"It was 'Pumpman' who shouted through the door, and threatened the deceased, saying, 'You owe me, you little shit'."

"No."

"How do you know if you weren't there?"

"I wasn't there, so I don't know what happened."

"When he would not let you in and you couldn't force your way in, you all started to leave?"

"No."

David picked up the phone records again. "As you were leaving, Mr Ward received a call, didn't he?"

"I wasn't there!"

David picked up the phone records again as he continued, "As we can see from the records, at 12:48am, Mr Morris used his home phone to call

Mr Ward. Mr Morris was obviously at home at that stage."

Tim's normal beaming smile turned into a frown as he looked at his junior and whispered something to him. Charlie's face was now quite white.

"I wasn't there. I didn't visit Danny's flat that night."

"I suggest you did and then you went off and no doubt collected your girlfriend's money. You then phoned Ward to see if he was still in the area."

"No, it didn't happen like that."

"You returned to the scene and met up with Mr Ward and Pumpman again?"

"No, it was just Ward."

"My client, Mr Morris, then appeared and so did Mr Williams?"

"No."

"Mr Morris started to leave the area as Ward, Pumpman and you, together advanced towards Mr Williams, forcing him into the alleyway where Pumpman stabbed him to death."

"No!"

"Ward took the knife from Pumpman and ran off to hide it. You also ran off, but in the direction that Mr Morris was walking."

"No."

"You caught up with him and you were both scared as a result of what you had seen. You both agreed to say nothing because you were both terrified of what Pumpman might do to you."

"No."

"It was only when you were arrested and the police started to accuse you of the murder that you decided to blame Paul Morris instead?"

"No."

"Did the Police tell you that if you said it was Mr Morris who committed the murder, they wouldn't charge you?"

Charlie looked alarmed and looked towards the prosecutor.

"No, it wasn't like that," he answered nervously.

David looked at him for a few seconds and, as he sat down, he added, "I suggest it was exactly like that."

CHAPTER 37

THE CO-DEFENDANT'S CROSS EXAMINATION

William Smythe looked across the courtroom at an ashen-faced Charlie Dickson. This was not a witness he wanted to rely upon as part of his defence but he had to ask him some questions in view of the accusations that had just been put about his client.

"Mr Dickson, I am going to ask you some questions on behalf of my client, Michael Ward."

William grinned at Charlie, as he thought that at least Charlie now knew he was representing his friend.

"No doubt Mr Dickson you have many friends?"

Charlie looked puzzled, "I have a few."

"No doubt you are in regular communication with close friends. I daresay you contact them more than two or three times a week by phone?"

"Yeah, I suppose so."

"Now there is no secret about it. You knew Mr Ward because he regularly supplied drugs to you?"

"Yeah."

"This was usually fortnightly?"

"Yeah, usually."

"You also met him occasionally socially?"

"Once or twice."

"So yours was not a close friendship?"

"No."

"Not so close that you would feel the need to lie on his behalf?"

"No."

"Now you have told us you were not present earlier in the evening when Mr Ward and Mr Morris went to Mr Williams' flat?"

David immediately rose to his feet, "There is no evidence that Mr Morris went to Mr Williams' flat that night, my learned friend should re-phrase the question."

William smiled, "Quite right, there is no such evidence, yet! I will re-phrase the question to keep Mr Brant happy."

He turned to Charlie. "Mr Dickson, you say you did not go to Mr Williams' flat that night?"

"No I didn't."

"You collected your girlfriend's money and phoned Mr Ward at 1:08am. You then met up a few minutes later in Saunders Road?"

"Yeah."

"Mr Williams then approached the two of you?"

"Yeah he did."

"He was aggressive?"

"Yeah."

"He attacked Mr Ward?"

"Yeah he did."

"Mr Ward managed to defend himself and knocked Mr Williams to the ground?"

"Yes."

"Then Mr Morris came from nowhere and stabbed him to death?"

"Yes, that's what happened."

"At no stage was Mr Ward aggressive?"

"No."

"He only acted in self-defence?"

"It looked like that to me."

"Mr Ward never had a knife?"

"I didn't see him with one."

"From what you saw, he could not have caused the fatal injury to Mr Williams?"

Charlie looked a little puzzled by the question so William tried again. "Mr Ward did not stab Mr Williams?"

"No."

Tim was already on his feet before William sat down. He immediately asked, "You were not one of the people outside Mr Williams' flat earlier that night?"

"No."

"Therefore you do not know what was discussed between those persons or what their purpose for being there was?"

"No."

"When you arrived in Saunders Road you saw Mr Ward?"

"Yes."

"You did not immediately see Mr Morris but clearly he was nearby because, as you told us, he suddenly appeared from nowhere?"

"I suppose so."

"Although it seemed to you that Danny Williams was aggressive, you had not seen what had occurred outside his flat a short time before?"

"No."

"What you saw was Mr Ward knock him to the ground and then almost immediately after, you saw Mr Morris get on top of him and bring his hands forcefully down upon Mr Williams' chest?"

"Yes."

"So from what you saw, Mr Ward and Mr Williams could have been acting together?"

Both David and William rose to their feet to object to the leading question. Tim made a pretence of an apology and withdrew the question. He noticed one or two members of the jury smile at him. He did not need say anymore, he had made his point.

CHAPTER 38

THE GIRLFRIEND

It was close to lunch, and Mr Justice Knight adjourned the court at the end of Charlie's evidence, with a stern warning that the accused man should not speak to any witness about his or their evidence over lunch. The judge was aware that the next witness was Charlie's girlfriend, Tracey Andrews, and he wanted to avoid any suggestion that they might collude before she gave her evidence.

At ten minutes past two, Tracey Andrews walked into courtroom three, conscious that all eyes in the courtroom turned towards her. She was an attractive young girl, wearing a tight pink suit that showed her figure off well. She had clearly worked on keeping herself trim after having a baby a few years earlier. David's immediate thought was to ask himself what she saw in a druggy like Charlie Dickson. He soon put the thought out of his mind as he thought, after all a few people might ask what Wendy saw in him!

Tracey took the oath and answered a few preliminary questions from Tim about where she lived, her youngster Jimmy and how long she had known Charlie for. Then he got to the point.

"Now, Ms Andrews, I understand that you claim benefit payments for yourself and your young child?"

She clearly looked a little embarrassed as she answered, "That's right. I don't have a choice, do I!"

Tim nodded as if he understood and cared, "We also understand that these benefits are paid into your bank account?"

"Yes, that's right."

"Can you tell us when these clear, sorry, when you have access to them?"

She frowned at him slightly, "The payments are made fortnightly on Monday evenings. The payment always CLEAR just after midnight on Tuesday morning."

Tim smiled, he should not have assumed she had a limited knowledge just because she was dating Charlie Dickson!

"What arrangements do you have in place to collect the money?"

"I have a lot of bills to pay and it's not easy living on benefits, particularly as Charlie doesn't work and doesn't claim benefits, so I need the money as soon as it clears. Charlie always goes and collects it after midnight on Tuesday morning."

"Do you know why Charlie does not claim benefits?"

"He's too proud."

Tim did not want to say the obvious and undermine Charlie in the jurors' eyes. "Does he always go at the same time, or does the time vary?"

"It's always around the same time, just after midnight."

"Does he bring all the money back to you?"

"No, I let him keep £10 to buy a draw for himself. He gets it from a friend of his called Afro and then usually smokes it with his friend before coming home."

She turned to the judge and quickly added, "I won't allow smoking in the flat around Jimmy."

Tim continued, "I want to ask you about the night of 5th-6th May of this year. Do you recall that night now?"

"Only because of this case," She said dismissively.

"I understand. Now did Charlie go to collect your money that night?"

"Yes."

"Can you recall what time?"

"The usual, it was around midnight."

David noticed a few jurors making a note of the time. Good they're listening, he thought.

"Did you look at a clock when he left?"

"No."

"So it might have been later?"

David was about to object to the leading question but Tracey quickly answered, "No, he always goes at that time."

"How long was he out that night?"

"I'm not too sure. I went to bed after he'd left. I knew he would smoke weed with his friend Afro and he wouldn't be back for about an hour, so I went to bed."

"Were you awake when he came back?"

"No, though I was woken up by Jimmy crying. I noticed the clock said 2am. I went to see Jimmy and then saw that Charlie was in the living room."

"What did he look like?"

"What do you mean?"

"Did he look like he normally does when he comes home from collecting your money or was he different?"

"He was really charged up, with adrenalin or something."

"Did he tell you why?"

"He said he'd witnessed a fight. He said it was between Afro and this other boy, called Danny, and then another man had come out of nowhere and stabbed this boy."

"Did he say stabbed?"

"Well, he said this other man hit him, but we know he was stabbed."

"You mean you know now but did not know at the time?"

"Yes."

"Did he describe this other man?"

"No."

"Did he tell you this man's name?"

"Yes, he told me he was called Paul. He ran after him to ask him what it was all about and Paul said he had a problem with this Danny and Danny got what he deserved."

"Did Charlie know if Danny had been stabbed?"

"No, he said he had seen Danny get up and walk away. He thought he was all right."

"When did he discover that Danny was dead?"

"The following day, Wednesday. I saw a memorial page on the internet for Danny Williams. I pointed it out to Charlie. He was shocked."

"What did he do?"

"He made a phone call and left the flat."

"Do you know where he went?"

"No."

"Did he return?"

"Yeah, later that night. Then he left the next day and didn't return for three weeks."

"We have heard he was arrested at your flat. Were you present?"

"No, I wasn't."

She scowled, "When I returned my flat was in a mess. The police had almost wrecked the place!"

Tim ignored the comment and asked her to remain where she was for more questions.

David had carefully watched her give evidence, she did not seem to be lying and he doubted the jury would think she was. He had to try a different approach.

"Ms Andrews, you are still in a relationship with Charlie?"

She smiled, "Yes, I am."

"No doubt you want that to continue?"

She looked down to her feet, "Yes."

"Not just for your benefit but for the benefit of your son, Jimmy. I take it Charlie acts as his father?"

"Yes."

"You spoke to Charlie about what he had witnessed in the early hours of 6th May?"

"Yes I did."

"Did you discuss it again with him?"

"Yes, a few times."

"Did he give you all the details the first night or did he give you a few details at first and then provide more as time went by?"

"It was late the first night so he didn't say much. He told me more as time went by."

"The first night he told you he had witnessed a fight?"

"Yes."

"Did he tell you who was involved?"

"He told me Afro and this "Danny" were involved."

"Did he mention at first, on that night, the name of the man who hit Danny when he was lying on the ground?"

"I think so."

"But you can't be sure."

"No."

"In fact, do you recall when he first mentioned the name 'Paul'?"

"I'm not sure. It may have been on the first night."

"Isn't it more likely he provided you more details when you discovered that Mr Williams was dead?"

"Probably."

"Now, once he discovered that Mr Williams was dead, he phoned someone and then went out. I have some phone records here. They show that at about 12 noon on the Wednesday, he phoned Mr Ward, the man you heard him refer to as Afro. Might it have been that time when he made the call?"

"I don't remember now."

"You've told us he went out. Do you recall when that was?"

"I think it was in the afternoon."

"Do you recall how long he was out for?"

"A few hours."

"Did he say who he had gone to see?"

"No, he didn't tell me."

"When he came back did he discuss the killing again?"

"I think we talked about it that night."

"Might it have been around then that he suggested that this 'Paul' was the murderer?"

"It might have been, I can't really remember."

"Do you know if he went out to see Mr Ward?"

"I don't know."

"He and Mr Ward were close friends weren't they?"

"I don't think they were that close."

"Do you know how they met?

"Charlie told me they were both living in the same hostel a few years ago."

David nodded and made a quick note on his papers before asking his next question.

"Mr Dickson had a business relationship with Mr Ward in that he bought cannabis from him but they would also socialise wouldn't they?"

"Sometimes."

"Has Mr Ward been to your flat?"

"No!" she replied adamantly.

Have you heard the name, 'Joey Talbot'?"

She paused before replying, "Yes."

"How have you heard that name?"

"He has a bit of a reputation in our area."

"What sort of reputation?"

"Well he's an armed robber isn't he?"

David nodded. "Does Charlie know him?"

"He knows of him, we all do."

"Do you know if they have ever met?"

"I think they have."

"Do you know if they met on the night Mr Williams died?"

She looked nervous, "I don't know, Charlie never said anything about him."

"Are you sure he never said anything about Joey Talbot, aka Pumpman, being there?"

"I don't think so," she said even more nervously.

"Has anyone threatened you not to say anything about this Ms Andrews?"

"No."

"Has anyone threatened Mr Dickson? Maybe to make him give this account to the police?"

"No."

"Very well, has he told you of any offer the police have made to him in this case?"

"What do you mean?"

"Has he told you that the police have told him he won't be charged with murder if he gives evidence against Mr Morris?"

"He's never said that."

"Is he the sort of person who would voluntarily give evidence in a murder case involving people he knows?"

She laughed, "No!"

"The night of 5th-6th May, Charlie left your flat just after midnight. He did not return for about two hours did he?"

"No."

"Did he leave just after receiving a call from Mr Ward?"

"I don't know."

"Try to remember. We have phone records that show he received a call from Mr Ward just before midnight. Had he just received a phone call before he left?"

She paused clearly uncertain of what to say. David tried again. "Had he just received a phone call just before he left?"

"I think so, I can't really remember."

"It would not take him close to two hours to leave the house, go to the cashpoint, buy £10 of weed and smoke it, would it?"

"No."

"In fact, earlier you said in evidence that you expected him to be about an hour, but he was away for nearly two."

"Yes."

"Did he tell you where he was going?"

"He said he was going out to get my money and meet someone to buy weed. He never said anything else."

"When he returned did he tell you where he had been?"

"He told me he had seen a fight."

"Did he tell you he had been to Danny's flat with Michael Ward and Joey Talbot?"

"He just told me he'd witnessed a fight between Afro and Danny."

"He didn't mention anyone else at that stage?"

"I'm not sure. I can't remember any more."

"We know that once Charlie discovered that Mr Williams had died, he left the area for a few weeks. Do you know where he went to?"

"He told me he had gone to London."

"Did you have any contact with him during that period?"

"No, he never answered his phone."

David sat down, he had achieved as much as he could, now he would wait for William and Tim to un-do his good work

It did not take long for this to happen. William stood up and referred Tracey to her statement.

"You see the declaration you signed at the start of your witness statement?"

She looked down at the statement and said "Yes."

It states, 'This statement, consisting of four pages each signed by me is true to the best of my knowledge and belief and I make it knowing that, if it is tendered in evidence, I shall be liable to prosecution if I have wilfully stated in it anything which I know to be false, or do not believe to be true."

"Yes."

"Clearly then you wanted to be accurate in the account you gave to the police, not least because you could be prosecuted if you lied?"

"Yes."

"Now, when you made the statement it was nearer to the time of the incidents you referred to and therefore more likely to be accurate than your recollection of events today, months after the event?"

She looked suspiciously at William, as she answered, "Yes."

"In your witness statement to police, made on 15th July, you stated that Charlie came home and told you there had been a fight. Let me read the relevant section to you.

'He said he had seen a fight between Afro and Danny. Danny had attacked Afro who had knocked him to the ground. He then said Paul Morris came from nowhere and hit Danny in the chest.'

"Can you see that Ms Andrews?"

"Yes."

"So is that what you were told in the early hours of 6th May?"

"It must have been."

William sat down, giving David another smug grin.

Tim only asked her about one matter, "Did Charlie ever tell you where he went when he left your address for a few weeks?"

"Yes, he said he went to stay with his Aunt in London."

"Might he have said his Aunt who lives in London Road, Brighton?"

Tracey paused, "I thought he said London but I'm not sure now."

CHAPTER 39

THE PRISON SNITCH

Wednesday finished with Tim reading a few statements from witnesses who nobody required to attend court for questioning. Now it was Thursday morning and he announced to the court that he was calling Joey Talbot.

The jury was sent to their room as Joey was produced from the cells via the dock where Paul and Michael were seated. It was the usual precaution observed for prisoners. It was thought better to have the jury absent at this time in case there was any attempt to escape custody. In fact, nothing so dramatic occurred, and not even a word passed between the prisoners who did not even acknowledge one another.

Joey swaggered into the courtroom with a large grin on his face. He clearly intended to enjoy the day out of his prison cell and his new role as a prosecution witness.

Once the jury had returned and Joey had taken the oath and given his name, Tim started with a few preliminaries. This was necessary as there were two heavily-built security guards sitting behind Joey and he knew the defence would make a point if he did not raise it first.

"Mr Talbot, it is right that you are currently in prison, awaiting trial?"

Joey looked at him with contempt, and simply replied, "No."

Tim was momentarily perplexed. "I understand that you are a serving prisoner?"

Joey smirked as he replied, "No, I'm not."

Tim became a little frustrated as he asked, "Where are you currently residing?"

Joey smirked again, "At the Scrubs."

"You mean, Her Majesty's Prison, Wormwood Scrubs, in London?"

"Yeah."

"So you are a prisoner?"

"Yeah, but I'm not a 'serving' prisoner. I haven't been sentenced yet."

Tim sighed, "You are awaiting trial then?"

"No, I pleaded guilty, so I am not awaiting trial," he answered smugly, clearly satisfied by outsmarting a lawyer in court. "The Judge has put back my sentence," he continued.

Tim nodded, realising he would have to ask more precise questions with this individual.

"Do you know the Defendants in this case, Michael Ward and Paul Morris?"

Joey looked towards the dock, "Yeah, I know them," he replied with a snarl.

"Are they friends of yours?"

"No!"

"How do you know them?"

"We all used to live in the same area, I saw them around."

"When were you arrested?"

Joey smirked again, "When? Which time?"

Tim tried to smile but he distinctly disliked this witness. "On the most recent occasion,"

"I was arrested on 8th July this year, at four in the morning, while I was asleep!"

"What were you arrested for?"

"Possession of a shotgun, ammunition and a knife."

"You pleaded guilty to these offences?"

"Yeah."

"And you are awaiting sentence?"

Joey narrowed his eyes as he looked at Tim,

"Yes. I've already told you. I'm awaiting sentence."

"After arrest, which prison were you sent to?"

"Lewes."

"It is not disputed that both Paul Morris and Michael Ward were in that prison at the same time as you. That's right isn't it?"

"They were both in there when I arrived. We were on the same wing."

"Did you ever talk to them?"

"Yeah, loads of times."

"Did you ever discuss this case with them?"

"Yeah, with both of them."

"Tell the court what Paul Morris told you about the case if you would please Mr Talbot?"

"He's a cocky little shit! I can tell the court that!"

The Judge looked at him sternly but Joey ignored him and continued, "He was always playing the 'hard man' around our area. He used to …"

Tim interrupted, "Mr Talbot, could you just tell us what he told you in prison?"

Joey looked at him coldly, but then noticed that there was a police officer in court, who was involved in his own case and who was making notes.

"Alright. I used to chat with him a lot. Sometimes in the dining hall, sometimes in his cell. Anyway, he was always boasting and acting like he was really hard. He told me he had cut his own Dad up for 'dissing' him."

Tim intervened, "Just in case the jury do not know, what do you mean, 'dissing' him?"

Joey looked surprised at what he thought was a stupid question. "You know, he thought his Dad was not showing him respect."

"Thank you. What else did Paul Morris tell you?"

"He told me that he had an argument with this lad called Danny and smashed his windows. Then Danny came round to his father's house and put a few bricks through his window."

Tim again intervened, "Did he say bricks?"

"Yeah, bricks or something like that."

"Very well, please continue."

Joey noticed a particularly attractive blonde girl on the front row of the jury and smiled at her, licking his lips. She immediately looked away with disgust and he frowned and continued with his evidence.

"Yeah, well anyway, he told me he was almost hit by the brick or by the glass from the window. He got angry and decided to go round with Afro to sort Danny out."

Again Tim interrupted, "Did he say what was agreed between them?"

Joey looked surprised at the questioning. "What do you mean?"

Tim tried again, "Did Mr Morris tell you what was agreed between him and Mr Ward?"

"No, he just told me they went round to sort Danny out."

"Did he tell you what happened?"

"Yeah, he said Danny wouldn't open the door so he tried to smash it in but he couldn't so they left."

"Did he say where they went?"

"Yeah Afro went to deal some weed. Morris told me that, about fifteen minutes later, he saw Danny Williams having a go at Afro. So he pulled out the knife he always carries and stabbed Danny in the heart."

"Did he say what Ward was doing?

"No."

"Did he say whether there was anyone else there?"

"Yeah, he said the kiddy who Afro had dealt some weed to was there."

"Did he describe how he stabbed Danny?"

"Yeah he showed me. He took the knife like this."

Joey Talbot made a gesture, holding his hands together above his head and then bringing them down rapidly on the stand before him, his hands making a thud against the wood.

Joey continued, "He stabbed him and then ran off."

"Did he say what happened next?"

"Yeah he said the kiddy ran after him and asked him what it was all about. He said he told him it was because Danny had thrown bricks through his windows."

"Are you sure he said bricks?"

"It was something like that, maybe bottles."

Tim nodded and looked towards the jury, checking to see that they were listening to this evidence. He then turned back to Joey.

"Did you also speak to Mr Ward in prison?"

"Yeah. I saw him a few times as well. He gave me the same story as Morris. They went round to sort Danny out but couldn't get in. He then went off to deal with the kiddy and later Danny came up to him. There was a scuffle and then he said Morris came from nowhere and stabbed Danny."

"Did he tell you what he meant by going round to 'sort Danny out'?"

Again Joey looked at Tim as if he was an idiot, "It's obvious, they were going to give him a good hiding."

"He told you that Mr Morris had stabbed Danny. Did he say what with?"

Again Joey looked at him as if he was mad, "With a knife of course!"

"Did Mr Ward say anything else about the knife?"

"Only that it's the one Morris always carries."

Tim smiled and asked Joey to wait there for more questions.

David rose to his feet quickly. He had been observing Joey throughout his evidence. It was clear Joey was not going to help him so there was no point in being subtle.

"What is your name?"

Joey now looked as if he thought all barristers were stupid.

"I've already given my name."

"You have given us the name, 'Joey Talbot', but you have another name as well, don't you?"

"What do you mean?"

"You are known amongst your associates as 'Pumpman'?"

Joey shrugged and David continued. "You are known as 'Pumpman'?"

"Some people call me that."

"Why?"

"I don't know," he paused and then smiled as he added, "it's probably because I lift weights. Some people call it 'pumping' weights, hence 'Pumpman'."

David smiled in return, "Please, Mr Talbot, don't be modest. You received the name from your associates because of your use of pump-action shotguns when you embark on armed robberies."

Joey smiled, "Maybe."

"There is no 'maybe' about it Mr Talbot. You were convicted of an armed robbery of a post office in 2000 when you were in possession of a sawn-off pump-action shotgun."

"Yeah well that was a long time ago, I've changed a lot since then."

"True, it was a few years ago now, but you only came out of prison in relation to that case in 2008 didn't you?"

"Yeah, I did my time."

"Yes, and you carried on committing armed robberies?"

"I've not been convicted of any."

"I didn't ask that, but let's move on. You have told the jury that you are awaiting sentence?"

"Yes."

"It's right isn't it that you are awaiting sentence for, amongst other matters, possession of a sawn-off pump-action shotgun with ammunition?"

Joey smiled at the jury again, as he answered, "Yeah."

"The gun and ammunition were found in the boot of your car?"

"Yeah."

"That's a black Mercedes motor car?"

"Yeah."

"Also found in the boot of your car was a hunting knife?"

"Yeah."

"That's a knife with an eight inch blade, a 20cm blade with a serrated edge?"

"Yeah."

"A very sharp weapon?"

"It's sharp."

"Also found in the car was some camouflage coloured body armour?"

"Yeah, there's nothing illegal about that."

"True, in itself, simple possession would not be an offence, any more than simple possession of the ski masks, also found in the boot of your black Mercedes would be."

"Yeah, that's right."

"Except of course the whole lot put together was a robber's kit. You were going equipped to commit an armed robbery, which is an offence."

Joey shrugged, "I wasn't charged with that."

"Was the decision not to charge you with going equipped to commit armed robbery, made before or after you agreed to give evidence in this trial?"

"I'd already been charged when I was sent to Lewes prison. Anyway, I wasn't going equipped."

"Why did you have a sawn-off pump-action shotgun, ammunition, a hunting knife, camouflaged body armour and a ski mask with you?"

Joey grinned as he replied, "My friend makes Rap videos and I was using them as props."

"Props? Why did you possess live ammunition?"

Joey hesitated before replying, then smiled again, "It makes a bigger bang! It looks better on the video."

"What is your friend's name?"

"He doesn't want me to say."

David quipped, "I doubt anyone is surprised about that!"

A couple of jurors laughed as David moved on. "The truth is, you were planning to commit an armed robbery when you were arrested, weren't you?"

Joey shook his head, "No, it was all for a video."

David looked down at a statement the prosecution had served from a police officer who had interviewed Joey about Paul Morris.

"Let me ask you, why are you giving evidence in this case?"

"I didn't like what I heard. Morris was boasting that he did the murder but there was more evidence against Afro than against him. He said he'd probably get off and Afro would go down. He was going to let Afro take all the blame. I didn't think it was right."

"Are there any other reasons that you have given evidence here?"

He paused before answering, "No, that's it."

"Mr Talbot, as you told us, you are awaiting sentence and that sentence has been adjourned until after this trial?"

"Yeah that's right."

"It has been adjourned so that you can give evidence at this trial. You were informed that by assisting the prosecution in this way, you will receive a significant discount in your own sentence?"

"No one has told me that."

"Come now Mr Talbot, you know full well that you will receive a discount of up to 50% off your sentence. That's the reason you have given evidence."

"No, I wasn't told that."

David picked up the witness statement he had been reading and held it so everyone could see. "Mr Talbot, you first approached the police and spoke to Detective Constable Bryant?"

"I don't remember the officer's name."

"He has recorded that the motive you gave for coming forward to give evidence was, and I quote, 'to obtain a reduction in my sentence'. That is the only reason you came forward isn't it?"

"No, the officer's got it wrong."

"You knew that by giving evidence for the prosecution you would receive a significant reduction in what would otherwise be a lengthy sentence?"

"No, that's not true."

"Of course, your evidence has to be favourable to the prosecution to receive that reduction, which is why you have made up these lies against Paul Morris?"

"No, I've told the truth."

"I suggest you were in prison with him and you did speak to him. However, he never said he had killed Mr Williams, did he?"

"He did."

"In fact, there could never have been such a conversation. You knew all along who killed Mr Williams didn't you?"

Joey Talbot gave him a suspicious look as he replied, "No, I didn't."

"You knew Mr Williams didn't you?"

"I might have seen him round the area."

"You did more than see him round the area, you supplied him with the drugs that he sold?"

Joey raised his eyes to the ceiling, "So I'm a drug dealer now as well, am I."

David picked up a copy of Joey's antecedents. "You do have a number of convictions for possession of drugs, don't you?"

"Yeah, look closely at my record, I've got convictions for possession, not supply."

"Yes, you've been lucky! Nevertheless you supplied Mr Williams with drugs and he did not pay you?"

"That's a lie. You're a fucking liar."

"Mr Talbot!" Mr Justice Knight intervened, "I will not tolerate that type of behaviour in my court. Counsel has a job to do. He must put his client's case, you will not address him like that again. If you do, you will be held in contempt, that means more prison time for you!"

Joey Talbot shrugged. Mr Justice Knight, continued, "Do you understand?"

Joey looked at him, "Yeah, but he's calling me a liar. He's the one lying!"

"Just answer the questions Mr Talbot." He turned to David, "Please continue Mr Brant.

David bowed his head slightly, "Thank you, My Lord," and then turned to Joey. "You supplied Mr Williams with drugs and he did not pay you and, indeed, he refused to pay you and owed you money for the drugs?"

"That's not true it's a fu..." he looked at the judge, "it's a lie."

"In the early hours of 6th May, you went to his address with Mr Dickson and Mr Ward didn't you?"

"No, I never."

"Ward was shouting, that he had almost been 'brained' the other night when Mr Williams threw bottles through Mr Morris' windows."

"I wasn't there."

"You were there and you shouted out to Mr Williams that he owed you?"

"No, because I wasn't there."

"You all tried to get into his flat but couldn't so you left. Mr Dickson then left and went to collect some money from a cashpoint. He then came back, purchased some cannabis off Mr Ward and as they were smoking it together, Mr Williams approached you all. It was at that stage that you probably saw Paul Morris arriving across the street?

"I wasn't there. How many times do I have to say it?"

"I suggest not only were you there, it was you who stabbed Danny to death?"

Joey squinted his eyes and looked aggressively at David, "No, it wasn't me."

"Did you use that large hunting knife that the police found in the boot of your car?"

Joey Talbot hammered his large fist onto the edge of the witness box, "This is rubbish, I wasn't there."

"Where were you then?"

Joey paused again, "I don't know."

"Come now Mr Talbot, you've had months to think of where you were, surely the police have asked you the same question to check if you had an alibi?"

Joey involuntarily looked away, before looking back, "No one's asked me that before."

David produced Joey's most recent police statement, served just before the trial. "Really, it says in your witness statement that was made just before this trial, 'I don't know where I was in the early hours of the 6th May.'

In order to give that statement someone must have asked you if you had an alibi for that time and place?"

Joey just shrugged.

"You must have some idea where you were on that day?"

"I've no idea."

"Mr Talbot, or shall I call you 'Pumpman'? You know full well where you were in the early hours of 6th May. You were in Saunders Road, Moulsecoomb, where you murdered Mr Williams!"

David immediately sat down before Joey had a chance to reply.

CHAPTER 40

THE PRISON SNITCH CONTINUES

William Smythe rose to his feet quickly to repair any possible damage to his case. "Mr Talbot, how well do you know my client, Michael Ward?"

Joey was quieter than before, "Not very well, I've seen him around the area and I met him a few times in prison, that's all."

"You have no reason to lie on his behalf?"

"None. I don't care what happens to him."

"Michael Ward played no part in your decision to give evidence?"

"None."

"And you do not seek to minimise his involvement in order to protect him?"

"No."

"Indeed, your evidence is that he told you he went round with Mr Morris to Mr Williams' flat in order to 'sort him out'?"

"Yeah, that's what he said."

"I just want to deal with that for a moment. He told you there had been a problem between him and Mr Morris, didn't he?"

"Yeah, Morris had smashed this Danny's windows and Danny had smashed his. So they went round to sort him out."

"In fact, didn't Mr Ward say he was going round to 'sort the problem out', not to sort Mr Williams out?"

"It's the same thing."

William shook his head slowly from side to side, "No, it's not Mr Talbot, one suggests sorting a problem out, possibly by discussion, the other suggests sorting an individual out, probably by violent means.

Is it fair to say Mr Ward never suggested to you that he intended any violence towards Mr Williams?"

"He never said anything about violence."

"Further, you told us that Mr Ward said that Mr Morris had used a knife to stab Mr Williams and it was a knife he had carried before?"

"Yeah."

"Mr Ward never suggested that he had seen the knife that night, before Mr Morris produced it and stabbed Mr Williams?"

Joey Talbot smiled as he answered, "No, he never."

"Nor did he say that he knew that Mr Morris was carrying a knife that night."

"No, he never said he knew."

"He told you he was surprised and shocked when Mr Morris produced the knife and stabbed Mr Williams."

Joey paused and looked at Michael Ward in the dock, "Yeah, that's right, I think he did say that."

William thanked him and sat down.

Tim rose to his feet, "Mr Talbot, you have told us that Mr Ward said they were going round that night to sort Mr Williams out?"

"That's what I remember."

"What did you understand him to mean?"

"I thought they were going round to give him a good hiding."

"A beating?"

"Yeah."

William made an audible sigh and raised his eyes towards the ceiling of the courtroom. A few members of the jury saw the gesture and smiled in support.

Tim grinned at the witness as he continued, "Now, both Mr Ward and Mr Morris explained to you that they went together to sort Mr Williams out?"

"Yes."

"You were not present?"

"No."

"Do you have any idea where you were in the early hours of 6th May?"

"No, I've no idea. I could have been anywhere."

"Did you have anything to do with the killing of Danny Williams?"

"No!"

"It is your evidence that both Mr Morris and Mr Ward told you, independently, that Morris committed the murder?"

"Yes, it is."

Tim thanked him and sat down. The court was then cleared and Joey was led through the dock back to the court cells. The jury was not present to see him smirk at Paul Morris on his way down the stairs.

As it was almost lunch-time, Mr Justice Knight announced that he was adjourning the case until 2:30pm, a bit later than usual as he was entertaining some local dignitaries over lunch. Although he said that he hoped this did not inconvenience anybody the smiles from those now granted a longer lunch hour demonstrated that it did not.

David and Graham changed out of their robes and went out to the restaurant next door to the court to order a three course lunch. As they eagerly awaited the first course, Graham commented on David's cross-examination of Joey Talbot. "I think you did a superb job David, you caught him out in a few lies, which should cast doubt on the rest of his testimony. The suggestion that he wasn't doing this to secure a discounted sentence was obviously nonsense. I doubt anyone on the jury believed that!"

David looked around to ensure no jurors or other people from the case were present in the restaurant. "We made some headway with Joey but I have to wonder, was it enough? He was quite adamant in his protestations of innocence of the killing and, apart from our clients' claims, there is no evidence that he was even at the scene. He is not seen on any CCTV, even though Morris, Ward and Dickson are. You would expect the CCTV to pick him up too if he had been present."

Lunch arrived and both munched silently at their prawn salads, the healthiest part of their meal. After the first course was fully enjoyed, David pondered out loud to his junior, "You know Graham, what really gets to me in this case is, even if we made any headway this morning, the prosecution are going to apply this afternoon, to put before the jury, Paul's previous convictions for wounding his father with a knife. There is no real basis for objecting especially as Joey Talbot referred to it already but when the jury hear details of that evidence, the prejudice will be such that any headway we made with Joey Talbot, will simply disappear. We desperately need to find something in this case that really helps our client, the proverbial 'smoking gun' which points to the truth. However, I'm beginning to wonder whether one exists!"

CHAPTER 41

THE BAD CHARACTER APPLICATION

As they returned to court, David and Graham were approached by Tim's junior, Sean, wearing a cheerful smile. "Hallo, David, Graham, I trust you've had a good lunch?"

David replied for both of them, "Yes, thanks Sean."

He was about to make his way to the robing room when Sean added, "Tim is busy at the moment, but he wanted me to tell you that not only does he want to adduce the evidence of your client's previous conviction and the facts of it, he wants to call your client's father as a prosecution witness."

David halted in his tracks.

"When did you make that decision? It's one thing to have the facts before the court, but the only reason for calling the father is to prejudice the jury. Really Sean, your team must be very uncertain about the quality of your case to want to take that course at this late stage."

Sean recoiled, he was not experienced enough to deal with this type of 'robing room banter' and looked worried. David had a momentary pang of guilt for treating a junior barrister in this way, particularly one from his own chambers. He personally disliked taking advantage of inexperienced barristers, but, then again, Sean had been particularly close to Tim recently and had become noticeably arrogant. With that in his mind, he could not help but add, "Sean, please be careful, you do have a duty to be fair when prosecuting. No doubt you will convey that thought to your leader and both reconsider whether you should call this evidence which has no real relevance to the current offence but is wholly prejudicial!"

David walked off to the robing room, followed by Graham, who was barely able to hide the smirk on his face. He enjoyed seeing uppity prosecutors put in their place.

At 2:40pm, Mr Justice Knight returned to court. He was clearly happy, and David concluded that he had enjoyed an excellent lunch, probably with a glass or two of wine. At least that might put him in a more reasonable mood when hearing the next application, he thought.

Tim addressed him first, "My Lord, the prosecution team has been consulting over lunch and we have an application to place before Your Lordship."

The Judge raised an eyebrow at him as Tim continued, "Whatever happens in relation to the application, we will not be able to present any further live evidence this afternoon and, in order not to waste their time, might I suggest that they be sent home and asked to return tomorrow?"

The Judge's demeanour visibly changed. "Mr Adams, I am surprised at such an application being made now. We broke for lunch before 1pm, almost two hours ago. If we were going to release the jury that was the time to do it, not now whilst they have been wasting two hours of their time!"

Tim was not put off at all by the comment, "My Lord, no one regrets that more than me but the prosecution team needed to discuss the progress of the case and the evidence called so far. We were not in a position to suggest that they be sent home before lunch."

Mr Justice Knight sat back in his chair, adopting a smile at the thought of an early day, "Very well," he said, as he turned towards his usher, "George, would you inform the jury that, with my regrets, we will not need them any more today and that I hope we have not inconvenienced them too much. Could they be at court tomorrow at 10 am please, when we will resume with the evidence."

He turned back to Tim, "Well, Mr Adams, what is this application about?"

Tim smiled, "My Lord, you may recall that at an earlier stage, I informed you that Mr Morris has previous convictions. The prosecution states that one of those previous convictions is relevant and we seek to put that before the jury under the provisions Criminal Justice Act 2003, on the basis that the evidence of the conviction is relevant to an important matter in issue between the defendant and the prosecution, namely, his propensity to commit offences of this type. Alternatively, the prosecution apply to put the previous conviction before the court on the basis that the defendant, through his Counsel's cross examination, has made an attack on another person's character, namely the character of Mr Dickson and Mr Talbot. The written application in relation to the first part of this application is already before the court, the second part of this application has only arisen during the trial.

The Judge looked through his papers and picked out the Bad Character application referred to and read it before stating, "I see that you want to adduce the evidence of this conviction through a police officer who will present the Court's memorandum of conviction."

He turned towards David. "Is there an objection to this Mr Brant?"

David answered quickly, "My Lord, I was only notified just a few minutes before coming into court, that the prosecution now wish to call Mr Morris' father to give live evidence."

The judge raised an eyebrow as he turned back towards Tim. "That is an unusual course to follow, Mr Adams, when there is a conviction and the facts can be related to the court through the police officer in charge of the prosecution case. Why have you altered your position?"

"As I indicated," Tim replied casually, "It is as a result of the recent consultation over lunch. As the prosecution will be adducing evidence of a telephone conversation between Mr Morris and his father, it has been decided that it would assist the jury to hear directly from the father about both the previous conviction and the phone call."

The Judge looked surprised. "Surely this was a decision that could, indeed should, have been made long before the trial?"

Before Tim answered the judge, he turned towards David. "In any event, Mr Brant, is this application opposed? It may well be you would rather have the father here to ask some questions of him?"

David responded quickly, "Thank you, My Lord, we do not want to trouble the father, who will be forced to give evidence against his son. In any event, we do object to these applications. Obviously that matter has to be dealt with first and, only if we are unsuccessful in our opposition, should we move onto how the evidence should be put before the jury."

The judge nodded, adding, "I can see you may object to the application dealing with propensity, but can you really argue that you have not made an attack on another person's character?"

David smiled, "No, I cannot, My Lord, but, of course, under the Criminal Justice Act 2003, evidence of this conviction must be excluded if it appears to you that the admission of the evidence would have such an adverse effect on the fairness of the proceedings, that you ought not to admit it. I certainly rely on that section in this case. This evidence is highly prejudicial and will have the effect of getting the jury to embark upon what the courts refer to as 'satellite litigation', necessarily determining the reliability of the father's evidence and whether the conviction is a valid one."

The Judge nodded and turned to Tim, "What do you say, Mr Adams?"

Tim shook his head, "The issue would hardly amount to, 'satellite litigation'. The issue has already been litigated. We are not calling the father to re-litigate the issue, only to deal with the facts of the matter as the previous court had accepted. The evidence will not take long and will assist the jury in determining the reality of this case. In relation to prejudice, my Learned Friend Mr Adams, clearly on instruction, has embarked upon an attack on a number of prosecution witnesses putting their character before the jury. It is only right that the jury see the character of the person on whose behalf this attack has been made. If there is any prejudice, then that can be adequately dealt with by giving the jury a suitable direction when Your Lordship sums up the case to the jury"

CHAPTER 42

THE RELUCTANT WITNESS

As David had predicted, the judge ruled that the bad character evidence was admissible and he would not exclude it on the basis of any perceived unfairness to the defence.

It was now Friday morning and the jury filed dutifully into court, to be told by Tim that the next witness was David Morris, Paul Morris' father.

David Morris was brought into court by the usher. He was clearly the most reluctant witness to date in the case. He slowly made his way to the witness box, glancing apologetically to his left to see his son in the dock, who in turn was facing forwards, trying desperately to avoid making eye-contact.

David Morris took the oath and turned towards Tim as he was asked to give his name. Tim wasted no time on pleasantries. "Mr Morris, you are the father of Paul Morris, the defendant in this case?"

Morris answered slowly and quietly, "Yes, sir."

"Please speak up Mr Morris, the jury has to hear your answers."

Morris raised his voice as he repeated, "Yes sir."

"Much better. Now, I want to take you back to 9th June of this year, in this Crown Court. Do you recall giving evidence in the trial of your son who was charged with wounding you?"

"I didn't know what he was charged with."

"Very well, we will prove what he was convicted of later, do you recall giving evidence?"

"Yes," he said, turning to look at Mark Crook, the officer in charge of this case, who was seated behind Tim. "He made me give evidence he threatened that I would be locked up if I refused."

Tim ignored the comment as if it were irrelevant and continued his examination. "Your evidence related to an incident that took place on Saturday, 25th January 2014?"

"I don't remember the date."

"That's not a concern, it is a matter of record."

Morris looked at him quizzically. Tim continued, "Tell us in your own words, what happened that day?"

"It's a long time ago, I've forgotten."

Tim looked at him sternly. "Mr Morris, you made a witness statement to the police about this incident didn't you?"

"I don't remember."

Tim showed him a copy of the statement, "Before I ask any further questions can you confirm that is your signature?"

Morris looked at the statement. "It looks like it."

"Does it record your recollection of this matter when you made this statement?"

"What?"

"Sorry Mr Morris, I am using an expression from an Act of Parliament which makes such statements admissible. Does it record what you told the police on that occasion?"

"I suppose so."

"You state that you cannot recall the incident now, does it follow then that your recollection of the matter was likely to have been significantly better at the time you made that statement, than it is now?"

Morris was clearly becoming resigned to the fact that he was going to have to give evidence of the incident. "Yeah, probably. Look, I had a fight with my son Paul. I told him to get out of the house and I got a cut across my knuckles. That's it."

He rubbed the knuckles of his right hand, as if to emphasise the point. He then quickly added, "But, he's a good boy, he always used to attend Church with us every Sunday, he wouldn't kill anyone."

Tim gave him a satisfied look. Finally he had got there. But he wanted more, ignoring the reference to Morris' alleged religious observance, he asked, "Did you have a weapon?"

Mr Morris looked at him strangely, "No."

"Had you attacked him?"

"No."

"Did he attack you?"

"I told you. I don't remember what happened."

Tim's smile rapidly turned into a frown. "Mr Morris, I am going to ask you to look at your witness statement."

Morris interrupted, "Yes he attacked me."

"Did your son Paul have a weapon?"

"Yes, he had a knife."

"What type of knife was it?"

"It was a kitchen knife."

"What type of blade did it have?"

David Morris looked confused by the question so Tim tried again, "You have told us it was a kitchen knife. Kitchen knives come in all sorts of designs. Was it a straight edge or a serrated one?"

"It was serrated."

David noted a couple of jurors making a note of this answer. Tim had also noticed. Satisfied he turned back to Mr Morris, "Thank you. Now, I want to move on to a time just before the trial of that case. Let me show you a transcript of phone evidence that we have in this case."

Tim produced copies of the evidence for the Judge and the jury and gave one copy to David Morris. "Your son Paul was remanded into custody after this allegation of murder was made."

He turned to the jury, "Members of the jury, as I mentioned earlier to you and as His Lordship will no doubt remind you in due course, being remanded into custody happens in virtually every case of murder and should not be held against Mr Morris."

Two older ladies on the front row of the jury, smiled at him, acknowledging his obvious fairness to the defendant. He turned back to David Morris. "You will see Mr Morris that your son Paul phoned you from prison on Wednesday, 4th June 2014.

The relevant part of that call has been transcribed and is in front of you. You will see that your son stated, 'Dad, please don't give evidence against me, you know I didn't mean you to get hurt.'

You then replied, 'I'll think about it, son. You know I still love you.'

He then replied, 'I love you too Dad.'

"Do you recall that conversation now Mr Morris?"

The reluctant witness looked down and quietly sobbed, "Yes"

Tim appeared to empathise with the witness, feigning a look of concern. "Mr Morris, I appreciate this cannot be easy for you, but it is important. You did attend the trial and were reluctant to give evidence weren't you?"

Morris wiped a tear from his cheek and replied, "Yes.".

"Just as you have been reluctant today.

"Yes."

Tim nodded again and continued. "If you turn over the page you will see that there was a further call to you from your son Paul. Again, it's from prison and this one was made on 19th June, 2014.

As you see, you said to him, 'Sorry son, they made me give evidence against you.'

Morris almost whispered in reply, "Yes."

He replied to you, 'It's alright Dad, I know you didn't have a choice.'

"Do you recall that conversation?"

"Yes."

"As we can see, later in the same conversation Paul talked to you about this case. He stated to you, 'I'm waiting for the results of the DNA. I'm worried it might come back positive.'

"Do you recall that conversation?"

"Yes."

"Thank you Mr Morris. Will you wait there?"

David noted how the jurors all turned to look at him to see how he was going to deal with this unhelpful evidence against his client. He assumed an air of confidence and looked at the jury first before turning to the witness thinking, he wished he knew how to deal with it!

CHAPTER 43

THE RELUCTANT WITNESS IS CROSS EXAMINED

David glanced at the statement in front of him. It was taken by police some months ago from David Morris. He also looked at the transcript of the prison calls before looking again at the witness.

Morris was clearly in a state. It had been difficult enough giving evidence in the first trial against his own son, but this was far worse. He was assisting the prosecution in a murder case against his son and he knew he was possibly helping to put his son away for life.

David waited as the witness blew his nose and tried to compose himself. "Mr Morris, I am asking questions on behalf of your son."

Morris nodded.

"As you told my learned friend, you were clearly reluctant to come to this court to give evidence, weren't you?"

"Yes."

"And, as you told him earlier, you were reluctant to give evidence in this Crown Court on the last occasion you gave evidence against your son?"

"Yes."

"The transcripts of the prison calls have been read out to you, and you seemed to recall them?"

"I remember them, yes."

"You stated in one of those calls, on 19th June 2014, that you were sorry for giving evidence, 'Sorry son, they made me give evidence against you', and Paul replied, 'It's alright Dad, I know you didn't have a choice.' You recall that now?"

"Yes."

"How did the police make you give evidence in this case?"

"They told me if I didn't they would arrest me and lock me up."

"Did they tell you that before you gave evidence today?"

"Yes."

"We know that there was a fight between you and Paul and you both got angry with each other, that's right isn't it?"

"Yes."

"We also know that during that fight, you received a minor injury didn't you?"

David emphasised the word 'minor' for the benefit of the jury.

"Yes."

"A scratch across your knuckles."

"Yes."

"Both you and Paul were angry and you wanted to throw him out of the house, which is what you did isn't it?"

"Yes."

"You made a statement to the police about how you had received this minor injury?"

"Yes."

"That statement contained a declaration that you signed, stating that it was, 'true to the best of my knowledge and belief and I make it knowing that, if it is tendered in evidence, I shall be liable to prosecution if I have wilfully stated in it anything which I know to be false, or do not believe to be true'."

"Yes."

"Did the police remind you of that declaration when they made you give evidence?"

"Yes, they did."

"Did they also tell you that if you went back on that version or gave a different version of events, that you could be prosecuted?"

"Yes, they said that."

"So, you had to follow what you put in the statement whether it was true or not?"

Morris looked at him, confused. "I don't understand?"

"That is my fault, Mr Morris. What I am suggesting is that you only gave evidence against your son because you were afraid that you might go to prison if you did not?"

"I've already said that."

"Yes, please bear with me. I am also suggesting that you only followed the version of events that was in your statement because you were afraid that, if you did not, you would go to prison?"

"I've already said that as well."

"Yes, but what I am suggesting is that there was a fight between you and your son, but he never had a knife. You made that up in order to get him out of the flat because you were angry with him?"

Morris was silent.

"Mr Morris, I suggest the minor injury you received over your knuckles was not as a result of Paul using a knife, but as a result of you hitting out at him and catching your knuckles on the sharp edge of a kitchen door. That is how the injury was caused, wasn't it?"

Morris looked down in the witness box, and after a pause of a few seconds, muttered an almost inaudible, "Yes."

David was not sure the jury had heard him. "I'm sorry Mr Morris, you will have to speak up. Is that a 'yes' to my question?"

Morris looked up and repeated his answer loudly.

"Why did you lie to the police?"

"I wanted him out of the flat. I was angry with him. We were always arguing, he wouldn't do anything to help around the flat, he wouldn't get a job, he was always rude to his mum and me. We'd had enough of it."

"So you lied in your witness statement to the police?"

"Yes, I didn't think they would charge him."

"And you lied in court at his trial?"

"I was scared of going to prison. My wife's ill. I look after her and the other kids. I couldn't go to prison. I didn't think they would do anything about the charge and I said I couldn't remember anything about it, but they forced me."

Again, he looked at Paul in the dock. "I really am sorry son."

Paul lifted his head and gave his father a half smile.

David was as surprised at the answers as everyone else in court, but he continued to show no expression on his face as he moved on. "Mr Morris, I want to deal with another part of the prison phone conversation. You will recall that you were asked about it by my learned friend, Mr Adams. Paul told you, 'I'm waiting for the results of the DNA. I'm worried it might come back positive.' Do you remember that conversation?"

"Yes."

"Did Paul ever discuss the allegation of murder with you?"

"A few times."

"He told you he hadn't committed this murder didn't he?"

It was a risky question, but his client had been adamant that he had denied the offence to his father.

"Yes."

"He told you this on several occasions?"

Tim rose to his feet. "I must object to this line of questioning. There is no relevance to establishing previous consistent statements and this line of questioning is inadmissible, as numerous Court of Appeal authorities state, the evidential value of such testimony is nil."

David quickly responded, "In fact, My Lord, it is relevant and the testimony does have considerable probative value to the issues before us. The Prosecution has led this phone conversation. I am simply putting it into its proper context by adducing evidence of conversations surrounding it."

Mr Justice Knight gave a friendly smile to David as he issued the warning. "Ask the question Mr Brant, but let's not dwell on this area for too long."

David gave a grateful bow and faced Morris again. "Your son told you on many occasions before this telephone conversation, and after it, that he had not committed the murder, didn't he?"

"Yes, he did."

"Did you ever ask him why he was worried about the DNA results?"

"I think it was during a prison visit, when he told me that he had visited this lad's flat a few times. He said he thought that his DNA might have got on the lad's clothes on one of those occasions. I didn't really know what he was going on about."

David thanked him and sat down. William Smythe rose slowly from his seat peering at Morris over the top of his spectacle rims.

"Mr Morris. You clearly love your son?"

"Yes, of course."

"As we know, he is facing a very serious allegation of murder, with serious consequences if he is found guilty?"

"Yes."

"You would do anything to help your son, your own flesh and blood, wouldn't you?"

"Not anything. I wouldn't lie!"

"Come now Mr Morris, you are telling us now that you did lie in court to save your own skin, surely you would lie in this court to save your son's?"

"I'm not lying. He didn't cut me with a knife, I made it up before."

"I suggest you did not make it up. You have made this version up now to protect your son. You have lied to this jury."

He sat down before Morris answered.

It was now Tim Adams turn to rise to his feet again, this time he asked that the jury to be sent out of court so he could raise a matter of law.

After the jury was excused and Mr Morris led out of court, Tim voiced his concerns to the judge in their absence. "Clearly the prosecution have been taken by surprise by the answers given by Mr Morris just now. He represents the classic 'hostile witness' and I must apply to treat him as such during my re-examination of his evidence."

Mr Justice Knight nodded and turned to David, "Do you have any objection in these circumstances?"

David thought about his response for a few seconds before answering, "There is a distinction to be drawn between a witness giving merely 'unfavourable' testimony and a witness giving 'hostile' testimony. I submit this was merely 'unfavourable' not 'hostile', and there is therefore no basis on which my learned friend can properly treat him as 'hostile' and cross-examine his own witness.

No doubt Your Lordship will recall that it was a last minute application by the prosecution to call this witness for their own purposes. They shouldn't complain now that his evidence has been unfavourable to them."

Mr Justice Knight nodded, but ruled against the defence. "Despite your brief, but nevertheless eloquent submission, Mr Brant, I am going to allow the Prosecution to treat this witness as hostile."

He turned to Tim. "However, Mr Adams that does not mean you have leeway to keep this witness here for a significant period. Put the issues to him that want to and then, please, let's move on."

Tim bowed his head graciously, "Thank you My Lord." He sat down and turned to Sean with a smirk as they waited for the jury to be brought back into court.

A few minutes later, the jury filed in, shortly before Mr Morris resumed his seat in the witness box. It was noticeable how Tim now made no pretence of having any empathy with the witness.

"Mr Morris, I suggest that you told the truth to the police when you told them your son had cut your hand with a knife, you told the truth, albeit reluctantly, when you were questioned at the previous Crown Court hearing and you told the truth earlier today when you answered questions from me and said your son had cut your knuckles with a knife?"

David quickly sprang to his feet, "My Lord, I do object to that statement, it is not actually a question, and it is based on a misconception. I have checked my own note and my junior's note of the evidence and Mr Morris did not allege today that his son cut him with a knife. What he said was, 'I had a fight with my son Paul. I told him to get out of the house and I got a cut across my knuckles.' He did not say how he received that cut."

Tim momentarily turned slightly pink in the face and turned round to consult with Sean. He turned back quickly and assumed his usual smile, "It appears my learned friend is right. Very well let me ask you to look at your witness statement Mr Morris."

He showed him the statement, "Does it state there that your son cut you with a long knife he was carrying?"

Morris looked at the statement and whispered, "Yes."

"Please speak up Mr Morris. In the statement you described the knife in detail, saying it was a kitchen knife with a serrated edge which you had noticed had gone missing weeks before and which you assumed your son was carrying with him on a daily basis?"

"Yes."

"You describe how he lunged at you, how you put your hand up to defend your face and how the knife was drawn across your knuckles, don't you?"

"Yes."

"That was the truth wasn't it?"

"No."

"You have lied today and made up an account that is favourable to your son simply to protect him, isn't that right Mr Morris?"

"No."

"If what you tell us is the truth, you would never have allowed him to be convicted of wounding and face a prison sentence for that. You would have owned up during that trial and said then that you had lied."

"No."

"You know full well that your son was regularly carrying a knife when he went out. It was the same knife that you noticed had gone missing from the kitchen. The same knife you said in your statement he used to cut you across the hand!

As was becoming the convention in this court, he sat down before Mr Morris could reply.

CHAPTER 44

THE PROSECUTION CASE CLOSES

Tim called his final witness in the case, Detective Sergeant Mark Crook at the recommencement of the trial on Monday 15th September.

The rest of Friday was taken up by Sean calling a series of police officers to deal with the arrests of the defendants and the reading out of various statements from witnesses who were not needed by either side to give evidence. The jury had listened with interest as Detective Constable Barry Nicholas had relayed how Paul Morris had responded when arrested, 'Fuck off you pig, I ain't done no murder. I don't even know the kid.'

Quite a few jurors had looked in Paul's direction with fixed frowns. They also listened to Detective Constable Darren Irvine relate that Michael Ward had given a more restrained response of 'Murder? What murder?' when he was told he was being arrested on suspicion of murder

There had been little cross examination by either leading counsel of any of these witnesses and the court finished at the timely hour of 4pm.

Mark Crook now walked into courtroom number three, and looked around. He was no stranger to Lewes Crown Court, and had been in this very courtroom several times before. He had also been allowed to sit in court during the trial as his evidence was not expected to be controversial. Nevertheless, he felt a degree of nervousness as he walked towards the witness box. He knew it was irrational as he had nothing to hide and he could not imagine the questioning would prove that difficult.

As if to prove the point, Tim eased him into his evidence. "Detective Sergeant Crook, you are the officer in the case, which means you are in charge of the investigation, have submitted all the necessary papers to the Crown Prosecution Service and are able to answer any questions about the investigation. Is that correct?"

Mark tried to adopt an expression of humility as he responded, "I will do my best sir."

Tim nodded and continued. "Officer, I want to take you through some of the steps of this investigation. I believe you first became involved in this matter on the morning of 6th May, 2014. Within three days of that date, both defendants were in custody and interviewed and both were charged with murder on 11th May 2014?"

Mark sat up a little, looking proud at a job well done, "Yes sir!"

"We have heard that, before this trial, Mr Morris faced another trial concerning an injury inflicted on his father with a knife?"

Mark assumed a serious expression, "Yes sir".

"He was convicted of that offence, wasn't he?"

"He was sir, on 12th June 2014, at this Crown Court. The sentence has been put back until the conclusion of this matter."

Tim smiled. That was all he wanted from this witness. He asked Mark to remain in the witness box and he turned towards David, as if to say, he's all yours, but you will get nothing from him. David rose to his feet thoughtfully.

Mark Crook watched him as he rose. He thought there were no possible in-roads into his evidence, but he was always apprehensive at this stage.

David smiled at the officer and asked, "Mr Crook ..." It seemed as good as anywhere to start. "... As you have already told us, you are the designated officer in the case and you are responsible for the investigation of this allegation and the compilation of the papers?"

"Yes sir."

David pulled out a witness statement.

"Whose decision was it to make Charlie Dickson a witness rather than a defendant?"

Mark hesitated slightly before answering, he wanted to get this right, "It was decided that there was no evidence against him. We could see, from the Cash point machine evidence, that he had gone and collected cash for his girlfriend, and this supported his account that he was just doing a drugs deal and not involved with the murder."

Mark smiled, he had been expecting that one and thought the answer was a good one

"Were you aware at that stage that the timings did not tally? That his girlfriend gave a statement to police suggesting he left their flat long before he claimed he did?"

Again Mark smiled as if it was irrelevant, "We were aware of minor discrepancies in timing, but you will be aware with your experience sir, that frequently happens in an investigation. People are frequently out on timings."

The officer assumed an air of calmness as he thought how easy this was!

"Isn't the reality that you made him an offer, if he gives evidence in this case then he wouldn't be charged with murder?"

"Certainly not sir." He continued smiling.

"Very well officer, let me ask you about 'Pumpman', otherwise known as Joey Talbot. He has an appalling criminal history doesn't he?"

"He most certainly has sir!"

"He is an armed robber isn't he?"

"He has been convicted of that offence in the past, yes sir."

"What deal has been done to encourage him to give evidence in this case?"

"There is no 'deal' as such sir. He offered to give evidence and of course we will inform his sentencing court that he has given some assistance."

"He will get a considerable discount for giving evidence won't he?"

"I don't know exactly sir, that will be up to the sentencing judge."

"Come now officer, you expect him to be given a considerable discount. For an early plea of guilty he will receive one third off his expected sentence, for giving assistance and evidence that discount will be a half or in some cases, even more?"

"If you say so, sir."

David smiled, "You are well aware of that officer, and you are also aware that he will receive that discount whether he told the truth or not?"

"I don't agree with that sir, we expect him to tell the truth." Mark assumed an almost hurt expression.

"Yes but there is no mechanism in place to ensure that he does!"

"I'm not sure that is the case, sir."

"Has there been any other offer made to him?"

"I don't know what you mean sir."

The 'sirs' were becoming a little sharper now.

David noticed this and decided it was time to press the officer. "You know exactly what I mean. Joey Talbot faces a criminal trial for being in possession of a robber's kit. A sawn-off, pump action shotgun, ammunition, camouflage body armour, a hunting knife and ski masks. He has pleaded guilty to possession of these items with what is called, 'a basis of plea'. In other words his lawyers have supplied a written document headed "Basis of Plea" and asked the prosecution to accept it. Joey Talbot claims he had these items with him for his friends 'Rap movies.' Has that basis been accepted for the purposes of his plea and sentence?"

"I believe the prosecution could not gainsay that basis, so it has been accepted."

"Really officer, a convicted armed robber is in possession of a robber's kit, and you say you could not disprove his claim that he was making Rap movies! A deal has been done hasn't it whereby he gives evidence and the prosecution accepts this absurd basis of plea, reducing his sentence even further."

Mark looked sternly at David, "No such deal has been done," he answered emphatically.

David noticed that the officer had dropped the 'sir' now.

"In any event, Mr Talbot gave a reason why he was giving evidence to a Detective Constable Bryant?"

"I believe so."

"In a note provided by Detective Constable Bryant, he has recorded that Joey Talbot told him the reason for coming forward to give evidence in this case was to obtain a reduction in his sentence?"

"Yes sir, he has recorded that."

"And you have no reason to doubt that is the case?"

"No I do not sir."

"So would you agree that he has a strong incentive to give evidence supporting the prosecution case?"

"We believe his account, sir."

"Like you believe his account of making Rap movies?"

"As I've said, we cannot disprove his account, so we have to accept it."

David realised he was getting nowhere with this line of questioning and decided to abandon it. There was just one last matter he wanted to deal with though. "Of course officer, Mr Talbot has another excellent reason to lie."

Mark looked puzzled as David continued.

What better reason than to blame Mr Morris for the killing if Mr Talbot himself was the murderer?"

Mark was about to answer when David interrupted him, "Officer, can you answer this. Did you check to find out where Mr Talbot was at the time this murder took place?"

Mark paused, "We did check sir. He told us he did not know."

"Apart from asking him, what checks did you carry out?"

"There weren't any other checks we could carry out. He only approached us months after the event and we had no reason to think he had been present. No one informed us until your client put it in his Defence Statement, ..." He paused before adding, "... many weeks after the event."

David smiled at the jibe and the fact the officer was reminding the jury that his client had made no comment to all the questions asked in interview. "I understand that officer, but did you check his phone records? Joey Talbot presumably had a mobile phone and you could have checked its location for the night of 5th-6th May 2014?"

Mark chuckled, "Mr Talbot is not the kind of person to keep a mobile phone that long. He's more likely to buy a pay as you go phone and dispose of it every day!"

David looked squarely at the officer and smiled. The officer's own smile, however, slowly disappeared from his face as he realised what he had said. David turned to the jury to make sure they had taken it in, and then turned back to the witness. "Really officer? What type of person disposes of mobile phones on a daily basis? An armed robber? A drugs dealer perhaps? Or both?"

Mark was annoyed with himself. He chastised himself mentally for going out the night before and consuming too many pints of beer. "I'm sorry sir, I've probably maligned him too much. I have no evidence to suggest he disposes of mobile telephones on a daily basis, I just know he informed us he uses 'pay as you go phones' and said he did not believe he still had the one he was using around that time."

"How convenient officer, how very convenient!"

"Not really sir, not really."

CHAPTER 45

THE DEFENCE CASE

There was no further questioning of Mark Crook, who returned to his seat in court behind the prosecution barristers, raising his eyes a little to the solicitor from the Crown Prosecution Service who had come into court to watch part of the evidence. She just looked at him contemptuously, thinking that an officer of his seniority should not have made such a damaging comment.

David wasted no time in announcing that he was calling his client, Paul Morris to give evidence. Paul came out of the dock with a burly uniformed security guard following him. It always made a bad impression and David had his usual thought at these times, wondering if the United Kingdom would ever allow the common practice in other countries of allowing a defendant to sit next to his lawyers. He then dismissed the thought. He didn't really want to sit next to Paul Morris for an entire trial!

Paul confirmed that he wished to affirm instead of take the oath, and the usher selected an appropriate card from which Paul read to confirm he would tell the truth to the court.

David eased him into his evidence by asking a few preliminary questions about his age, where he lived, and some background details before moving onto the issues for trial.

"Mr Morris, can you tell the ladies and gentlemen of the jury how long you have known your Co-Defendant, Michael Ward, and where you met him?"

Paul Morris looked at the jury as he had been advised to do by David. Unfortunately he also adopted an involuntary scowl, which he had not been advised to do.

"Yeah, I was having problems with my parents a few years ago and I went to live in a hostel. I met Afro there."

"You know Mr Ward as Afro?

"Everyone knows him as Afro."

"When did you first meet him?"

"A few years ago."

"Can you remember the date, just approximately, no one expects an exact date?"

"I think it was 2012, I was 17. I stayed there a few months and then I went back home."

"Did you deal with your problems with your parents?"

"Yeah, everything was fine."

David looked towards the jury wondering how they would take the next piece of evidence.

"Mr Morris, I want to take you back to earlier this year when you had a further problem with your father. We have heard that there was an incident on Saturday 25th January of this year. Tell us in your own words what happened?"

"I had an argument with my Dad about playing loud music in my room. He told me to turn the volume down and I got annoyed at him nagging me about it so I turned it up. He then told me to get out of the house and I wouldn't."

"Where did this argument take place?"

"At first, it was in my bedroom, then he told me to come downstairs. I did and we both went into the kitchen."

"Then what happened?"

"I swore at him and he lost his temper and swung at me with his right hand. I ducked out of the way and he hit the side of the kitchen door, cutting the knuckles on his hand."

"Did you have a knife at any stage?"

"Definitely not, no."

"Did you cut him?"

"No, I did not."

"What happened next?"

"He shouted that 'was it' and said he was going to get the police onto me and get me thrown out of the house."

"And that is what happened?"

"Yes."

"You were charged with wounding him and were bailed to stand trial. Where did you live after this?"

"I went to live with my Uncle Dan who lives a few streets away in Old Street in Moulsecoomb."

"How long did you live there for?"

"Just a few weeks, he threw me out."

David noted a few jurors give enquiring looks at the last comment.

"Did you have a disagreement with your Uncle?"

"Yeah, he lives in a small flat and we got on each other's nerves, so I went back to my Dad's house."

"Was it a condition of your bail that you stay at your Uncle's address and do not visit your father's address?"

"Yes, but I had nowhere else to live and my Dad said I could come back and live with him."

David looked across at the jury. A few were taking notes, most were looking impassively although one older lady had a scowl that rivalled Paul's.

"Let us move on for the moment to the trial of that matter. We know it took place in June of this year. Just before the trial, you were in custody for this current matter. We have seen a transcript of a phone conversation you had with your father on Wednesday, 4th June, when you said to him, 'Dad, please don't give evidence against me, you know I didn't mean you to get hurt.' Firstly, did you say that to him?"

"Yes, I did."

"Secondly, why?"

"I was scared. I was facing a murder charge and I was scared they'd use my Dad to say I used a knife to hurt him when I didn't."

"Very well, let's move on now to Mr Williams. When did you first meet him?"

"I met him a few weeks before he was killed."

"In what circumstances?"

"I met him through Afro."

"How did Mr Ward know him?"

"They were both drug dealers in the area. They sold a bit of weed. They got to know each other because they bought their supplies from the same person."

"Do you know who that was?"

"Yes, Afro told me it was Joey Talbot. He was a friend of his."

"Did you know Joey Talbot?"

"I did by sight, but I didn't have anything to do with him."

"Why not?"

"He's a violent man. Everyone in the area knows that he's done a few armed robberies."

"Did you ever visit Mr Williams' flat?"

"Yeah, I did."

"How many times?"

"A few times."

"What did you do there?"

"We just chatted and smoked weed."

"Was it just the two of you?"

"No. Whenever I was there, Michael was there as well and also some friends of Danny's were round."

"What was your relationship like with Mr Williams?"

"Alright, we never had any real problems."

"Was there a time when Mr Williams' windows were damaged?"

"Yes."

"Did that have anything to do with you?"

"No."

"What happened then?"

"Afro and I went to Danny's to smoke some weed. Everything was ok until Danny and Afro started arguing over the streets they were selling in. Afro said the area around the High Street in Moulsecoomb was his patch. Danny said he could sell wherever he wanted. Both of them got up and Afro pushed Danny back down and left. I left with Afro and, when we were outside, he picked up a couple of bricks and smashed Danny's windows. Some neighbours started to look out of their houses so we legged it."

"We have heard that Mr Williams went to your parent's address and threw some bottles through the front window. Why did he do that if you had nothing to do with smashing his windows?"

"I don't know. I guess he thought Afro and I had both smashed his windows. I don't know if he knew where Afro lived, but he knew where I lived because we walked past my address together once and I pointed it out to him."

"Did you get injured when the bottles came through your window?"

"Yeah. A bit of glass from the window caught me in the face and cut it."

"What about Afro?"

"One of the bottles came right through the window and almost hit him in the head."

"Was he injured?"

"No, he was lucky."

"How did he react?"

"He swore and said he had almost been brained."

"Do you ever use that expression, 'brained'?"

"No, never."

"We heard that the police came to your address as a result of a neighbour's call and you told them it was Mr Williams who had put bottles through your window and you took the police to his address?"

"Yes, that's right."

"Mr Williams wasn't in or wasn't answering his door when you arrived with the police. What did the police tell you?"

"They said they would come back and they would arrest him."

"What did you think they meant by that?"

"I thought they would be round every day till they nicked him."

"Had you any intention of going round to Mr Williams' address again."

Paul looked towards the jury, "No, not after he put my Dad's windows in."

"Let me ask you about Charlie Dickson. Did you know him before the night of Mr Williams' death?"

"No I'd never met him. I only met him that night."

David took a quick look at the jury to see how they were reacting to Paul's evidence. Although there were a few blank expressions, a few were taking notes, which meant they were at last listening. It was now time to move on to more important matters.

"Mr Morris, lets deal with the night of the 5th to 6th May. Where were you that night?"

"I was at my parents' home."

"Did you go out at all?"

"Not till later. I was bored and I used my parents' home phone to call Afro to see what he was doing. He told me he was selling a little weed but he was running out and we could hang around together after he'd made his last deal."

"Do you know what time this was?"

"Yeah it's on the telephone schedule."

David asked the jury to pick up the schedule and then stated, "We can see that at 12:48 you made a call to Mr Ward. Is that the one you are referring to?"

"Yeah, that's the one."

"What did you do?"

"I left the house a few minutes after the call and came across Afro selling cannabis to Dickson."

"Was there anybody else there?"

"Yeah I saw that Joey Talbot was with them."

"What happened next?"

"Danny came from an alleyway and started mouthing off to Afro. He was complaining about Afro dealing on his patch."

"Did you hear Mr Williams say anything else?"

"I heard something about, 'why were you banging on my door', or something like that."

"Tell us what happened next?"

"A fight broke out between Afro and Danny. I didn't see who started it. I saw Danny knocked to the floor and then Joey Talbot just jumped on him and stuck a knife into his chest."

"Did you see the knife?"

"I saw something glinting under the street light so I assumed it was a knife."

"Were you able to tell what type of knife it was?"

"No."

"What did you do?"

"I just walked away quickly. I didn't want to run, but I walked quickly."

"Were you alone?"

"At first then that Dickson lad joined me."

"Why did he join you?"

"He just came up and said something like, 'Did you see that?' I said I did.

I told him I didn't want anything to do with it. He agreed and we both said we'd keep our mouths shut because we knew Joey Talbot and his reputation and didn't want to end up dead!"

"We have seen some CCTV images of you walking with Mr Dickson past various shops. Was that when you were discussing this?"

"Yeah."

"We have heard that a few days later you were arrested by a Detective Constable Nicholas at 4:55am on 9th May 2014 at your father's home. He cautioned you and you replied, 'Fuck off pig, I ain't done no murder. I don't even know the kid.' Did you say that?"

"I did and I'm sorry, I just thought the police were hassling me at the time."

"Why did you say you did not know who the 'kid' was?

"I knew Danny just as Danny. I didn't know his last name at that time."

"You were taken to the police station and were given the opportunity of taking advice from a solicitor. You were then interviewed by the police and you made no comment to every question asked. Why was that?"

"The solicitor advised me to make no comment, so I didn't."

We have further heard on 11th May that you were charged with the murder of Mr Williams and again cautioned and your reply was 'I didn't do it.' Did you say that?"

"I did."

"And was that the truth?"

"Yes, I had nothing to do with the killing. They've all fitted me up."

"We have a transcript of a telephone call from you to your father on 19th June 2014 when you stated, 'I'm waiting for the results of the DNA. I'm worried it might come back positive.' Did you say that?"

"I did."

"Why were you worried about the DNA results?"

"I'd been to Danny's a few times. I thought I might have left my DNA all over and they might find it and think I'd killed him."

"We have heard you were remanded in Lewes prison where you have remained since. Did you meet Joey Talbot in there?"

"Yeah I did."

"Did you have any dealings with him?"

"I tried to avoid him but he did come up to me a few times and try to talk to me."

"Did you ever say to him you had killed Danny Williams?"

"No, of course not, he knew who killed Danny Williams. It was him!"

CHAPTER 46

PAUL MORRIS CROSS-EXAMINED

William Smythe pushed aside a few papers on the bench in front of him and pulled on the lapels of his gown before turning to Paul Morris.

"Mr Morris, we heard from your father, when he gave evidence, that you were a regular Church-goer, along with your family?"

"Yes sir."

"Were you still attending Church at the time of this incident?"

"Yes sir."

"Do you believe in God?"

"Yes of course I do sir".

"Do you belief it is important to tell the truth when you take an oath on the New Testament?"

"Yes sir."

"Then why did you affirm before giving evidence, rather than swear on the New Testament?"

Paul froze for a moment, "I don't know, I thought I had sworn on the Bible."

"No. You did not. We all saw you answer the usher when he asked you whether you wished to swear or affirm. We all saw him produce the card for witnesses who wish to affirm."

David noticed the usher nodding and looked at him sternly until he stopped. William continued, "I do not criticise anyone who takes an affirmation."

He looked towards two jurors who had affirmed when they were selected, and he smiled at them.

"However, if you are a regular Church-goer, who claims to believe in God, and was going to tell the truth in this court, you would have taken an oath on the New Testament. The fact that you affirmed suggests you knew that you were going to lie, or that you are not a church-goer at all. In either case, you appear to be dishonest."

"That's not true. I'll swear on the Bible now."

William Smythe looked at the faces of the jurors, and moved on, he had made his point "You met Mr Ward when you were in a hostel together?"

"Yes," replied Paul, still reeling from the last exchange.

"You had been thrown out of your home by your parents?"

Paul's eyes narrowed angrily as he replied with a tight mouth, "Yes."

"You went back, and, as we have heard, were thrown out of your home once again?"

"Yes."

"For attacking your father with a knife?"

"No, it wasn't like that."

"Did a knife go missing from your parent's address?"

"Not that I know of."

"Is your father a liar?"

"No."

"He would not have made a story up about you cutting him with a knife unless it actually happened?"

"He did."

"You got to know Danny Williams and visited his flat from April onwards?"

"Not every day."

"But on quite a few days?"

"A few, yes."

"You had a falling out with him and you put some bricks through his window?"

"No, that was Afro."

"It was you. You, Mr Ward and Danny were all smoking cannabis in Danny's flat. Everything was fine between you and then you suddenly started shouting at Danny that he had been dissing you. Danny told you both to leave his house which you did and then you threw bricks through his windows?"

"That's not true. It was Danny who started arguing with Afro, telling him not to sell weed on his patch. Afro got angry at Danny and we were both thrown out. It was Afro who threw the bricks through Danny's window."

"So you say. However, Danny did not do anything to Mr Ward. It was your parents' window that Danny targeted and threw bottles at. Wasn't it?"

"Yes."

"You were hit by flying glass?"

"Yes."

"You must have been close to the window when the bottles came in?"

"I was."

"Almost 'brained' by them?"

"No. I was hit by glass from the window, Afro was almost brained by a bottle."

"You must have resented Danny treating your parents' home like that."

"No."

"Oh, come now, it's only natural you must have felt resentment. You certainly told the police his address and even took them there, no doubt hoping he would be arrested?"

"So, what."

"Well, when the police did not arrest him, did you decide to take the law into your own hands?"

"No."

"I suggest you arranged with Mr Ward to go to Danny's address in the early hours of Tuesday, 6th May in order to 'sort things out'?"

"No, I never."

"You told Mr Ward you wanted to just talk to Danny?"

"No, I never, I never said anything about going to Danny's."

"You had a different intention. You were going to make him pay for what he had done to your parents' windows and because you thought that he had 'dissed' you?"

"That's not true."

"You phoned Mr Ward at 12:48am as we can see from the phone records?"

"Yeah, I did."

"Why?"

"I was bored, I wanted to go out."

"You arranged to go to Danny's with him?"

"No I never."

"You told Mr Ward you just wanted to talk to Danny?"

"That's rubbish."

"You went there with Mr Ward and another boy?"

"No, I never."

"Once there you made threats to kill Danny if he didn't let you in?"

"That wasn't me."

"You were the one trying to smash his door down?"

"No, I wasn't."

"You failed to do so and then you all left and went your separate ways?"

"No, I wasn't there."

"Mr Ward went off to deal some cannabis to Mr Dickson?"

"I saw him dealing to Dickson when I arrived. I wasn't there earlier on."

"Danny then appeared out of nowhere and attacked Mr Ward didn't he?"

"It looked like that to me."

"Mr Ward only acted in self-defence, and knocked Danny to the ground?"

"It looked like that to me, yeah."

"You then came from nowhere and plunged a knife deep into Danny's heart, killing him."

"No I never, that was Joey Talbot who did that."

"I suggest that Mr Talbot was not even there Mr Morris, and you are making that up to try and get yourself of this serious charge.

"Yeah, he was there."

"You then walked off and got rid of the knife just before you were joined by Mr Dickson?"

"I walked off because I could see there was going to be trouble. Dickson joined me a few seconds later."

"Why would he go up to you, a perfect stranger, if you hadn't been involved?"

"Well, why would he go up to me, a perfect stranger, if I'd just stabbed someone?" Paul smirked at what he saw was his own cleverness.

William frowned at Paul, "Mr Morris, you are not here to ask questions. I suggest that he went up to you to ask you why you had just attacked that young man?"

"No, he never, because I didn't attack him!"

William sat down and nodded at Tim. Tim remained seated as the Judge announced that it was past 4pm and Tim would cross examine Paul Morris the following day. Tim nodded at the judge in agreement, whilst thinking how much he enjoyed a good cut-throat defence like this. Not only did that mean half his job was done by co-defending counsel, but it also meant the jury usually didn't believe any defendant and convictions were almost guaranteed.

CHAPTER 47

PAUL MORRIS CROSS EXAMINED AGAIN

The following morning Paul returned to the witness box. Tim rose to address the court, but as he spoke, he looked straight at the jury, and not at Paul.

"Mr Morris, it is your case that you had nothing to do with this terrible murder. That you were in fact an innocent bystander. Is that right?"

Paul looked at him wary of committing to any answer, but eventually settled for, "Yeah."

Tim nodded, "It must have been a terrible scene to observe, from what you tell us. Mr Talbot producing a large knife and stabbing young Danny in the heart?"

"Yeah, it was."

"Obviously, you are aware that the police need to investigate all manner of crimes, but with particular care in serious ones like murders?"

"Yeah," answered Paul, looking very puzzled now.

"When the police question a suspect, you must be aware it is to determine whether that person is innocent or guilty or whether someone else might have committed the offence?"

"Yes." Paul was looking worried now as he felt himself falling into a trap from which he could do nothing to escape.

"The police need all the help they can get don't they?"

"I suppose so," he answered, not that this had ever occurred to Paul before. Helping the police? What a ridiculous idea, he thought. They never helped him!

"Did you have any difficulty giving your account to this jury yesterday?"

Paul was truly puzzled now, "What do you mean?"

"Well, you didn't have any difficulty in recollecting events, you never slurred your words, or seem to be overcome with nerves?"

"No," he answered tilting his head quizzically at the annoying barrister.

"You have found it quite easy to answer the questions put to you by both of my learned friends, and under the scrutiny of the jury, the judge and members of the public?"

"Yeah, that's right. I have nothing to hide!" Finally, he thought, a clever answer. He lent back in the witness box smugly.

"So why didn't you answer any of the police officer's questions when you were in the police station?"

That's easy, thought Paul, "My solicitor advised me not to."

"Obviously, I will not ask you what your solicitor advised as that is covered by legal professional privilege."

Paul looked questioningly at him.

"It means that legal advice you received is confidential and you do not need to answer any questions about it. However, it is correct that, although your solicitor MIGHT have advised you to make no comment, the decision whether to answer questions or not, was yours, wasn't it?"

"Yeah, but I took his advice."

"On your account you were an innocent man?"

"Yeah."

"You knew who had committed the murder?"

"Yeah."

"You could have told the police there and then but you didn't. Why not?"

"Because my solicitor advised me not to."

"You are still a young man, but you are old enough to know that it was your decision and you were warned by the officer who interviewed you, that it could harm your defence if you did not answer police questions."

"I know, but I took my solicitor's advice."

"The reality is, that you knew you were guilty of murder and could not think of a cover story at that stage. You waited until all the prosecution evidence was served and then you concocted an account to fit that evidence, didn't you?"

"No, that's a lie."

"No Mr Morris, it is the truth.

"No, it's not."

"How long have you known Mr Ward?"

"A few years now."

"Are you close friends?"

"Not really."

"Did you tell Mr Ward what happened between you and your father?"

Paul hesitated, "Yeah, I told him my Dad hurt his hand on a door frame."

"Door frame? Your barrister, Mr Brant QC, put it was the edge of a door, not the door frame. Which was it?"

"It's the same thing."

"No its not, but let's move on. Didn't you tell Mr Ward that you had cut your father with a knife across his knuckles?"

"No, I never."

"That's what happened isn't it? You got angry and resorted to using a knife to deal with your anger?"

"No, I never."

"A knife with a serrated edge."

"It's not true."

"That's what happened to Mr Williams as well. You got angry and used your knife with the serrated edge to wound and kill him?"

"No I never, it was Talbot."

"What reason do you say Talbot had to kill him?"

"Because Danny owed him money and wouldn't pay him."

413

"That's not a reason to kill someone is it? The better, though still inexcusable, reason would be because they put a bottle through your window and almost 'brained' you?"

"I didn't kill him."

"You have told us that you did not want to go to Danny Williams address again. Why was that?"

"Because he'd put bottles through my Dad's windows and I thought the police were going to be there."

"If that is true, why did you go to his address that night?"

"I didn't."

"Mr Morris, on your own account you went there. According to what you have told us, you went to meet Mr Ward in Saunders Road, where Danny lived. Why did you go there if you were trying to avoid him?"

"It's where Afro suggested we meet."

"It is right, isn't it, that you only live a few minutes away from Saunders Road?"

"Yeah."

"On foot it would probably take you no more than five minutes to get there?"

"About that."

"We know that you called Mr Ward at 12:48 according to the phone records, so assuming you left straight away, you would have met up with Mr Ward at just before 1am?"

"I didn't leave straight away."

"Why not, you said you were bored, surely as soon as you arranged to meet Mr Ward you would have left your house?"

"Not straight away."

"Well, shortly after 1am, then?"

"I wasn't looking at the time."

"The next time we can be certain of, is 1:25am when you are seen on the CCTV with Mr Dickson in Saunders Road. What had you been doing for twenty to twenty five minutes?"

Paul was clearly getting annoyed now, "I just fucking told you, I didn't leave straight away."

Mr Justice Knight intervened, "Mr Morris! You have heard me tell Mr Talbot, please just answer the questions. There is no need to swear unless you are repeating a conversation you heard or took part in."

Paul, looking slightly embarrassed dropped his head and apologised.

Tim smiled, he would have preferred it if the judge had not interrupted his cross-examination and allowed Paul to become angrier and abusive, it would have made a useful impression on the jury.

He looked at Paul with a steely glance before asking, "The reality, Mr Morris, is that you got there just before 1am. You met with Mr Ward and a third person, and visited Danny Williams at his address?"

"That's a lie, I never. Anyway, that bloke said it happened at 12:45, I was at my Dad's at that time."

Tim did not even pause as he had been waiting for this opportunity, "Mr Morris, I presume you are referring to the evidence of Mr Brook. Others put the incident at around 1am." He turned to the jury and smiled, "We can all make mistakes about time."

Paul was clearly agitated. "It wasn't me, I didn't go to Danny's that night."

"Yes, you did and you threatened to kill him unless he let you in didn't you?"

"It wasn't me."

"You told him he had almost brained you the other night. You then tried to smash your way in, probably hammering against the door with the butt of the large knife you always carried. That's what happened isn't it?"

"No, I wasn't there."

"When you couldn't get in, you left, going in different directions, but you didn't go far?"

"I wasn't there."

"You then returned, saw that Danny Williams had left his property. Mr Ward knocked him down for you as you jumped on top of him and stabbed him to death. That is what happened isn't it?"

"No."

"Danny Williams had 'dissed' you that is why you killed him?"

"No, I didn't kill him."

"I suggest you left the scene and discarded the knife, possibly in a drain or a bin and you were then joined by Mr Dickson who asked you what it was all about."

"No it didn't happen like that."

"You told him it was because Danny had put some bottles through your parents' windows and the bottles had almost hit you. You told Mr Dickson that 'Danny had it coming'. That is what happened isn't it?"

"No, it's a lie."

"Either a great number of people have lied about you or you are the liar. Why would these people all allege that you were the killer unless that was true?"

"I don't know. They're just fitting me up."

"The truth is, you not only committed this murder, you were proud of it. You boasted about it to Joey Talbot in prison didn't you?"

"No I didn't. That's a lie so that Talbot will get a lighter sentence. This is a fit-up."

"You even boasted that the evidence was stronger against Ward than it was against you and he would be convicted and you would be acquitted?"

"I never!" Paul was getting visibly angry now.

"It must have been a big shock to you when you read the statement of Joey Talbot?"

"It was, because it was all lies."

"No, I suggest it was the truth. That is why you had to think something up to deal with it. Is that why you invented this lie that he was the murderer not you?"

"It's not a lie, it's the truth."

"Like all defendants you had to submit a Defence Statement in this case outlining what your defence is. Yours was out of time and only served after you received Joey Talbot's statement. Was it because that was the time you first came up with this lie about Joey Talbot being the murderer?"

"No, I saw him kill Danny. I knew he was the murderer when I was arrested."

"If that was true you would have told the police the moment you were arrested and not waited so long. The truth is you killed Danny Williams, you believed you were getting away with it and it is only when your friends and acquaintances started to tell the truth about what happened that night, that you came up with this monstrous lie?"

"That's not true. I didn't kill him."

Tim sat down with a last look of utter contempt towards Paul which was clearly noticeable to the jury and in reality was entirely for their benefit.

David was now in a slight quandary. Tim had laid the groundwork for the judge to give an 'adverse inference' direction about Paul's failure to answer questions in interview. The jury could draw an adverse inference if they were sure that he had not answered questions because he had no answer to give at the time or had invented his evidence since. Sometimes that could be countered by a defendant waiving legal professional privilege and calling his solicitor to give evidence that his client had given this version of event to the solicitor at the police station. Of course here the account about Joey being the killer had only been given after Joey Talbot's statement had been served, so waiving privilege would have potentially supported the prosecution case. In any event, the thought of calling Jimmy Short to give evidence sent shivers down David's spine. He had to re-examine his client now, but he had to be careful.

"Mr Morris, you have been asked a lot of questions over the last day or so and I only have a few more. Firstly, you were asked about taking an affirmation rather than swearing on the New Testament. Does that make any difference to you? Have you told lies because you affirmed rather than swearing an oath?"

"No."

"Would you be willing to swear an oath now and repeat all your evidence?"

"Yes."

"I doubt anyone will want you to do that," he paused looking at Tim and William, "No, then let's move on. It has been alleged that you have invented your account and did not answer questions in the police station because you had not made this story up yet. Is that true?"

"No."

"Why did you not answer questions in the police station?"

"I was scared and I relied on my solicitor's advice who told me to say nothing."

"Did you kill Mr Williams?"

"No."

"Who did?"

"Joey Talbot."

"Have you found it easy to give evidence against Joey Talbot?"

"No."

"Why not?"

Paul looked genuinely afraid for the first time in his evidence, "Because I'm scared of him. He's a violent man and he has friends in prison as well as on the outside. I'm scared every single day that I will be attacked when I take a shower or when I'm alone in my cell."

CHAPTER 48

MICHAEL WARD GIVES EVIDENCE

William Smythe asked for a little time to consult with his client, before calling any evidence and the judge adjourned proceedings to break for an early lunch at 12:30. At 14:05 the court re-assembled and William announced that he was calling Michael Ward.

The same procedure was carried out with Michael as had been with Paul. He came down from the dock to the witness box, flanked by two large prison officers who gave the clear impression he had been remanded in custody and was an escape risk.

William asked him a few preliminary questions before taking him through his background and how he had met the various people in this case. He then moved onto the night of Thursday, 1st May.

"Mr Ward, we have heard, that on Thursday, Danny Williams had bricks thrown through the windows of his new flat. Did you have anything to do with that?"

"No, sir."

"Do you know who did?"

"Yes, it was Paul Morris."

"Tell us what happened that night?"

"Me and Paul had visited Danny that night. We were all smoking weed."

"Where did you get it from?"

"I had some of my own, Danny gave some to Paul and then smoked his own."

"What was the atmosphere like?"

"It was good, everyone was fine at first then Paul kicked off."

"What do you mean?"

"He started arguing with Danny that he was dissing him, not showing him enough respect. Danny just told him to fuck off and Paul got up and looked like he was going to have a fight. Danny told us both to leave and we did. As we did, Paul picked up a couple of bricks and put them through Danny's windows."

"Did Danny see that?"

"Yes, he shouted after Paul, but we both legged it."

"Why did you run away?"

"Because I thought Danny would think I had something to do with it."

"Did Danny ever say anything about you dealing drugs on his turf, or words to that effect?"

"No, he'd only been dealing cannabis in that area for a couple of weeks. I'd been dealing there for a lot longer than that."

David noticed as an old lady on the front row of the jury frowned at that answer.

William had not noticed and he continued with his questioning, "Let's move on to Saturday, 4th May, at just before midnight. Were you present at Paul Morris's address when two bottles came through the windows?"

"I was there."

"Did you know who had thrown them?"

"Yeah I saw Danny running away."

"Did you almost get hit by a bottle?"

"No. I was well away from the window. It was Paul who got hit and got a cut from some broken glass."

"Why didn't you call the police?"

"I had some cannabis on me and, anyway, Paul had thrown bricks through Danny's windows. We didn't think the police would care."

"We have heard that the police were called by a neighbour and you eventually answered the door to them. Why did it take so long?"

"I thought they might arrest me and I had a lot of bags of cannabis on me. I flushed them down the toilet before I answered the door."

"The police say you weren't very cooperative with them, is that true?"

"Yeah, I was shocked by what had happened and I didn't want to talk to them."

"Why?"

"I wasn't going to grass Danny up. He'd had his windows smashed as well."

"However, Mr Morris did tell them who had smashed the windows and took them round to Danny's address. Were you surprised?"

"Yeah, I didn't think he would grass Danny up."

"I want to ask you about Monday, 5th May now. Did you go round to Danny's address?"

"Yeah I did."

"Who was with you?"

"There was Paul and another white lad."

"Who is the other white lad?"

"I don't want to say. He didn't do nothing."

"When did you arrange to go round to Danny's?"

"I got a call earlier in the day from Paul. He said we should go and sort things out with Danny."

"What did you think he meant?"

"I thought he meant to just talk to him, not make it worse."

"Did you know or believe that Paul was going to attack Danny?"

"No."

"Did Paul have a knife on him?"

"Yeah."

"Did you know that at the time?"

"No. I know he sometimes carries knives. He told me he had cut his father across the hand with a knife, but I didn't think he carried them all the time and I didn't think he had one that night because I thought we were just going to talk to Danny."

"Tell us about that night, what were you doing in the early evening?"

"I was selling cannabis."

"Were you with anybody?"

"I was joined by my mate, around midnight."

"Is that the white man you do not wish to mention?"

"Yeah."

"How did you meet up with Paul?"

"He called me just before 1am…"

William interjected, "We can see from the schedule, this is the call at 12:48."

"Yeah that's right. He asked if I was ready to go round to speak to Danny. I said I was. I was in the area anyway, selling weed, so he agreed to join us. He arrived within about five minutes and we went straight to Danny's."

"So this would be around 1am?

"Yeah."

"Who knocked on Danny's door?"

"Paul did, he got really angry saying he was going to "fucking kill" Danny. He then produced the knife and started banging on the door with the end of it. He was trying to smash his way in when there was no answer. I looked at my mate and we were both shocked. We decided to leave and Paul came after us. We then all split up."

"We have heard that Mr Dickson phoned you at 1:08 in order to buy some weed from you. Is that right?"

"Yes."

"Or was he the man who was already with you?"

"No why would he phone me if he was with me?"

"Quite, now did you and the others separate?"

"Yeah, I waited for Dickson and then sold him some weed. As I was doing that, Paul appeared. He was really angry. He started shouting at me, asking me what I was doing banging on his door. I tried to tell him it wasn't me but he just went for me."

"Did he say anything to you about you selling drugs on his turf?"

"He did. I was surprised, he'd never said anything like that before."

"What did you do?"

"I defended myself and knocked him to the floor."

"Were you intending to hurt him?"

"No, I was just protecting myself."

"What happened then?"

"Paul came from nowhere and thrust a large knife into Danny's chest."

"Did Paul say anything?"

"Yeah, he said something like he was going to kill Danny."

"What did you do?"

"I was in a shock, I just ran off."

"Did you have a knife at any stage?"

"No."

"We have heard that you were arrested a few days later on suspicion of murder. You were cautioned and said, "Murder, what murder?"

"Why did you say that?"

"I was shocked that I was being arrested. I hadn't done anything."

"You were taken to a police station and allowed to see a solicitor and then interviewed. You made no comment to every question asked. Why was that?"

"I was advised to make no comment by my solicitor. Anyway, I knew Paul had been arrested and I didn't want to grass him up."

"Mr Ward we have heard that you were remanded in custody to Lewes prison. The same prison as Mr Morris. Did you see him in there?"

"Yeah, he was on the same wing."

"Did you talk to him at all?"

"No."

"Why was that?"

"He'd killed Danny, I didn't want to have anything to do with him."

"Did you meet Joey Talbot in that prison?"

"Yeah."

"Had you known him before?"

"Yeah, I'd seen him around the area."

"Was he present the night Danny got killed?"

"No."

"Did he kill Danny?"

"No, it was Paul."

"Did you speak to Mr Talbot in prison?"

"A few times."

"Did you discuss this case?"

"A couple of times."

"What did you say to him?"

"I told him Paul killed Danny and I had nothing to do with it. I told him we had gone round there to sort out the problems between us, not to sort Danny out."

William smiled and nodded. He then adopted a serious expression as he asked the next question. "Did you have anything to do with the death of Danny Williams?"

"No."

"Did you assist Paul or encourage him in any way or plan Danny's death together?"

"No."

"You have told us you did not want to 'grass' Paul up, yet that is what you have done by giving this evidence. Why have you now 'grassed' him up?"

"Because he killed Danny, I had nothing to do with it and I don't want to spend the rest of my life in prison for something I didn't do."

CHAPTER 49

MICHAEL WARD CROSS EXAMINED

William finished asking questions just before 4pm, and the case was adjourned until Wednesday for David to cross-examine.

He spent the evening looking over his own notes and a few supplied by Graham, in order to prepare for this moment. His main concern was that Michael Ward had given his evidence confidently and looked like he was telling the truth about Danny's involvement. Disconcertingly, some members of the jury had taken notes and nodded at parts of his evidence concerning Paul.

As David arrived at court on Wednesday morning, he was still contemplating his best approach. Half an hour later he was in court when Michael Ward took his place in the witness box.

David decided to start with a simple question, "Mr Ward, how long did you know Mr Williams for?"

"Just a few weeks, since he came into the area."

"Would you describe yourself as friends?"

"Not really."

"Nevertheless, you met up a few times and went to his address a few times to smoke cannabis."

"Yeah."

"Before he arrived in the area, you used to sell cannabis in the Saunders Road area, didn't you?"

"Yeah, but I did after he arrived as well."

"That must have caused some friction between you?"

"No, it was never a problem. I used to run out of stuff, I could have always sold more in that area."

"Clearly it was a problem between you on the night he was killed?"

"What do you mean?"

"According to your version of events, he came up to you that night complaining that you were dealing on his turf?"

"Yeah, but he'd never said that before."

"It is right, isn't it, that, from the moment Mr Williams came to the area, he started dealing cannabis near his address?"

"Yeah."

"As far as he was concerned that was his area wasn't it?"

"I don't think so."

"That's why you fell out that day in his flat, the day his windows were broken?"

"I never fell out with him."

"On 1st May, 2014, you and Mr Morris visited Mr Williams in his flat?"

"Yeah."

"You and he started arguing over the streets you were selling in?"

"No we never."

"The argument got heated and you both got up from your chairs and he pushed you back down?"

"It never happened like that."

"He told you and Mr Morris to leave, which you did?"

"Yeah, but that's because Paul told him he was 'dissing' him."

"That's an invention by you. The argument was about you and him selling drugs in the same streets. The same argument you had with him the night he died?"

"No, it wasn't."

"It was you who put the bricks through his windows, not Mr Morris, wasn't it?"

"No, that's rubbish."

David quickly looked at the jurors and noticed most of them were following the questioning intently.

"Mr Williams didn't know where you lived, did he?"

"I don't know."

"He had never been to your address?"

"No."

"You were there when Mr Williams put bottles through Mr Morris' window weren't you?"

"I've already said I was."

"You were seated near to the window?"

"No, I wasn't."

"It's a small living room, wherever you were seated was near to the window wasn't it?"

"I wasn't that close."

"How far away do you say you were from the window?"

"About two metres."

"So, six feet or so?"

"I don't know."

"You told us you saw Mr Williams running away, you must have been closer to the window than that!"

"I wasn't"

"The bottles came in and one almost hit you on the head, didn't it?"

"No."

"You were the one who said you had almost been brained?"

"No, I never. That was Paul."

"When the police came, you were not cooperative with them were you?"

"I was shocked."

"You were not cooperative with them because you knew that if you told them it was Mr Williams who had put bottles through the window, Mr Williams would tell them that it was you who had put bottles through his?"

"That's not true."

"Paul Morris did tell the police who had thrown the bottles, and he took them to Mr Williams' address. He would never have done so if he had been the person who threw the bricks, would he?"

"He did throw the bricks."

"When the police arrived, you flushed your stash of cannabis down the toilet. How much did you lose?"

"Not a lot."

"How much? £100, £200, £300 worth?"

"It wasn't as much as that, probably £60-£70."

"You must have resented that?"

"I've lost more."

"Did you blame Mr Williams for your financial loss?"

"It wasn't his fault."

"If he had not thrown the bottles, the police would not have been called to Paul Morris' address and you would not have thrown your cannabis down the toilet! You blamed Mr Williams for the loss, didn't you?"

"No."

"Is that one of the reasons you went round on the Monday night to his flat?"

"No."

David decided to try a different tack, "How long have you known Charlie Dickson for?"

"A few years."

"You met when you lived in a hostel together?"

Michael hesitated before answering, "Yeah, but I met Morris in a hostel as well, so what?"

"Obviously you not only regularly supplied him with cannabis, but you also socialised together, didn't you?"

"We met a few times, but we weren't really friends."

"You would smoke cannabis together and you would meet up regularly?"

"It wasn't regularly, once or twice, now and again."

"You would phone each other regularly wouldn't you?"

"Not that often."

"As we have seen, it was a lot more than once a fortnight, to arrange a drug deal, wasn't it?"

"Yeah, but it wasn't that often."

"I suggest you were very good friends, more than just a dealer and a customer?"

"We weren't good friends."

"Why did you phone him at 11:56pm on Monday night?"

"I wanted to see if he wanted some cannabis. He usually buys off me around that time."

"The reality is, he is a friend of yours. You asked him to go round to Mr Williams' address with you and with Mr Talbot, didn't you?"

"No."

"How well do you know Mr Talbot?"

"I know of him, I don't know him well."

"You bought your drugs supplies off him didn't you?"

Ward looked uncomfortable and turned to the judge, "Do I have to answer that question?"

Mr Justice Knight looked up from his notebook where he had been taking a detailed note of the evidence. "Yes Mr Ward, you must."

Ward looked unhappy and shrugged, "I'm not saying where I got my supplies from."

David smiled, "Mr Ward, I didn't ask you where you got your supplies from, I asked you if Mr Talbot was the supplier. Your refusal to answer that question is an answer in itself!"

Michael looked confused as David continued, "Joey Talbot also supplied Mr Williams with his cannabis, didn't he?"

"I don't know where Danny got his from."

"You know it was from Joey Talbot, the same supplier you had. You know that Mr Williams hadn't paid for them and Joey Talbot, aka Pumpman, agreed to go round with you because Mr Williams owed him money and wouldn't pay. That's the truth isn't it?

"No, it's not. Neither Joey nor Charlie were there."

"I notice you use their first names, is that because they were both good friends?"

"No."

"Who do you say was the third man with you?"

"I'm not willing to say."

"That's because the three men were you, Mr Dickson and Mr Talbot, weren't they?"

"No."

"The three of you went to Mr Williams' address and tried to persuade him to let you in."

"No."

"You were the one shouting to him that you'd almost been 'brained' the other night weren't you?"

"No."

"You were the one who threatened to kill him if he didn't let you in?"

"No, it was Paul."

"Joey had a knife with him and banged on the door with it didn't he?"

"He wasn't there."

"Was it Mr Dickson banging on the door?"

"He didn't do nothing."

"Sorry, are you saying he was there?"

Michael paused, looking nervous, "No, he wasn't there."

"As you were leaving, you received a call from Paul Morris, asking if you wanted to meet up, didn't you?"

"No, I received a call from Charlie, about drugs."

"I suggest when you couldn't get in, Charlie went off to the cashpoint so he could collect his girlfriend's money, he then phoned you to see if you were still around and came back to meet you. Is that what happened?"

"No, this is all rubbish."

"You did meet up with him and with Joey and the three of you came across Mr Williams again?"

"Joey wasn't there."

"The three of you forced Mr Williams into an alleyway and Joey stabbed him, didn't he?"

"No. it never happened that way."

"He gave you the knife and you ran off with it and dumped it somewhere?"

"I never touched the knife."

"When was the next time you were in contact with Mr Dickson?"

"I don't know, a few days later."

"We can see from the phone evidence that you were in contact the very next day, after the murder. On the Wednesday, he phoned you at about 12 noon. We have heard from his girlfriend that he went out immediately after that call, for a few hours. Did he meet you?"

"Maybe, I can't remember."

"I suggest you can. Is that when you concocted your lies about what happened, blaming Paul Morris, who you knew was innocent?"

"He's not innocent, he done it."

"Later, when you were remanded in Lewes prison, you met up with Joey Talbot didn't you?"

"Yes."

"Is that where you finalised this story together, Joey even adding a false confession to try and make the case stronger against Mr Morris?"

"That's not true."

"I suggest that is the truth."

Without a further word, David sat down. The Court room was silent for a few seconds before Tim stood up and commenced his cross-examination for the prosecution.

Tim gave his usual disarming smile to the witness. "Mr Ward, it has been put to you on behalf of Mr Morris that the person who wielded the knife that morning was Joey Talbot. Is there any truth in that suggestion?"

"No."

"Are you a close friend of Mr Talbot?"

"No."

"Have you any reason to lie to protect him?"

"No."

"It is your case that it was Mr Morris, yourself and a third man who you refuse to name, who went round to Mr Williams' flat that night?"

"Are you willing to name that third man now?"

"No."

"Very well, let me ask you about a few other matters. Firstly, we are not dealing with drug dealing charges here, so let's not worry about that. Did you and Danny Williams have any arguments about whose patch it was before that morning of 6th May?"

Michael shook his head and answered, "No."

"So, it must have been a surprise when Danny Williams suddenly complained that you were dealing on his patch?"

"Yeah, it was."

"Is that really true? Drug dealers are notoriously protective about their territories?"

"Not everyone."

"Drug dealing is a dangerous business isn't it?"

"Yeah."

"There are rival dealers, rival gangs, even some buyers can cut up rough and attack a lone dealer?"

"Yeah."

"That's why many dealers have protection, isn't it?"

"They either carry weapons or have a body guard?"

"Not everyone."

"Were you carrying any weapons that night?"

Michael was looking worried, "No."

"Did you have a bodyguard, or perhaps, two, with you that night?"

"No."

"At the time you were friends with Paul Morris weren't you?"

"Yes."

"You met quite frequently?"

"Yes."

"No doubt you discussed personal matters with each other?"

Michael looked confused, "What do you mean?"

"The type of things that friends usually discuss with each other. You would discuss such things wouldn't you?"

"I suppose so."

"For example, he no doubt discussed with you why he was thrown out of his house?"

"Yeah."

"What did he tell you?"

"That he had cut his father's hand with a knife."

"Did he say why he did that?"

Michael smiled, "Yeah, he said it was because his father was dissing him."

Tim could not resist grinning at the witness, "Thank you. Can you tell me, did Paul Morris regularly carry knives around with him?"

Michael smiled in satisfaction as he answered, "Yeah, he did."

Tim was visibly pleased with his cross-examination, "Now, I want to move on to 1st May when Danny's windows were broken. You say it was Mr Morris who did it, and he says it was you."

"It was him."

"You both say there was an argument in Danny's flat. Why then, if it was between Danny and Paul Morris, did you have to leave? Surely the fact he asked you both to leave was because you were both arguing with him?"

"No, it was just Paul. Maybe he felt I would take Paul's side I don't know."

"You were there when you say Mr Morris put bricks through Danny's windows?"

"Yeah."

"Did you try to stop Mr Morris?"

"No."

"Did you encourage him to throw the bricks?"

"No."

"Did you throw a brick?"

"No."

"Anyway, Danny went to Mr Morris' flat when you were both there and he threw bottles through his window."

"Yes."

"That must have annoyed you both?"

"I was shocked, not annoyed, they weren't my windows!"

"You were almost hit by flying glass. That must have angered you?"

"Maybe a little, at the time, yes."

"According to you, the next day you arrange with Paul Morris to "sort" Danny out?"

"No, it was to sort the problem out."

"How did you think Paul Morris was going to sort this problem out?"

"By talking to Danny."

"Really? The same Paul Morris that regularly carries a knife, the same Paul Morris who had cut his own father with a knife for 'dissing' him, the same Paul Morris who had thrown bottles through Danny's windows for 'dissing' him?. This Paul Morris was going to just "talk" to Danny after he had thrown bottles through Paul's parent's windows and cut him with broken glass?"

Michael looked uncomfortable, "Yeah."

"Come now, you knew he was going to 'sort him out' in a violent way and you were there to help him, weren't you, as was your friend, the man you won't name?"

"No, that's not true."

"You couldn't get in so you left. You received a call from Mr Dickson and you went to supply him cannabis. As you were doing so, Danny appeared and again started arguing with you about supplying on his patch?"

"No, that's not how it happened."

"Paul Morris was there as well and you all moved into the alleyway as Danny backed away. You knocked Danny to the ground and Paul Morris pulled out the knife you knew he was carrying and stabbed Danny through the heart. That's how it happened, isn't it?"

"No, it wasn't like that."

"You then went your separate ways as we have heard?"

"Yeah, but the rest isn't true."

"You and Mr Morris both had issues with Danny Williams that night. You both wanted to 'sort him out'. You knew Mr Morris regularly carried a knife and would or at least may use it on Danny and you were there to help him."

CHAPTER 50

THE PROSECUTION CLOSING SPEECH

The remainder of Wednesday was taken up with the barristers discussing the law with Mr Justice Knight to try and agree the legal directions that he would give the jury. It was a standard practice and was useful to the barristers to know the judge's directions before they addressed the jury. It had the advantage to the Judge that it also tended to reduce appeals.

It was now Thursday morning and once the jury had taken their seats, Tim stood for the final time to address them.

He looked at each member of the jury in turn before addressing them. "Ladies and gentlemen, I am sure that we can all agree on one thing from Counsels' benches, namely, just how attentive you all have been to the evidence in this case. Of course that is important in all cases but particularly in one as serious as this. As you will recall, at the beginning of this case, you took an oath, or an affirmation, to try the case according to the evidence, and it is that evidence and not anything I say, or my learned friends say, that is evidence. The purpose of all our speeches is to present our cases to you. If we make points that you consider are helpful, all well and good, if we make points that you do not think are helpful, then you are at liberty to reject them.

In this case, there are clearly a number of conflicts in the evidence. As I anticipate his Lordship will direct you in due course, it is not every conflict that you will have to deal with, only those which you consider are relevant to the charges in this case. Please remember at all times, the defence does not need to prove anything in this case, it is for the prosecution to prove to you these men's guilt, and to do so to a high standard, you must not convict either of them of any offence unless you are sure of their guilt.

It is a high standard and intentionally so and it is only fair that I, as the prosecutor, mention this to you."

A few of the older ladies on the jury were nodding at how reasonable this was of Tim to concede.

"Now defence counsel will no doubt remind you of the burden and standard of proof..."

He paused before continuing, "..and they might possibly remind you of it several times! No doubt their stance will be that you cannot be sure of anything in this case. Please be wary of this. The defence will no doubt raise some good points, but they may also suggest some fanciful notions to you. However, you are expected to bring your combined common sense into the jury room and put aside fanciful notions that really will not help you with your deliberations, but only serve to confuse you and raise unnecessary doubts.

What I say on behalf of the prosecution is that this is a case where you can be and should be sure of both men's guilt on the charge of murder. The prosecution say that the evidence has clearly established that Morris was the person who wielded the knife and took away that young man's life and Ward was a willing accessory to that murder.

As I stated in opening this case to you, even though it is not suggested that Ward wielded the knife or even had a knife, he is equally guilty of murder on the basis he was party to a joint enterprise, and not even one necessarily to kill. The prosecution do not need to prove that was the intention of either of them, it is sufficient to prove the offence of murder if the intention was to cause really serious bodily harm. I suggest that was, at the very least, the intention here.

In fact, the prosecution state that it was undoubtedly the killer's intention to murder young Danny Williams. It is just common sense isn't it that, if anyone uses severe force to plunge a knife through a breast bone and into someone's heart, their intention must be to kill.

In this case we do have a number of conflicts. Issues arising both before and after the time of the murder, but of one matter there is no real issue between the prosecution and the defence, and that is that it is clear that this was a murder.

In the early hours of 6th May, 2014, Danny Williams was murdered. There is no issue about that. No one challenges that. It is not said by anyone that the person who plunged that knife into Danny's heart was acting in self-defence or that it was a bizarre accident! It was an act of cold-blooded murder.

The only real issues are, who committed it and what role did Mr Ward play?

There is an important conflict here that you will have to resolve. Mr Morris claims that Mr Talbot committed the murder. Both the prosecution and Mr Ward state that it was Mr Morris.

The issue in relation to Mr Morris is, did he plunge the knife into Danny Williams' heart? If you are sure that he did, then it is clear that he intended at the very least to cause really serious harm and that he is guilty of murder.

The issue in relation to Mr Ward is slightly different. Was he part of a joint enterprise to kill or cause really serious harm even though he did not use a weapon himself? Was he there to lend support if it was needed or was he there expecting a lesser offence to be committed, for example a beating? As his Lordship will direct you, even if that was his intent, if he was aware that Mr Morris had a knife and at the time and believed that he may use it to cause really serious injury or death, he would still be guilty of murder.

In his case and his case alone, there is a further consideration, there is the alternative charge of manslaughter. Again, his Lordship will direct you about this. If you are sure he was part of a joint enterprise to cause some harm to Danny Williams but not death or really serious harm, then he would be guilty of manslaughter. Nevertheless, rest assured that, despite my comments about manslaughter, the prosecution's case is that this was a murder and both are guilty of it.

Let us look briefly at the evidence against these two. An important starting point, I suggest, is to look at what was happening between the parties at the time this murder occurred.

The evidence is clear that Danny Williams only went to live in that area a few weeks before his death. You might think it is also clear from the evidence of the social worker, Lisa Thomson, or whatever she calls herself these days ..."

David noticed that the old lady on the front of the jury smiled at this comment and was listening intently to every word Tim uttered.

"... that Danny was not ready to live alone. Within a short time of moving in, his flat was in a disgusting state, attracting all manner of undesirable people to smoke cannabis and generally make a nuisance of themselves, including these two defendants.

At first, the relationship between these two defendants and Danny appears to have been a good one, but clearly things changed on 1st May 2014, a couple of weeks after Danny moved in. Was there an argument about Mr Ward dealing drugs on Danny's patch? Was the argument about Mr Morris thinking he had been 'dissed' or disrespected by Danny? Was it a combination of the two, perhaps? It probably does not matter because it is clear that, whatever happened, Danny told them BOTH to leave his flat and, after they left, one or both of them threw bricks through his windows.

Now we know Danny retaliated. It appears he did not know where Mr Ward lived. However, he knew where Mr Morris lived and he went there and threw some bottles through his window.

That behaviour is clearly not to his credit, but no one can possibly suggest that he deserved to die for it.

We know that Mr Morris was injured by flying glass, or almost 'brained' as he put it. Mr Ward was not injured, but it must have been a frightening moment for him and undoubtedly caused him to become angry. Even he agrees he was shocked. You may think that these two wanted revenge. Mr Morris, who cut his father's hand with a knife for 'dissing' him, was hardly likely to leave this matter in the hands of the police. You may think it clear that an arrangement was made by them to go to Danny's to 'sort him out'.

Of course, Mr Morris says there was no such arrangement. He says he arranged to meet Mr Ward in the middle of the night, just to hang around the streets, for no purpose whatsoever. He tells you that he had no intention of going back to Danny's flat.

Is that really credible? On his own evidence, that is where he ended up that night, in Saunders Road, outside Danny's flat.

Of course, Mr Brant has made a good point that Mr Brooks, in his evidence, stated that he heard the initial noises outside Danny's flat at 12:45 and we know that Mr Morris was at his parent's home at that time because it was at 12:48 that he phoned Mr Ward.

Mr Brant will no doubt remind you that I opened this case relying on Mr Brook's evidence. Clearly I was wrong. We can all make mistakes about the time and I suggest that Mr Brooks did make a mistake. It is likely that the first incident outside Danny's flat took place closer to 1am, than 12:45. As we have heard, it would only take five minutes or so for Mr Morris to get there from his address.

You have heard evidence that Mr Morris was outside Danny's flat that night. Mr Ward has told you that they did go to Danny's flat. Of course, Mr Ward could hardly claim he was not there because he knows he was picked out during identification parades by the neighbours as being one of the youths who were present!

You will want to be careful about his evidence when considering the case against Mr Morris, but I suggest that part rang true. Why would Mr Ward lie about Mr Morris' presence? Mr Brant will no doubt suggest that it was to protect Mr Talbot, but really is that the reason? Mr Ward did not need to say Mr Morris was there in order to protect Mr Talbot. He told you Mr Morris was there for a simpler reason, because it was the truth!

They went round to Danny's address that night to sort him out. Now Mr Ward has told you that what he thought Mr Morris meant to do was talk to Danny. Really! Ask yourselves whether it is credible that Mr Ward believed that? At one in the morning, three people were going round to Danny's, unannounced, uninvited, to just chat to him. If they had wanted to do that, why not phone him first? Or arrange to meet at some more sociable hour, like during the daytime?

Mr Ward knew that Mr Morris wounded his own father with a knife for 'dissing' him. He knew Mr Morris regularly carried a knife. Did he really think that the same Mr Morris, who had bottles thrown through his parents' windows by Danny, and was cut by the flying glass, just wanted to talk? I suggest not. No, it would have been obvious what Mr Morris meant to do, and Mr Ward went along with him to support him if needs be.

You also have the evidence of Joey Talbot that Mr Morris told him he was there and confessed to killing Danny Williams. Mr Brant will no doubt make a few comments about Mr Talbot's evidence and no doubt you will want to be careful when you consider it. Mr Talbot does have criminal convictions including one for armed robbery. He was arrested in possession of a sawn off pump action shotgun with ammunition and a wickedly lethal knife. You will want to consider his evidence carefully. Obviously, he has a motive to lie in that he will undoubtedly receive a reduction in his sentence for giving evidence for the prosecution, but the question for you is, did he lie? His evidence could not have been invented, it ties in perfectly with the prosecution's case because it was told to him by the people who were there, Mr Morris and Mr Ward.

What do you make of the allegation made by Mr Morris, that Mr Talbot killed Danny Williams?

If there was any truth in that, surely Mr Morris would have told the police about it in interview, rather than stay quiet and wait till he received all the prosecution evidence before fabricating his account.

We know that Morris and Ward were not able to get into Danny's flat that night so they left. Ward received the call from Charlie Dickson undoubtedly witnessed by Shereena Bennett and sold him some cannabis after 1:08am, the time Charlie Dickson called him.

It was then that Danny appeared on the scene probably complaining that Mr Ward was dealing on his 'patch'. All the evidence points to Mr Ward knocking him to the ground and Mr Morris then coming over and using severe force to stab him through the breast bone, into the heart, killing him. Noticeably, the wound caused had a 'fish tail' type shape, the type caused by a serrated knife. As we heard from Paul Morris' father, such a knife went missing from his address, taken by Paul Morris.

What do you make of Charlie Dickson? Of course, Mr Brant will no doubt properly draw to your attention that Mr Dickson was originally arrested on suspicion of being a party to the murder. Mr Brant will no doubt suggest that Mr Dickson has a motive to lie to incriminate Mr Morris in order to draw suspicion away from himself. He will no doubt identify apparent conflicts between the evidence of Mr Dickson and his girlfriend. Again, it will be a matter for you how important, if at all, these matters are.

Remember this, despite the suggestion made by Mr Brant, there is no evidence whatsoever that Mr Dickson was there that night outside Danny's flat with others trying to force their way in.

You may not think highly of Mr Dickson, apparently taking £10 every fortnight from his partner's benefits to waste on cannabis. You might not think highly of him apparently living off her when she has a young child to feed. But this is not a court of morals, it is a court of law. Mr Brant will no doubt try and persuade you that Mr Dickson's evidence is simply not credible, but is there in fact any basis for that?

There is no evidence whatsoever that Mr Dickson was a party to the murder, everything points to him being simply an eyewitness.

The defence for Mr Morris will have you believe that Mr Dickson, just like all the other witnesses in this case have lied about what happened that night. Is that really the case? Have so many people really conspired to come to court and lie on oath about Morris, or is it far simpler, there is only one liar in this court when it comes to the part Mr Morris played that night and that is Mr Morris himself.

I suggest to you when you consider the evidence carefully, as I know you will, there is only one proper verdict in relation to both Defendants, they are both guilty of murder.

CHAPTER 51

THE CLOSING SPEECH FOR PAUL MORRIS

David rose solemnly to his feet. He knew it would be no easy task persuading this jury of his client's innocence or at least to raise a reasonable doubt in their minds. He hated it when prosecutors predicted what he was going to say, particularly when they got it right! He would have to change tack to gain some support from this jury. Looking at the faces before him, that was not going to be an easy task.

He looked at the old lady on the front row who frowned at him in return, but he could see her face soften slightly as he smiled at her. No doubt she enjoyed the attention, he would address her a few times during this speech.

"Ladies and gentlemen, you have heard an excellent speech from my learned friend Mr Adams, and you will no doubt want to consider the points he makes carefully.

On one matter I can agree with him. It is the evidence that is important in this case, not our speeches, however well delivered they are. Mr

Adams suggested to you that I would dwell on certain matters, that I would say to you that ultimately you cannot be sure of anything. Let me put your minds at rest. I want to deal with the actual evidence in this case, not just the evidence the prosecution rely upon, but all the evidence you have heard, as it is upon that evidence that you arrive at your determination. There are in fact a number of facts that you can be sure of in this case and they all support Mr Morris' case.

Mr Adams has, quite fairly, told you twice now that the burden of proving this case rests entirely on the prosecution's shoulders. He has also quite fairly told you that burden is a heavy one. You cannot convict Mr Morris of murder unless you are satisfied so that you are sure that he is guilty. Nothing less will do. It used to be referred to as being satisfied beyond a reasonable doubt. It's the same test, merely expressed in different words.

That is an important starting point in this case. Also in this case you heard Mr Morris give evidence. He didn't need to do so, as he has nothing to prove in this case. It is a further important point that by doing so he assumes no burden of proving anything, that burden still lies entirely with the prosecution from start to finish. Further, as he chose to give evidence, the prosecution have the added burden of proving that he has lied to you. He does not have to prove he told the truth.

You will want to consider his evidence carefully in this case, tested as it was by two very experienced and able advocates. Did they really make any in-roads into that evidence? Did they really undermine it? Certainly they made suggestions to him, but did any of those suggestions strike home as being true? That will be a matter for you but I suggest that they did not.

Let's look at that evidence carefully together.

Mr Adams is right that there is no issue here that Mr Williams was murdered that night. The sole issue in relation to that is, are you satisfied so that you are sure on the evidence you have heard that Mr Morris was the person who struck the fatal blow?

It will come as no surprise that I suggest you cannot be so sure on the evidence you have heard

In considering the evidence do please put aside any emotions. It is tragic that a young man has lost his life, particularly in circumstances such as these, and it is natural for us to feel sympathy for him and his loved ones. Of course, those sympathies can play no part in your verdicts. It is natural that all right minded people will want to see the person guilty of this crime convicted and punished. But again, a need for a reckoning plays no part in your deliberations.

Let us look together at the suggested motive in this case. The prosecution do not have to prove a motive, but the lack of a credible one should cause you concern. I suggest that the motive suggested by the prosecution in this case is simply not credible.

If Mr Morris' motive was to pay Mr Williams back for throwing bottles through his parents' windows, you might think that he would not have told the police about the incident and then pointed out Mr Williams' address to them. He would have kept it a secret waiting for an opportunity to take revenge without raising the obvious suspicion that it was him. As a result of telling them, he knew the police might be at that address anytime of the day or night looking for Mr Williams. It would be the height of stupidity to go round there carrying a large knife.

When properly analysed, I suggest the evidence in this case is really divided into two parts: What I will call the 'credible' and the 'incredible' witnesses!

Let's begin with the 'incredible' witnesses upon which the entire case for the prosecution relies.

These are the witnesses like Mr Dickson who was lucky not to be charged with murder, Mr Talbot, a witness who carries firearms and commits armed robberies, and then the prosecution even rely on the evidence of Mr Ward, a person they say is guilty of murder!

When you look at it like this you will see that the whole of the prosecution case against Mr Morris relies upon witnesses of dubious character who have many reasons to lie and very few to tell the truth.

Let's look at Mr Dickson first. He was originally arrested on suspicion of this murder. It is only after he implicated Mr Morris that the prosecution dropped the murder investigation against him. He has every reason to lie to deflect attention from himself. In any event, does his evidence even add up?

He received a call at 11:56pm on the Monday night from Mr Ward. We do not know what it was about but we know that, according to his girlfriend Tracey, he left the house at his usual time just a few minutes after the call, at around 12 midnight. We also know that, unusually, he did not come back for over two hours. We do know he phoned Mr Ward at 1:08am and we know they met up shortly after that time from their own evidence. Did they meet up earlier? May they have done? What was Mr Dickson doing for over an hour? It doesn't take that long to go and collect Tracey's benefits. What does he say he was doing for that hour? Well he tells us there wasn't an hour, he says that for a change he went out nearer 1am that night.

Who was more credible? Mr Dickson who was trying his best to escape a charge of murder when he first provided this explanation or his girlfriend Tracey, who has no reason to lie about the time he left? Was he or may he have been one of the two men with Mr Ward outside Mr Williams' flat?

When did Mr Dickson find out that Mr Williams was dead? He was adamant that it was on the Friday when he heard about it on the TV, however, his girlfriend was equally adamant it was the Wednesday when she pointed out that Mr Williams' death was announced on a social media website. What was his reaction? He phoned Mr Ward and went to meet him. Is that when they concocted this case against Mr Morris in a desperate attempt to protect themselves?

We know that the next day Mr Dickson disappeared. He left the area for a number of weeks. Why? On his account, he had done nothing, he had no reason to flee. But as we heard, he not only fled the area, he threw away the clothes that he had been wearing the night of the murder. Why would an innocent man do that?

I suggest that you be very careful about his evidence, he has every reason to lie. He is a friend of Mr Ward's and as such has a reason to support him. He is not a friend of Mr Williams and therefore has every reason to lie about him in order to save his own skin.

Let us move on to the other main witness for the prosecution, Mr Talbot, aka Pumpman. What did you make of him? Isn't it a sign of true desperation when the prosecution have to resort to calling and relying on the evidence of a jailhouse snitch who has such an appalling criminal record. What did he say his reason for giving evidence was? Because he didn't like the idea that Mr Morris was suggesting he would be acquitted and Mr Ward would be convicted.

Nonsense, do you really think that was credible reason? The reason for being the jail house snitch is for one reason and one reason only. There is one matter that is more important to all prisoners than anything else and that is their date of release. Long term criminals like Pumpman, know there are two ways to get an early date of release, firstly to plead guilty, secondly, and more importantly, to give assistance to the police.

Every prisoner knows if you do both, you get a hefty discount off your sentence, up to half the expected sentence, if not more in some cases. You can get it reduced even further if you get the prosecution to accept an absurd basis of plea, namely that a convicted armed robber had a pump-action, sawn-off shotgun with ammunition, balaclavas and camouflage coloured body armour in order to make Rap movies!

All prisoners know this and it is nonsense for an experienced criminal like Talbot to claim he did not give evidence for that reason. Indeed, we know that he confirmed this with the police that the sole reason he was giving evidence was for a reduction in sentence. No other reason was given then. Only in subsequent months does he come out with other reasons to pretend that he has some morals.

What evidence does he have to give in order to obtain this hefty discount in his sentence? It has to be evidence that supports the prosecution case against Mr Morris and to a certain extent against Mr Ward. Only then will the police inform his sentencing judge that he has given 'assistance'.

But it goes further, Pumpman has a further reason to lie in this case. Probably the best one.

He was the murderer.

What better reason to support a police

prosecution and get an innocent man convicted so that the police never come knocking at your door.

I ask you not to rely upon such an untrustworthy witness who has every reason to lie.

Let us look at the final witness the Crown rely upon in this case. Like the other 'incredible' witnesses, Mr Ward, has every reason to lie. In his case, unlike Dickson, he is actually charged with the murder.

Mr Ward admits he was outside Mr Williams' flat in the early hours of 6th May when threats were made to kill him. He also admits to striking Mr Williams shortly before he was stabbed to death. Of course he only made these admissions when he was picked out on an identification parade by civilian witnesses who saw him there that night. Nevertheless, the prosecution try to rely on a major part of his account claiming he told the truth whenever he blamed Mr Morris, but equally they say he has lied when he seeks to exonerate himself.

They cannot have it both ways. Either he is telling the truth and is a reliable and accurate witness in relation to all the matters he has given evidence about or he is not.

Mr Ward has every reason to lie to lay the blame

on Mr Morris' shoulders. He knows what really happened. Has he really told you the truth? Did he look like he was telling the truth when he squirmed around in the witness box whilst being questioned?

I suggest he looked very uncomfortable giving his evidence because he knew he could be caught out in his lies at any moment. When you are considering the case for and against Mr Morris, I ask you to please be careful when weighing-up his evidence. It will be a matter for you, but a possible way of doing this is to look for supporting evidence from an independent credible source.

Of course, when you do look for that credible independent evidence in this case, you rapidly discover that it simply does not exist.

Let us now turn to the independent and credible evidence in this case. Namely, the evidence of the wholly independent witnesses, the law-abiding honest neighbours who gave evidence before you. They have no reason to lie and although they may have made minor mistakes, one matter does stand out in this case from their evidence.

Not one of them gives any evidence against Mr Morris.

No one says they saw him outside Mr Williams'

flat that night. None of the honest, independent witnesses ever identified Mr Morris as being there.

Equally, none of those honest witnesses saw Mr Morris with a knife. None of those honest witnesses saw him wield a knife and kill Mr Williams. None of those honest witnesses identified Mr Morris as even being present when the fatal blow was struck.

Indeed, when you look at it closely, as I know you will, their evidence taken together rather than implicate Mr Morris, tends to point directly away from him.

Consider the important evidence of Mr Brook. He was adamant that he heard the noises outside Mr Williams' flat at 12:45 that night. He gave you evidence about the accuracy of his clock."

David looked down at his notes as he read a quote, "He said, 'It's set by radio signals that come from Rugby I believe, so it's never out by more than a few seconds or so'.

In those circumstances you may think he could not have made a mistake about the time. If he is right, or may be, because that is the standard to apply in the case of Mr Morris, then Mr Morris was not outside Mr Williams' flat because we know from the phone evidence that he was at home. He called Mr Ward from his home at

12:48. He could not be in two places at once and if he was not outside Mr Williams' flat at 12:45, then the whole case against him starts to collapse.

Mr Adams in addressing you, correctly predicted I would remind you of what he said in opening about this evidence. He said this, 'Mr Brook was awoken by loud noises which sounded like someone kicking at a door. He looked at his clock and noted that it was 12:45am. He did not look out at that stage for fear that whoever was causing this noise might direct their attention towards him, but he did hear someone say words to the effect, 'You almost brained me the other night, let me in or I'll fucking kill you.'

The prosecution were relying on that time as being accurate. They had not realised, at that stage, that evidence gave Mr Morris an alibi so it is only now they suggest that Mr Brook has got his timings wrong, even when there is no real basis for doing so save that it fits their case as they now present it.

However, instead of being wrong, Mr Brook's evidence is supported by another prosecution witness, Shereena Bennett. She also supports Mr Morris' case. Firstly in a minor way, she told you she did not see a white man outside Mr Williams' flat. She certainly did not identify Mr Morris as being there. Nor did her son, Lloyd.

Admittedly, he said the men with Mr Ward were white but he did not identify Mr Morris as being one of them.

Shereena Bennett also gave very important evidence in favour of Mr Morris. She saw Mr Ward receive a phone call as he was leaving Danny Williams' flat. She accepted in cross examination that she was not looking at a clock and this call could have been before 1am. On that basis it could have been the call made by Mr Morris at 12:48 which further supports his case that he was not present at Mr Williams' flat that night.

What else is there? In reality, there is nothing.

The prosecution have scraped the bottom of the barrel relying on the 'incredible' witnesses, but they carry on scraping the very sludge of that barrel and rely on two additional pieces of evidence. Firstly, the fact that Mr Morris has a previous conviction for assaulting his father. Secondly, the fact that Mr Morris did not answer questions in interview when the police questioned him.

Mr Adams in his final address to you frequently reminded you that Mr Morris has a criminal conviction for cutting his father's hand for 'dissing' him. As he put it, what would Mr Morris do to a man who threw bottles through his father's window and cut him with broken glass?

It is true that Mr Morris has this previous conviction recorded against him, however, Mr Adams forgot to remind you of the evidence you actually heard. You will recall the evidence of Mr Morris' own father who admitted to you that he had lied in court on a previous occasion because he was embarrassed and he caused the injury to himself by striking the edge of a door. I suggest you do not put any reliance on this allegation because of the father's admission that he perjured himself. The Prosecution called him as a witness of truth but they now ask you to disbelieve the evidence they called before you and rely on evidence he gave in the past.

I suggest the only fair way to deal with this conviction is to please put it out of your minds.

The second matter the prosecution rely upon is that during his questioning by police he made no comment to all the questions asked. Of course you have heard two important matters about that interview. Firstly, that was his right and secondly, he was advised by his solicitor to make no comment.

Mr Morris had never been arrested for something so serious in the past. He sought the advice of a professional experienced solicitor and it was given. Can you really hold it against him that he relied upon that advice? Wouldn't any of us rely upon the advice of an expert in that situation? I suggest that it would be wrong to draw any adverse inference against Mr Morris in the particular circumstances of this case."

David paused and looked around the faces of the jurors before continuing. He noted with satisfaction that virtually all of them were listening to him, some were even nodding and one or two, including the old lady at the front, were even smiling at him. He continued, "Ladies and gentlemen, I am not going to suggest this is an easy case. You will shortly hear from Mr Smythe on behalf of Mr Ward who will no doubt suggest that the evidence is overwhelming against Mr Morris and yet there is none against Mr. Ward. As you will probably have noted, being in this position ..."

David pointed to where he was standing, "... is rather like being sandwiched between two prosecutors! No doubt you will want to consider very carefully what Mr Smythe has to say and so you should. However, what I suggest to you is that when you look at all the evidence closely in this case, the evidence against Mr Morris is weak and there is in reality no credible evidence to gainsay or contradict his account that he had nothing to do with this murder.

I suggest that in those circumstances there is only one proper verdict in the case of Paul Thomas and that is, not guilty."

CHAPTER 52

THE CLOSING SPEECH FOR MICHAEL WARD

There was a break for lunch before William Smythe began his address to the jury.

"Ladies and gentlemen, I am conscious that you have heard two excellent speeches from my learned friends this morning. I'm sorry to say that you now have to suffer a speech from me. It is at moments like this I tend to feel like Henry VIII's sixth wife on her wedding night, I know what to do but how do I make it interesting!"

There was a slight murmur of appreciation from the jury who in reality had had enough of listening to speeches. William waited a few seconds before carrying on. "Having started with a reference to an historical figure, it only seems appropriate to refer to another. This time a quote from Shakespeare's Henry IV part 1, Act 2 scene 2, 'A plague upon it when thieves cannot be true one to another!'

You might think that is an appropriate quote in this case, and, as I am dealing with quotes, perhaps Mr Morris will remember the famous quote by Oscar Wilde, 'Always forgive your enemies - nothing annoys them so much'."

The jury was now grinning at William so, having had the impact he wanted, he moved on. "Of course, although I introduce some levity into the proceedings, no one can doubt this is a serious case. It is a serious case with serious consequences for both these young men and therefore must be treated with great care by us all. Fortunately, like Mr Adams has said, we have all noticed how conscientious you have been in carrying out your duties during this case and listening attentively to the evidence.

Mr Brant in addressing you suggested that he felt he was sandwiched between two prosecutors. Let me dispel that myth straight away. As you know, I am here to represent Mr Ward and present his case to you. It is no part of my function to prosecute Mr Morris and the verdict you bring in relation to him is no concern of mine. However, of course the interests of Mr Ward are different to those of Mr Morris and I would be failing in my duty if I did not draw some of those differences to your attention and demonstrate that some of the matters raised on behalf of Mr Morris do not really make any sense and indeed tend to defy common sense."

David looked up slightly at this point and adopted a slightly bemused expression so that the jury could see. William expected this and ignoring him, continued, "Let us begin with one fact that everyone in this court can agree on. Danny Williams was brutally murdered that night by someone wielding a knife. Someone you may think who regularly carried knives and knew how to deliver a blow accurately enough to both incapacitate and kill a man.

It is important to note that no one is suggesting that it was Michael Ward who wielded that knife. The Prosecution do not say that, they clearly say it was Morris. Even Mr Morris, when he gave evidence, never suggested that it was Mr Ward, he said it was Joey Talbot.

Now some of you may think that Mr Morris' evidence was hard to believe, particularly his efforts to explain why he had avoided swearing on the New Testament. Nevertheless, no one was able to twist his evidence to suggest that Mr Ward was the knife-wielder in this case.

You may think the knife-wielder is undoubtedly a person who has previous experience of using a knife to wound someone and we all know who that is in this case. Mr Morris has a previous conviction for wielding a knife against his own father.

Clearly you will want to consider Mr Brant's speech carefully on this issue. There is no doubt that the father went back on his previous evidence in this court, but it is important to note that he did not do so at the last trial. It's perhaps understandable that he chose to lie on his son's behalf when he faces a murder charge, but there is no doubt that he originally told the police that Mr Morris had cut him across the hand with a knife. He even added that the knife had gone missing some time before and described it having a serrated edge. Was that detail really an invention or was it the truth?

Mr Morris senior repeated that evidence in the Crown Court when his son was tried for that offence. Now it might be possible to argue that he lied to the police originally to get his son out of the house but what about in court, when he said his son had cut him with a knife? We know from the transcripts of the prison telephone calls that he had reconciled with his son by that stage. Was he really likely to lie in those circumstances?

No, I suggest the truth is obvious here. He did not lie originally, he did not make up a story about a knife going missing, and he did not make up a story about being cut by his own son in court. The truth is clear. Mr Morris cut him with a knife. It is Mr Morris who was handy with a knife and knew how to use one.

You may think the evidence is overwhelming that Mr Morris was present the night Danny

Williams was killed and was the killer. Of course it is right that Mr Brant, on behalf of Mr Morris, relies heavily on Mr Brook's looking at his remarkably accurate clock. Of course the clock may well have been accurate to a few seconds but that does not mean Mr Brook was!

Please remember what Mr Brook stated when he first gave evidence before you. He said, 'I had gone to bed at about 10:00 pm and I was woken at just before 1am when I heard loud noises coming from that man's flat.'

'I was woken at just before 1am'. That accords with the evidence of Ms Shereena Bennett who told you, 'It was about 1am when I was woken by a loud noise'.

Mr Brant managed skilfully to get them both to say it could be earlier, but we all know that people are seldom accurate on times. Mr Ward says it was around 1am and so do the prosecution witnesses. There is very little in a few minutes here and in reality it does not provide the alibi that Mr Morris craves.

What then is the case against Mr Ward?

The prosecution put their case against Mr Ward, not on the basis that he wielded the knife, not that he supplied the knife, not that he disposed of the knife, not that he was encouraging Morris to use it, but on the basis that he was involved in a 'joint enterprise'. They say he was part of a scheme to kill or cause really serious injury to Danny.

What is their basis for suggesting this? It appears solely to be on the basis that he was present that night, although, as they accept, he was clearly unarmed. The prosecution appears to rely heavily on Mr Talbot and his evidence that Mr Ward told him that they went round to 'sort Danny out'. It is not clear but they also appear to rely upon the fact that Mr Ward acted in self-defence when Danny attacked him that night.

The prosecution say that these men were acting together intending to kill Danny or cause him really serious harm.

As you heard, Mr Adams dismisses the suggestion that Mr Ward thought they were going round to Danny's at 1am in the morning in order to discuss their problems. He says that if that had been their intention, they would have called first and arranged a visit when he would be in during the day.

Mr Ward's case and his evidence on the other hand is very simple. Yes there had been a previous incident where Danny had thrown bottles through Morris' window. That was because Morris had earlier thrown bricks through Danny's window. That was the payback. Despite what the prosecution suggest, it did not really concern Mr Ward. Yes he was present when the bottles were thrown but there is no evidence to suggest he had almost been hit by a bottle, save for the comment of Mr Morris and the prosecution can hardly rely on him as a witness of truth. On the other hand, we know that Mr Morris was 'almost brained' by a bottle that night because we have the physical evidence that he received an injury to his head from flying glass. You may think it obvious in those circumstances that it was Morris who made the comment about 'almost being brained'.

The suggestion that they would not have gone round at 1am just to chat ignores the reality of the life style these people had. It's clear that they were night owls. Mr Dickson said he had bought drugs off Danny in the past which must have been soon after midnight because that is the only time he ever had any money. You may think on the evidence that we have heard, that after midnight is the time these people sold drugs. One am is just normal business hours to them.

Now, at this stage, I should say something about drug dealing. Mr Ward admits he is a drug dealer. You will not like that fact, and no one expects you to, but this case is not about drug dealing. It is about murder and the fact he is a drug dealer will not assist you in any way in determining whether he was party to a murder.

Please put any such prejudicial thoughts out of your mind and concentrate on the evidence.

When you look at the prosecution evidence carefully, it actually supports everything that Mr Ward has told you. Even the suggestion that he went round to 'sort Danny out' is dealt with when you consider that Mr Talbot did not seem to understand the difference between dealing with a problem by conversing and physically assaulting someone. That perhaps says a lot about Mr Talbot.

There is no evidence that Mr Ward was aggressive that night. Yes, he defended himself but there is no suggestion he went over the top, he exercised restraint. He was assaulted and he forced his attacker to the ground. He took no further action after that. Hardly the actions of someone who the prosecution suggests went there to kill or cause really serious harm to Danny.

Noticeably, the first incident outside the flat was over when Danny appeared in the street. Everyone was going their separate ways. Mr Ward defended himself and was not demonstrating any intention of harming Danny when later, out of nowhere, Morris appeared and stabbed Danny in the heart.

That was not a joint enterprise, a pre-planned mission to cause serious harm or death, that was a one man show and that one man was Morris.

What other evidence is there against Mr Ward?

There is none. No one claims to have seen him cause any injury to Danny, no one claims to have witnessed him pre-planning this incident with Morris. When you look at the evidence against him carefully there is only one proper verdict and that is not guilty to both murder and manslaughter.

CHAPTER 53

THE DELIBERATIONS

"There you are members of the jury that is the evidence in the case, you will hear no more so please do not ask for any."

Mr Justice Knight had spent part of Thursday afternoon and most of Friday directing the jury on the law to be applied in the case and summarising the facts before they were permitted to retire to consider their verdicts. It was now 2:30pm and he was finishing his summing up of the evidence.

"I suggest that one of the first things you do is elect a jury foreman." He smiled and looked at a few of the female jurors, "That means a man or a woman. Then after the jury bailiffs have been sworn please retire to your rooms. You may have heard of majority verdicts, please put them out of your mind. Your verdict must be unanimous. Should the time come when I can take a majority verdict from you, I will send for you."

He looked away from the jury and towards the jury bailiffs who took their oaths to keep the juries in a private and convenient place and not to allow anyone to speak to them. After the formalities were over the jury picked up their papers and followed the jury bailiffs to their retiring room.

They had no problem selecting a jury foreman, Michael Greenslade, aged 64, a former company director, had already suggested himself for the job and no one objected. He seated himself at the head of the table as everyone took seats around it. When everyone was seated, he got straight down to business.

"I see there's a kettle in the room with some tea and coffee."

He looked around the room before his eyes fell on Lesley Babb, a twenty two year old administrative assistant from a Brighton Wholesalers' firm. He gave her a big beaming smile, "Lesley, would you be a love and put the kettle on? I'll have a tea please."

Lesley looked around the room to see if she had any support against this obviously sexist treatment, but no one would look in her direction, and she shrugged and got up to put the kettle on. She noticed one sachet of tea had a hole in it leaking tea leaves. She smirked as she placed it in Michael's cup.

Soon they were all busy in debate sipping at their tea and coffee. Michael had quietened down after initially taking the lead. It had not helped that he was now trying surreptitiously to remove tea leaves from his mouth.

Gareth Alexander, a 37 year old business man, was annoyed that he was still there at all. He had not expected to spend more than the two weeks referred to on his jury summons. Now he could see there was a big chance this case would go into the following week and he had a number of important business meetings in his diary. He decided to cut through the arguments, "Look, this is an easy case, Moulsecoomb is such a horrible area. They're all criminals there! I have no doubt they're both guilty of murder."

Gary Smith, an unemployed 24 year old, looked up from the doodle he had drawn on his jury notebook. He had taken no part in the discussions yet but now felt the need to comment, "I live in Moulsecoomb."

Gareth looked at him with contempt and an expression that clearly conveyed that Gary had just proved his point for him. This clearly annoyed Daphne Whitchurch, a 34 year old teacher. "I live in Moulsecoomb too. Not everyone there is a criminal! There are some very nice parts of Moulsecoomb and a lot of very nice people live there."

Gareth's face dropped. He had not spoken to Daphne as she kept to herself during the adjournments but he had thought she was quite attractive and that he might approach her after the trial to see if she fancied going out for a drink with him. He decided it might be better to keep quiet for now and as soon as possible, retrieve his mobile phone from the usher and cancel Monday's appointments.

Michael Greenslade spat the last of the tea leaves into his cup with a quick glance at Lesley, who was smiling at him and added, "Really, I think we should concentrate on the evidence, rather than make general unhelpful comments about where people live."

Gareth looked down in despair as he thought it wise to cancel Tuesday's appointments as well.

Doris Hornsbury, a 62 year old retired librarian, had been relatively quiet throughout the meeting. She looked at Michael with admiration, having decided early on that he was the most intelligent man on the jury. "I agree with Michael we should concentrate on the evidence. I think that prosecutor summarised the evidence perfectly in his final address. He was so fair to the defendants throughout this case and he made some excellent points."

Thomas Finley, a 29 year old accountant at a local Brighton firm, quickly responded, "I thought the prosecutor was far too theatrical and smarmy. That gesture he made with the knife when he first addressed us, was wholly unnecessary and clearly meant to prejudice us."

Soni Akhtar, a 36 year old business woman from Hove, also joined in. "I agree, I think that Morris's defence counsel made some excellent points in this case. He made them fairly, he did not resort to theatrics. He put all the facts properly before us without resorting to emotion."

Thomas Finley looked straight at her. "I disagree, he kept on noisily underlining throughout the case to emphasis a point as if we weren't capable of seeing it for ourselves."

There were a few nods around the room, from those who did not know what he was talking about.

Thomas warmed to his theme, "And I wasn't impressed with his junior who made that loud and I thought improper comment when Dickson was giving evidence."

There were a few blank expressions around the room. "You know, when the prosecutor said to the judge that Dickson was not going to be charged with possession of cannabis, he shouted out, 'nor with murder'."

There were a few nods but an equal number of blank expressions. Thomas was not deterred,

"And I didn't think much of Ward's barrister either!"

Jonathon Yates, a TV repairman from Lewes, interrupted, "Did you like anyone?"

Thomas replied defensively, "I thought the Judge was ok" He paused before adding, "Albeit a little long-winded!"

Jonathon responded, "Well I thought Ward's barrister was very good. He was funny and he made some good points as well."

Michael Greenslade felt that control of the meeting was slipping away from him. "Can we please concentrate on the evidence and not what we think of the barristers and the judge?"

Doris was supportive, "I agree with Michael. I'd like to say I think the prosecutor made an excellent case. I think there is no doubt that Morris and Ward went round to 'sort Danny out'. They were annoyed with him for the bottle throwing incident. Morris clearly had a knife and Ward knew it and they both planned to kill or at least seriously hurt Danny."

Soni Akhtar shook her head. "I disagree, Morris' defence barrister made an excellent point in relation to timing. The prosecutor relied on Brook's timings at the start of the case no doubt because Brook had that clock that was accurate to within a few seconds. Brook was adamant that he had looked at the clock, which is quite natural when you are woken, and he had seen the time of 12:45am when he heard noises outside Danny's flat. That couldn't be Morris because we know he was home at that time. Also, Morris had given the police Danny's address. He was expecting them to turn up any day or night at any time. He is hardly likely to have taken a large knife round there knowing he might bump into the police."

There were a few nods around the room and a few jurors shaking their heads.

Michael had been shaking his head, "I think the pathology evidence is quite important in this case, particularly the evidence about the fish tail wound."

Gary Smith's face drained of colour as he thought about the wound, "Do we have to discuss that, I felt quite ill in court when that evidence was given."

Soni Akhtar immediately supported Gary, "I cannot see how the pathology evidence is important, it cannot tell us who committed the murder! I think we should concentrate on the so-called eye witnesses.

That Dickson's evidence does worry me. His girlfriend clearly said he left the flat just after

12am. What was he doing for an hour till he got her money?"

Lesley Babb now joined the discussion, "I didn't like that 'Pumpman', I didn't like the way he looked at me. It gave me the creeps."

Gary immediately looked away from her and down at his hands.

Doris added, "But he may have been telling the truth. It is possible he was giving evidence because he didn't like Morris boasting that he was going to get off and Ward was going to get convicted."

Michael shook his head, "No Doris, he was obviously doing it for a reduction in his sentence, that's what he told the police. However, that does not mean he wasn't telling the truth."

Doris looked at Michael with a hurt expression and remained quiet for a few seconds before adding, "I don't like that Morris, remember what he said to the police when he was arrested."

Gary looked at her now, the colour returning to his cheeks, "Yes but the police can be annoying around there. I've been stopped a few times by the police when I've been minding my own business. You have to remember that Morris had been arrested previously for assaulting his Dad with a knife and he has always said he did not do it."

Doris was not going to be persuaded, "I think it's appalling that he attacked his own father with a knife. I think it shows just what he's like. If he was prepared to use it on his own father then he would definitely use it on a drug dealer who he had fallen out with!"

Gary raised his eyes to the ceiling, "Did he attack his father with a knife? I think he and his father could have been telling the truth about that. The father could have been embarrassed and made it up that his son attacked him and then finally told the truth in this court.

Doris was not to be beaten, "What about him claiming he believes in God and then affirming!"

Gary shook his head, "You can't hold it against him that he affirmed, I affirmed."

Michael now intervened, "I don't think Doris' point is that he affirmed. It's that he claimed to be a devout Churchgoer and then affirmed. Surely he would have taken the oath on the New Testament if he was so religious and the fact he did not suggests he knew he was going to lie."

Gary was adamant now, "I disagree, he said he would swear an oath on the New Testament and then repeat his evidence."

Michael assumed a supercilious air, "Yes but only when he was caught out!"

Doris now felt she had some support again, "What about Ward? He's a criminal, a drug dealer. He deserves what he gets."

Michael shook his head, "Yes, but we are not dealing with him for supplying drugs, he admits that. He is charged with murder."

Gareth Alexander looked up from his jury pad where he had been calculating how much he was losing financially by being here. He looked at the animated faces around the room and decided to cancel Wednesday's appointments as well.

CHAPTER 54

THE VERDICT

The jury was sent home on Friday at 4:30pm and resumed their deliberations on Monday at 10:00am. As they had not reached any decisions they were sent home again at 4:30pm. On Tuesday morning, 23rd September, they recommenced at 10:00am and at 11:00am, Mr Justice Knight called them back into court and gave them a majority direction telling them he would now accept a decision on which at least ten of them agreed.

At 12:30pm, the jury filed back into Court. As they did so, David quickly looked back towards the dock. Paul Morris was leaning forward and gripping the edge of his seat and clearly looking nervous. Michael Ward on the other hand did not seem to have a care in the world.

Once they were seated, the court clerk stood and asked the jury foreman to stand. Michael Greenslade rose to deliver the verdicts. David looked at the jurors closely, trying to guess what their decision was. However, they were giving nothing away. Some were looking towards the defendants others were looking away. David knew there were a few people out there who claim that you can tell a verdict by whether the jury look at a defendant or not. If they will not look, it's a guilty verdict, if they look it's a not guilty. However, in his experience, this was unreliable, for he had noticed over the years that some jurors would look at a defendant and gladly pronounce him guilty, others would look away, still uncertain perhaps, and declare that he was not guilty.

The clerk addressed the jury foreman, "Have you reached verdicts on which at least ten of you are agreed?"

Michael looked at the other jurors before replying, "Yes".

"On count one of the indictment do you find the defendant, Paul Morris, guilty or not guilty of murder?"

David tried to remain calm, even though, after all these years, he still got butterflies in his stomach when verdicts were delivered.

Michael spoke slowly, loudly and it seemed to David, proudly. "Guilty."

"Is that the verdict of you all or by a majority?"

"By a majority."

"How many of you agreed and how many dissented?"

"Eleven agreed and one dissented." David noticed an Asian lady on the jury frowning and assumed she was the dissenting vote. At least he persuaded one person, he thought to himself.

The clerk went through the same procedure regarding Michael Ward. Again, the foreman shouted out the word "Guilty", though this time the majority was ten to two.

David looked at William Smythe who nodded at him. He then turned to Tim who was positively beaming. David smiled as it struck him that this could mean he would be a lot busier in the future. Tim would be in great demand from the Sussex CPS and David would probably be covering a few of his silk returns soon!

Mr Justice Knight also smiled briefly, the decision had been exactly what he had predicted on day one of the proceedings. In his mind this trial had been a waste of time and of public money. This simply would not be allowed in Commercial Courts. He stopped smiling as Tim addressed him.

Tim took him through both defendants' previous convictions and asked whether he was going to sentence then and there.

The judge looked at defence counsel and asked if there was any reason to postpone sentence. Both said that there was not. They had advised their clients that there was only one sentence for murder, life imprisonment. The only issue now was the length of the minimum time they would spend before they could apply for parole.

David went first and put forward what little mitigation there was. In this case it was mainly Paul's youth and immaturity. William followed and used the same mitigation but emphasised that Michael Ward had not wielded the knife.

Mr Justice Knight listened carefully to both Counsel and took a few notes. When they had finished he asked the defendants to both stand. As they did, David noted that Michael Ward was looking shell-shocked. He had clearly convinced himself that he was not going to be convicted.

"Paul Morris and Michael Ward you have been found guilty by this jury of the crime of murder. In the early hours of Tuesday 6th May 2014 you both went to visit Danny Williams at his flat. I do not doubt for one moment that your joint intention was to kill him. You Morris carried the knife, a knife which you had previously used to cut your own father with. You Ward were not armed but you knew that Morris was in the habit of carrying knives and I do not doubt that you knew he had a knife with him that night and was intending to kill Danny Williams because Danny Williams had thrown bottles through

Morris' window in retaliation for you two throwing bricks through his.

Danny Williams would not let you in and you both tried to force entry. When you failed you left, although you both stayed in the area. Unfortunately for Danny Williams he left his flat a little later and came across you two. He may have been aggressive because of what had happened to him, but he did not deserve the treatment you meted out to him.

You Ward knocked him to the ground and when he was incapacitated, you Morris took advantage of the situation and used severe force to plunge a knife through his chest, damaging his sternum and passed on through to his heart. A fatal blow and in my judgement a deliberate one carrying with it an intention to kill.

You then both left the area and you Morris clearly discarded the knife somewhere.

Neither of you has shown any remorse for your actions. You Ward blamed Morris for the killing without owning up to your own role in this murder. You Morris tried to blame a prosecution witness for the murder. Although he has an appalling criminal record I do not believe he played any part in this incident and it was particularly devious of you to seek to blame him.

There are few mitigating circumstances in this case. I am sure your joint intention was to kill rather than the lesser intention of intending to cause really serious harm so there is no mitigation there. The only mitigating features I have discovered, with the aid of your counsel, is your young age and the fact that you Ward were not armed yourself and did not wield the fatal blow.

The sentence for murder is fixed by law, it is life imprisonment. I must set the minimum term, namely the term that you will serve before you can apply for parole. It is important for you both to appreciate that you will not be automatically released at the end of that period that will only happen if the parole board considers you safe to release you from custody. Even then you will be on licence for the rest of your life. You will have to obey the conditions of your licence otherwise you may be recalled to prison.

Parliament has decided that in cases where a knife was taken to the scene as was the case here, the starting point is a minimum term of twenty five years. The use of knives to cause injury and/or death has become a major menace in this country. That starting point can be increased if there are aggravating features or decreased if there are mitigating ones.

In your case Morris, I consider there are no major aggravating features in this case and the only mitigating feature is your young age. Accordingly in your case the minimum term you must spend in prison before you can be released is one of twenty-two years less the time you have already spent in custody. I have to sentence you for the assault on your father and I pass a concurrent sentence of three and a half years. You will therefore serve a minimum sentence of twenty-two years.

In your case Ward, the same starting point applies. Again there are no major aggravating features in this case and you have the mitigation of age and the added mitigation that you did not wield the knife although that can be little mitigation in the circumstances. In your case the minimum term I set is one of twenty-one years."

He looked at the prison guards, "Take them down."

David looked back towards the dock to see that surprisingly Morris had a smirk on his face whereas Ward had almost collapsed.

CHAPTER 55

THE SILK RETURNS

Fifteen minutes later David and Graham were in the cells of Lewes Crown court facing Paul Morris across a small table. Normally they found moments like this to be very difficult. It was never easy talking to someone who had just been sentenced to life imprisonment and was facing a couple of decades in prison before he could apply for parole, but in this case it was surprisingly easy. Paul was not in the slightest concerned about his conviction and seemed to be almost relishing his new found status as a convicted murderer.

David looked at the smiling face in front of him for a few seconds before he spoke, "Graham and I will look at all the papers and our notes to see if there are any possible grounds of appeal."

Paul just nodded as David asked him, "Paul, you seem surprisingly cheerful for someone who has just been found guilty of murder. Is there any reason why?"

Paul nodded again, but this time added, "I'm just glad they potted that lying bastard Afro. I thought he was going to get away with it and it was just going to be me doing life!"

After a few minutes, David and Graham left the cell. They could not be 100% sure of course, but they felt that the Lewes' jury had probably dispensed justice today.

At 5:30pm, they both walked into the Clerks Room to see a happy John Winston who greeted them both cheerily. "Good day Mr Brant and Mr Martin. We got a good result for chambers today."

David looked puzzled. "But we were convicted."

John kept on smiling "Precisely, but Mr Adams and Mr McConnell got a conviction in a murder. The Sussex CPS has already rung up, they want Mr Adams to lead in another murder starting at the end of October. That's good news for you Mr Brant."

David still looked puzzled. "Why is that good news for me?"

"Well Mr Adams is going to return a two week murder trial to you in the Bailey."

David smiled, "I see, another silk return for me then."

John nodded, "They're hard to come by these days but we seem to have got a few for you this year. Oh, and there's someone to see you in your room Mr Brant. I think it will probably be more good news."

David looked at him quizzically for a second before going to his room.

He opened the door and walked towards his desk when he noticed James Wontner QC, his former Head of Chambers, sitting at it reading through some papers.

James immediately looked up, "Hello David, it's good to see you!"

David smiled in return, "It good to see you too James. I have to say you are looking well. Everyone in chambers will be happy to see that you have made a good recovery."

James got up slowly from the desk and joined David by the window overlooking the Inner Temple Gardens.

"Well, it was touch and go David. I thought I was on my way to argue my final case with St Peter at the Golden Gates."

David laughed, "That's probably one argument you wouldn't win!"

James looked slightly hurt by the comment so David quickly added, "Only joking James. I'm glad to see you're back."

James gave a slight grin, "Yes, I'm glad to be back too. The doctors have said I should not stress out too much, but what do they know. I've told John to fill my diary with some good quality work."

David smiled as he inwardly thought that was goodbye to his own practice.

James continued not noticing David's expression, "Anyway David, I'm glad I've met you first as I wanted to raise a couple of matters with you before I talk to anyone else."

David gave him a curious look. "Certainly James, what is it?"

"I've been contacted by an old university chum of mine, Geoffrey Petford-Williams, an Oxford rowing blue. Anyway, his daughter has been called to the bar and is looking for a pupillage. I said I'd see what we can do for her. She's apparently very bright and would be an asset to chambers."

David paused for a second before replying, "James, you know we are bound by certain rules now, we have to have 'open' competition. We have signed up to the 'Pupillage Gateway' and as you know, potential pupil barristers have to apply through that system and be judged against all the other candidates out there. We cannot just take someone on after a chat over a coffee. It's not like it was in our day."

James nodded, "Of course, David, I understand, I wasn't suggesting she should have any preferences over other candidates, just that we should keep an eye out for her application and at least interview her."

David did not point out the obvious that that was showing preference over other candidates. He simply replied, "Well let's see what happens with her application."

James nodded and returned to David's desk and looked down at some papers in front of him. It was clear he was not going to move so David sat down at the desk opposite. He opened his bag and pulled out some papers and placed them on his desk. He was about to look at them when he had a thought. He looked up and said, "James, you said there were a couple of matters you wanted to raise with me, what's the other one?"

James looked up quickly, "Of course I almost forgot. I wanted to thank you for taking over the reins as Head of Chambers in my absence. I know it's a thankless task and by all accounts you've done an excellent job. Anyway, I am ready to resume my old role. I'm going to suggest we have a party in your honour to thank you for your services. I have no doubt everyone will whole-heartedly agree."

David looked at him and could not help the involuntary dropping of his jaw. This was one silk return he had not expected!

Books by John M. Burton

THE SILK BRIEF

The first book in the series, "The Silk Trials." David Brant QC is a Criminal Barrister, a "Silk", struggling against a lack of work and problems in his own chambers. He is briefed to act on behalf of a cocaine addict charged with murder. The case appears overwhelming and David has to use all his ability to deal with the wealth of forensic evidence presented against his client.

US LINK

http://amzn.to/1bz221C

UK LINK

http://amzn.to/16QwwZo

THE SILK HEAD
The Silk Tales volume 2

The second book in the series "The Silk Tales". David Brant QC receives a phone call from his wife asking him to represent a fireman charged with the murder of his lover. As the trial progresses, developments in David's Chambers bring unexpected romance and a significant shift in politics and power when the Head of Chambers falls seriously ill. Members of his chambers feel that only David is capable of leading them out of rough waters ahead, but with a full professional and personal life, David is not so sure whether he wants to take on the role of *The Silk Head*.

US LINK

http://amzn.to/1iTPQZn

UK LINK

http://amzn.to/1ilOOYn

THE SILK RETURNS

The Silk Tales volume 3

David Brant QC is now Head of Chambers at Temple Lane Chambers, Temple, London. Life is great for David, his practice is busy with good quality work and his love life exciting. He has a beautiful partner in Wendy Pritchard, a member of his chambers and that relationship, like his association with members of his chambers, appears to be strengthening day by day.

However, overnight, things change dramatically for him and his world is turned upside down. At least he can bury himself in his work when a new brief is returned to him from another silk. The case is from his least favourite solicitor but at least it appears to be relatively straightforward, with little evidence against his client, and an acquittal almost inevitable.

As the months pass, further evidence is served in the case and begins to mount up against his client. As the trial commences David has to deal with a prosecutor from his own chambers who is determined to score points against him personally and a co-defending counsel who likewise seems hell-bent on causing as many problems as he can for David's client. Will David's skill and wit be enough this time?

UK LINK

http://amzn.to/1Qj911Q

US LINK

http://amzn.to/1OteiV7

THE SILK RIBBON

The Silk Tales volume 4

David Brant QC is a barrister who practices as a Queen's Counsel at Temple Lane Chambers, Temple, London. He is in love with a bright and talented barrister from his chambers, Wendy, whose true feelings about him have been difficult to pin down. Just when he thinks he has the answer, a seductive Russian woman seeks to attract his attention, for reasons he can only guess at.

His case load has been declining since the return of his Head of Chambers, who is now taking all the quality silk work that David had formerly enjoyed. As a result, David is delighted when he is instructed in an interesting murder case. A middle class man has shot and killed his wife's lover. The prosecution say it was murder, frustration caused by his own impotency, but the defence claim it was all a tragic accident. The case appears to David to be straightforward, but, as the trial date approaches, the prosecution evidence mounts up and David finds himself against a highly competent prosecution silk, with a trick or two up his sleeve.

Will David be able to save his well-to-do client from the almost inevitable conviction for murder and a life sentence in prison? And what path will his personal life take when the beautiful Russian asks him out for a drink?

UK LINK

http://amzn.to/22ExByC

USA LINK

http://amzn.to/1TTWQMY

THE SILKS CHILD

The Silk Tales volume 5

This is the fifth volume in the series, the Silk Tales, dealing with the continuing story of Queen's Counsel (the Silk), David Brant QC.

Their romantic Valentine's weekend away in a five-star hotel, is interrupted by an unexpected and life-changing announcement by David's fiancé, Wendy. David has to look at his life afresh and seek further casework to pay for the expected increase in his family's costs.

The first case that comes along is on one of the most difficult and emotionally charged cases of his career. Rachel Wilson is charged with child cruelty and causing the death of her own baby by starvation.

The evidence against Rachel, particularly the expert evidence appears overwhelming and once the case starts, David quickly notices how the jurors react to his client, with ill-disguised loathing. It does not help that the trial is being presided over by his least favourite judge, HHJ Tanner QC, his former pupil-master.

David will need all his skill to conduct the trial and fight through the emotion and prejudice at a time when his own life is turned upside down by a frightening development.

Will he be able to turn the case around and secure an acquittal for an unsympathetic and abusive client who seems to deliberately demonstrate a lack of redeeming qualities?

UK

https://goo.gl/YmQZ4p

USA

https://goo.gl/Ek30mx

THE SILKS CRUISE
The Silk Tales volume 6

This is the sixth volume in the series, the Silk Tales, dealing with the continuing story of Queen's Counsel (the Silk), David Brant QC.

After a difficult, exhausting but highly remunerative fraud trial, David and Wendy decide to take their young daughter Rose on a cruise to Norway to get away from cases, chambers and city life.

A chance meeting leads to David being instructed in a particularly difficult murder trial. The case appears straight forward at first, even though the defendant's own friends give evidence against him. However, a series of surprising developments in the case make David wonder what his strategy should be and whether he should ever have taken the case on in the first place.

UK LINK

https://amzn.to/2VD6bPh

US LINK

https://amzn.to/2VfZoMo

PARRICIDE

VOLUME 1 OF THE MURDER TRIALS OF CICERO

A courtroom drama set in Ancient Rome and based on the first murder trial conducted by the famous Roman Advocate, Marcus Tullius Cicero. He is instructed to represent a man charged with killing his own father. Cicero soon discovers that the case is not a simple one and closely involves an important associate of the murderous Roman dictator, Sulla.

UK LINK

http://amzn.to/14vAYvY

US LINK

http://amzn.to/1fprzul

POISON

VOLUME 2 OF THE MURDER TRIALS OF CICERO

It is six years since Cicero's forensic success in the Sextus Roscius case and his life has been good. He has married and progressed through the Roman ranks and is well on the way to taking on the most coveted role of senator of Rome. Meanwhile his career in the law courts has been booming with success after success. However, one day he is approached by men from a town close to his hometown who beg him to represent a former slave on a charge of attempted poisoning. The case seems straight forward but little can he know that this case will lead him on to represent a Roman knight in a notorious case where he is charged with poisoning and with bribing judges to convict an innocent man. Cicero's skills will be tried to the utmost and he will face the most difficult and challenging case of his career where it appears that the verdict has already been rendered against his client in the court of public opinion.

UK LINK

https://goo.gl/VgpU9S

US LINK

https://goo.gl/TjhYA6

THE MYTH OF SPARTA
VOLUME 1 OF THE CHRONICLES OF SPARTA

A novel telling the story of the Spartans from the battle of the 300 at Thermopylae against the might of the Persian Empire, to the battle of Sphacteria against the Athenians and their allies. As one reviewer stated, the book is, "a highly enjoyable way to revisit one of the most significant periods of western history"

UK LINK

http://amzn.to/1gO3MSI

US LINK

http://amzn.to/1bz2pcw

THE RETURN OF THE SPARTANS

VOLUME 2 OF THE CHRONICLES OF SPARTA

"The Return of the Spartans" is a sequel to "The Myth of Sparta" and continues from where that book ends with the capture of the Spartan Hoplites at the battle of Sphacteria.

We follow their captivity through the eyes of their leader Styphon and watch individual's machinations as the Spartans and Athenians continue their war against each other. We observe numerous battles between the two in detail, seen through the eyes of their most famous and in some instances, infamous citizens.

We follow the political machinations of Cleon, Nicias and Alcibiades in Athens and see how they are dealt with by the political satirist at the time, Aristophanes, who referred to all of them in his plays.

Many of the characters from "the Myth of Sparta" appear again including the philosopher Socrates, the Athenian General Demosthenes and the Spartan General Brasidas whose campaign in Northern Greece we observe through the eyes of his men.

The book recreates the period in significant detail and as was described by one reviewer of "The Myth of Sparta", is, "a highly enjoyable way to revisit one of the most significant periods of western history".

UK LINK

http://amzn.to/1aVDYmS

US LINK

http://amzn.to/18iQCfr

THE TRIAL OF ADMIRAL BYNG

Pour Encourager Les Autres

BOOK ONE OF THE HISTORICAL TRIALS SERIES

"The Trial of Admiral Byng" is a fictionalised retelling of the true story of the famous British Admiral Byng, who fought at the battle of Minorca in 1756 and was later court-martialled for his role in that battle. The book takes us through the siege of Minorca as well as the battle and then to the trial where Byng has to defend himself against serious allegations of cowardice, knowing that if he is found guilty there is only one penalty available to the court, his death.

UK LINK

http://goo.gl/cMMXFY

US LINK

http://goo.gl/AaVNOZ

TREACHERY – THE PRINCES IN THE TOWER

'Treachery - the Princes in the Tower' tells the story of a knight, Sir Thomas Clark who is instructed by King Henry VII to discover what happened to the Princes in the Tower. His quest takes him upon many journeys meeting many of the important personages of the day who give him conflicting accounts of what happened. However, through his perseverance he gets ever closer to discovering what really happened to the Princes, with startling consequences.

UK LINK

http://amzn.to/1VPW0kC

US LINK

http://amzn.to/1VUyUJf

Printed in Great Britain
by Amazon